Going BLACK HOME

patris gordon

Going BLACK HOME

patris gordon

Dedicated to self-motivation.
Thanks for sticking around.

ISBN: 978-1-9163132-7-9

Printed in the United Kingdom

Published by Blank Screen

Chapter 1

1996

There wasn't much to distinguish this terrace cottage from the others within its vicinity, but Boy A couldn't have cared less. Its chiselled refinery, potted brickage and well-laden structure ran as oblivion across his young mind. To gauge the scene with an air of cinematic reference and a cool music soundtrack, but the reality felt too dull. Maybe due to being so quiet that you could hear a pin drop, or maybe he had vetted this street so much that all romance with it had been lost. Either way, he wasn't sure, but he caught Boy B staring at his unpopular trainers as if disappointed with the choice of attire, and he wondered what he was doing there to begin with. He waited, patiently, like his mum did when she knew the answer already and was pressing on him to confess any misdeeds he had undertaken and she normally disapproved of. He eventually met Boy B's eyes, bright and round, and he was right, he knew. The level of respect and acceptance his friends had with Boy B wouldn't be achieved overnight. Or perhaps it would.

"What?!" said Boy B. "We doing this?"

Boy A nodded. It was the best approach. His head fell towards his new Filas, and then moved closer to Boy B, sighting the black trackbottoms and hooded top inside the soft-padded leather jacket. Boy B dressed almost identical to him, but had a better build and loved the gym. Boy A didn't, frowning.

"Let's go!"

Boy A followed Boy B to the corner of the road, leading to the back of the terrace cottage. Inhaling, trying not to absorb the disconnect he was having with the area, the peaceful surroundings didn't match the reality of his and Boy B's high-rise council flats. It didn't share its grotty stairwells or rundown lifts. And Boy A knew the irony of it all. He only lived five minutes walk away from the good life, where the better income households and higher moral values resided.

"You sure about this?" His voice trying not to quaver. "I mean..."

Boy B didn't make eye contact. He had his own objectives and he wouldn't put them at risk now. Faced down to Boy A's trainers, he laughed as he spoke, unsure if it was the kicks or Boy A's statement.

"We've been through this, blud. Let's get it done and then talk about it tomorrow. Yeah?"

Boy B met Boy A's eyes. "Yeah?!"

Boy A rose his eyebrows in agreement.

"There you go," said Boy B. "There's a pot of gold at the end of the rainbow..."

2018

Rebecca wiped the water off her face with a paper tissue. Feeling its disappearance, she had to deal with something else. Almost pretending it wasn't there. She raised her head to the cheaply encrusted and poorly painted mirror in front of her and made eye contact with her reflection. A strange game to play but the only way to deal with her unsteady conscience. The mirror's pretty woman looked back at her, smiled and Rebecca returned the gesture wearily. Questioning her appearance even more, she knew it was too late to make any changes. Her makeup rubbed off with the water, and allowed her skin to exude a radiance uncommon for her at that time of day. From her lithe wrist, she checked her watch, noticing time had passed. Her phone vibrated. She sighed, at her black jumper and blue skirt, and black tights, with despair at her style, remembering the rush in the morning to get ready for work. It turned out to be a text from her mum and it zapped her energy. The screen dissolved in her vision as she held the phone for a matter of seconds before lifting her jumper slightly. A few severed scars bore position just above her hip, and served as reminders of the past. The clinic, the hurried procedure, the comforting nurse. The small scars, she pressed them firmly. The toilet entrance door opened, and she reacted quickly, dropping her top. Through the mirror she tried to recognise the person coming in. The young temp. Straight out of sixth-form college, nodding her head before the girl closed a toilet door. Rebecca thought about the text, deciding to reply later. Michael then took residence in her mind and she imagined him thinking of whether she was coming or not to his drinks' night in Shoreditch. Something was stopping her from leaving the office. Her work was done, the day had officially ended. She headed back to her desk and put her phone in her bag. Her colleague, Jason, crossed her mind, and if he'd approach her before he left. *Whap!* As if by magic, a pair of suede shoes hindered her vision.

"You got somewhere to be?" Voice husky as shit, and she loved it. Not as good looking as Michael, though, not even close. He had the body of an unattractive footballer, the strapping physique of a guy that enjoyed being on grassland, kicking an object or two, breathing heavily on a cold Sunday morning. Rebecca moved the attention from his shoes, and summoned a direct gaze with his eyes.

"Kinda. Supposed to be meeting Michael."

His posture awkward, a loose hand on her desk, and trying to simmer the disappointment at the announcement of her boyfriend. Jason had met Michael at the Christmas party.

"Ah, forget him, babe," he coughed. "You'll have a much better time with us." He attempted a penetrative stare, which Rebecca tried to ignore. This behaviour from Jason was predictable, but indicative of her confused stance with Michael, and the mixed signals she thought she was sending. Jason leaned forward and Rebecca became aware of how quiet the office was. Friday evening and everyone was down the pub. Sitting up, her eyes fought contact and control of the situation. Implicitly expressed, deep down Rebecca didn't want to show what she was thinking. *Crikes, what am I doing?*

"I'm not going to pretend I like the dude," said Jason, "but least let me show you what kind of fun we can have, yeah?"

Her head was nodding in agreement, her mouth forming a shy smile. A vibration from her bag sounded. Another text message.

For no apparent reason, Michael walked back to the table on tip-toes. It was as if he wanted to be taller than he already was. He stood six foot six, a solid build, partly achieved from playing professional basketball in his twenties. Strangely, there were times when he wished he had a couple of extra inches to his name. He could barely see Allen and Paul at the corner table across the sea of cigarette smoke and poor lighting. The others were to join them at any minute and he figured he'd be making the journey again very soon. Carrying three pints, two full, one half, balancing them carefully, careful not to spill anything through the narrow gaps of space people barely allowed. He tutted to nobody in particular, sure he was going to be "that guy" etched on everyone's Friday memory. Someone about to pull out their phone from a pocket.

"Sorry, mate," said Michael.

The bearded man had a glass in his hand and swung around, taking out his phone at the same time with his other hand. He bumped Michael, apologising before he sought recognition. "Sor... Shit."

A momentary sense of fear exuded from the man and Michael picked up on it. An assumed domination of height and build, sure, but the guy looked twice at Michael as if he had something else he wanted to say.

"Yeah."

Michael realised nothing else was going to happen and kept it moving. The guy held his phone near his face like some form of protection. Michael sighed and continued to squeeze his way through the pub until he reached the table. Allen and Paul saw the exasperation but both ignored their thoughts to question it.

"This place is crazy," said Michael as he put the beers down. His suit felt tight around his arms. Too many business lunches and too few scrimmages, he thought.

"You pick it every time," said Paul, absorbing the clamour of noise. He noted the unpleasant decor with its outdated colour scheme, poor vintage design, oddly selected and arranged props hanging from the ceiling and on the shelves. It didn't enhance the experience there at all. But there *was* still something warm about the pub: comforting; homely; even though smack in the middle of the city. And with more people coming in, the finite details of the surroundings became distant. Michael caught his eyes.

"Yeah, but it's usually not this busy. And it's *not* happy hour."

"What you mean?" said Allen, scratching his pleated trouser leg, worried the material was too thin.

"That's what I said. These three beers cost £15.75."

"£15...?"

"Sound like happy hour to you?"

Allen didn't respond. This question didn't warrant an answer. He observed Michael for a split second, analysing what he could from his friend. The handsome face, childish looks, smart dress. The aura of cash money and confidence. But experience with Michael signalled a deeper understanding, a deeper alliance of the goals and dreams, and the successes and failures. He threw Michael a look of acknowledgment, understating life's uncertainties and the reason why happy hour was applicable to this. His mobile phone vibrated in his pocket but he declined against pulling it out. It was probably from his fiancée.

As if sharing the same message, Michael pulled out his phone and sat next to Paul, waiting for the conversation to continue. There was a delayed silence, a short pitstop of opinion and expression.

Michael looked at his phone then laid it on the table. He picked up his drink and waved it at Allen and Paul. They followed suit and held up their glasses.

Paul queried the meaning. "To what are we celebrating?"

"Nothing, just the fact that we're all good. Lucky to have friends that care and support each other and we can still have a drink when we need to catch up."

"I hear that," said Allen, tired of holding his drink and desperate to quench his thirst. "To..."

"Hold on, hold on," said Michael. He glared at Paul and had second thoughts. "Ah, never mind. Thanks. Thanks for coming, guys. Cheers!"

The glasses clinked loudly as they resonated a shared belonging. Paul pulled away first. His face indicating curiosity.

"So, who else is coming?"

Michael reached to his phone, tempted to call Rebecca and find out if her plans included passing by as they'd earlier discussed that very morning. Her attitude was blasé, hinting at an escape clause if she needed one.

He caught eyes with Allen before moving over to Paul.

"Madyson and Daniel. Not sure if Lawrence is..."

Allen raised his eyebrows. "Oh, I think he is."

"What?"

Michael followed Allen's stare. He smirked at seeing his younger, shorter and only brother squeezing through the pub like he'd done moments earlier. It was a pleasant surprise to see Lawrence, although Michael doubted if his brother would stay around for long. He stood up and he held out his arms as Lawrence moved closer.

The embrace is strange, thought Allen, watching as a mix of distance and love surrounded the reunion. He knew they had had their difficulties but it was good to see they were making the effort. It was unlike his own immediate family. Catch-ups were only reserved for weddings and funerals, and it often frustrated Allen. He had two elder brothers and they were too wrapped up in their domestic and social situations to communicate regularly with him. He noticed the lingering release between Michael and Lawrence and understood the bond they had. He nodded his head when Lawrence looked in his direction and said something. A combination of increasing people, distorted banter and painful background music meant he didn't hear what Lawrence said.

Lawrence didn't realise this but moved his eyes over to Paul. Paul had found something more interesting in his drink than to acknowledge Michael's brother. Lawrence huffed, looked at Michael, who hadn't noticed anything and was now sitting. Lawrence motioned for Allen so he didn't sit on Paul's side of the table.

He wasn't sure what Paul's beef was, but the last time they'd all got together, for Michael's promotion a month ago, the conversation had circled around the women in their lives. He didn't appreciate Paul's stance on relationships with the opposite sex as, "what you make them, they're not beyond our control". Of course, Lawrence was drunk, and hadn't been in a long-term relationship since splitting up with one of the mothers of his children. The failure of these relationships seemed to confuse him, and were indeed beyond his control. It was all right for Paul, he thought then, the guy had cash. And that *is* the real deciding factor for the relationships with the opposite sex.

Lawrence soon left after that because he didn't say what he was thinking. He knew it would upset the night, and Michael's night, especially as the plan was to try and get them together at least once a month, but Paul's social analysis and 'worldly' views riled Lawrence. Just because...

"You all right, bro?" asked Allen.

Lawrence knew his status within the group, and hated projecting this perception, as easy as it would have been. The question made him the centre of attention.

"I'm doing good," Lawrence smiled. "Just started a new contract job at a small agency in the city. Keeping me busy..."

"Oh yeah," said Michael. "When you start? We know them?"

Paul focused his eyes towards Lawrence with interest but withheld his thoughts of disbelief. Lawrence would make anything up to present himself in a good light next to his brother, he thought.

"Oh, you won't know them. Very tiny," said Lawrence.

Allen leaned forward. "Go on."

Lawrence wanted to grab his phone at that moment, lodged in his inner jacket pocket, to distract him from answering. Almost pretend his life was undeserving of the attention.

"They're called Distinction. Near Finsbury Square, Moorgate way."

A waft of bemusement ran across his brother and his friends' faces.

"Okay," said Michael.

"Never heard of them," said Allen, "but sounds good."

Lawrence nodded.

"I will look them up," said Paul, missing the look of disapproval from Michael. Paul kept his eyes firmly on Lawrence to see if he would change his story. He waited a moment and pulled out his phone from his blazer pocket. *Is this company online? Had anyone written anything about it?*

"Paul, there's no need..." said Michael, staring at Lawrence. He sensed a similar angst as per the last time they all were together, especially if Lawrence was telling porkies. Lawrence had a terrible temperament, and Michael remembered their teenage scuffles, and how their parents were forced to throw the closest object at hand to help intervene. Their dad wasn't confident with his English and it served as a hindrance during these moments. Lawrence needed a father that could slap him straight, thought Michael, but their dad didn't believe in replicating violence as a means to stop their squabbles, even though he still had remnants of bruises from their fights all these years later.

Lawrence had a violent streak, and it had continued throughout his adolescent years to his early adulthood and landed him a stint in prison for six months for battering an ex-girlfriend. His background was well known by the group and whilst Lawrence and Paul didn't fight the last time, an undercurrent of anxiety seemed to surround them.

Allen picked up his beer and took a swig. Lawrence didn't have a drink and Allen knew a welcomed distraction when he saw one.

"Hey, man," Allen said loudly. Thry turned their attention towards him. "You want something to drink, dude?"

The language wasn't right but its meaning was spot on. Paul stopped typing on his phone, Michael duly smiled, appreciating the move, and Lawrence heistated before giving a certified head nod. Allen grinned, paused and moved about in his seat.

"What's, what's up, girl?"

Confusion reigned until a shapely shadow covered their view and a well-dressed woman entered their sights. Their heads rose, their faces lighting up with familiarity. There stood Madyson. Tall and vibrant. The backdrop of the pub a blur, her figure noticeably wrapped in a thin jumper, leather jacket and jeans, an overt confidence in her appearance. She smiled at Allen first as he had signalled at her. She extended her warmth towards the others.

"What's good?!" she laughed, teeth perfectly aligned and visible. Michael stood up first being the closest.

"Hey, hey," Michael said, standing. He gave her a hug. "I didn't think you were coming. Thought you were working."

"No, today is rehearsal, but then the big show starts next week. Need a break. It's been intense..."

Allen nudged at Lawrence to indicate he wanted to stand up. Lawrence moved over and stood up, finding himself next to Madyson. She looked Lawrence up and down, as if his presence was an amonaly among them.

"You all right?" Madyson asked Lawrence quietly. He nodded, before coughing and clearing his throat. Allen squeezed past him and approached Madyson.

"What up, sisthren?" Allen grabbed Madyson's waist, jolting her from her position and closer towards him. She obliged with the maneourve, accidentally stepping on one of Lawrence's feet. She hugged Allen tightly as their friendship revealed security. He released her softly, studied her outfit and muttered that he was impressed. "How's Hollywood?"

She raised her eyebrows. "Ha, ha. so funny, Allen. How's the 20-year-old secretary? Still picking up Post-Its from under your desk."

"Woooo," said Allen. "You have jokes. Someone's ready for a long night. And *who* told you about the secretary?"

Madyson turned her head, smiling, back to Lawrence and saw he was sitting back down. A sullen expression rendered his face. She didn't give it much thought as Paul was slowly waiting his turn.

"Hey, Madyson. Looking good." He reached over, holding her arm and kissed her cheeks. He didn't do hugs.

"Thank you, Paul. You, too. How's Helen?"

"She's doing well, thanks."

"She here?" asked Madyson.

"No, she's home, watching Jamie."

Squashing her lips, Madyson figured she'd be the only woman with them tonight as Helen, Michelle or Rebecca rarely ever came along. The wife, fiancée and girlfriend were, at times, uncomfortable with her friendship with the men, but she'd been friends with them for years; knowing Michael and Lawrence since secondary school.

The space between them standing (except Lawrence) was limited, and the proximity awkward. Michael saw a notification on his phone, which sat on the table. He'd offer to buy Madyson a drink but to visit the bar again was off the cards, and the path hadn't deflated. Paul wondered if she was going to ask about Helen again, but her interest waned on the subject. Allen spoke first, knowing somebody had to.

"I was just getting a drink for Lawrence, you want one?" asked Allen.

"Err, yeah. We're at a bar. Thanks." Madyson said, smirking.

"And..."

"Oh, a Jack D and Coke is good. Thanks." She playfully slapped at his arm, as Michael and Paul squeezed back down by the table, snatching at their drinks.

"Oh, Lawrence," shouted Allen, before he forgot. "What you on?"

He shrugged his shoulders: "Just a pint of whatever."

Allen wanted to keep the vibe cheerful and didn't push Lawrence for specifics. "Okay."

He churned his way through the bulging noise and bodies on his journey to the bar. Madyson took off her jacket and flung it next to Lawrence. Everyone stared at each other.

Michael slid his phone into his pocket. The message was from his car insurance company stating it would renew his policy automatically, but he didn't want this. *It's going to be more expensive than the previous year, strangely.* He caught eyes with Madyson and she was feeling good, he could tell. At his promotion drinks last month, she was nervous. Unsure of her role in her new theatre show and if she was really an actress at heart, self-doubt lingered and she suspected the director would pick up on it. It was clear to Michael this was no longer the case. Her show was starting next week — and the press preview would point out in its various mediums a captivate and damaged persona, skilfully portrayed by Madyson Peck. It had been a unique and interesting road for Madyson and to see her smiling as she was, Michael quietly saluted her.

"So, what's the gos?" said Madyson. "I feel like we haven't met up for donkeys."

"I know," said Michael. "It's like, our lives are getting too busy. Even for a get together."

"Mate, I met you last week. With Daniel," said Paul.

"Yeah, I know that," said Michael. "But not the whole gang..."

"C'mon, Mike," said Paul. He didn't mean to dispel the drama, but he couldn't help himself. "We all linked up like a few weeks ago, right?"

As if in a warmly-embroiled coma, Michael closed his eyes and swayed a bit on the chair. He bumped Paul with his shoulders, and smiled.

"You know I'm right..." said Paul.

"Oh, you guys, the fun never stops," said Madyson, peeking over to Lawrence, then back to Michael. "No Becky?"

Even with his phone lodged away, he knew the answer. "She said she was, but busy at work."

"Even now?"

"It's an internet-funded start-up with dodgy venture capital so she gotta put in those extra hours..."

Lawrence picked up the word 'internet' and as the attention had moved away from him for the moment, he wondered if Paul would try to revert back to the internet search effort and discovery of his new agency. There was a buzzing in his pocket and he ignored the phone.

Madyson felt the vibration, but decided not to get involved. She liked Lawrence; she just didn't like his story. She gazed across the table at Michael, his appearance dashing as he'd always been. He was virtually unchanged, apart from stress lines on his forehead and a sprinkle of random grey hairs. The attraction towards the opposite sex was still a puzzlement for her, but she acknowledged her growth in beauty, too. Her appearance was routine to them now and she appreciated that. She didn't need any unwanted attention. That came with work. Not only Michael, though, she thought when they'd meet up, all the guys were still handsome in their own way. The slight weight gain could only be noticed through looking at old pictures of them together. She had gone up a dress size and their waists were slowly expanding. Subconsciously, this was their shared acceptance: getting older and putting on weight, but being around people who didn't think twice about it. It wasn't explicitly addressed unless someone was wearing something that made them stand out.

The eyes around the table wandered for a moment before circling back to Michael. "Yeah, she might come, I don't know."

Madyson felt a tinge of concern. "Everything okay with you both?"

Coming from Madyson, and even around the guys, it was okay for her to ask. She had earned the permission to do so. Paul made a strained expression, wondering if his domestic situation would be vilified by Madyson. For an actress, he noted, she loved talking about other people's lives and not her own.

"We're good. Just keep getting caught up in our stuff with work and whatnots," said Michael, his head facing his drink for a second before rising his eyes to make contact. "I know you can't know everything about a person but it seems, at times, I miss the crucial parts of the puzzle that will make her happy. We're in a weird place but gonna be all right, I think."

"Rebecca's sweet, dude, you know that," said Paul, missing Madyson's frown.

"Thanks, bro," said Michael. "I just like to have things perfect, but I guess it doesn't work like that."

Lawrence looked at Michael to see if he was aware of what he said. He wanted to shake his head in disgust, but it was just a slip of the tongue — and he shouldn't think deeply on it. Paul isn't his "bro", although you would think they were at first glance. The usual disconnect Lawrence experienced with Michael was happening again. He stared around at the pub's interior, watching a pretty woman in a low cut top squeezing past a couple of guys and smiling as she did so. *Amazing grace.*

"You guys are perfect," said Madyson. "You'll be fine. We all go through ups and downs." She took a quick gaze at Lawrence and could sense he wasn't listening to the conversation. She followed his eyes and saw two guys whispering and staring at an average-looking woman. She ignored the scenario and returned to Michael.

"Anyway, change the subject, please," said Michael. "I don't want her to feel awkward or sense we were talking about her when she comes down."

"Don't be silly, bro," said Paul. "We know the rules."

Lawrence stared over at Paul again to see if he was trying to wind him up or something. He knew he couldn't sit there without saying a word.

Lawrence coughed. "Is Rebecca coming down, then?"

Michael shook his head as if to signify disgust. "Where are you, man?" There was a quiet laugh from Madyson and Paul. "I just said..."

He spotted Lawrence blushing. The cheeks appeared darker, but only Michael would have known it. He reached out his hand to Lawrence. "... she's coming down."

Looking at his brother's hand, he took it into his grip and felt the embarrassment lifting. "Oops. Sorry, mind's everywhere lately."

"No worries, dude," said Michael, taking his hand back.

Paul shot a quick gaze over to Madyson and tried to read her thoughts. She appeared uneasy and a change of subject was due.

"Madyson," said Paul. "You must be getting a nice bit of money for your new show?"

She laughed. Paul smiled, knowing Lawrence's strangeness would be instantly forgotten. "You always ask this."

"I know," Paul said, grinning.

Michael watched Lawrence and hoped his brother was doing okay. It'd been a few weeks since they had a real long chat. He took a sip of his drink and noticed Lawrence was without his. He raised his head up, and across the pub, but couldn't see Allen. His eyes stopped to a man in his 50s or 60s, speaking with a younger woman. His two top shirt buttons were undone and he had a hairy chest. The lady appeared unfazed and Michael wondered their relationship status. Rebecca shot into his mind and he looked at his phone to see if there were any new notifications. He turned back to Lawrence and a weary look engulfed his brother. It wasn't the place nor time for any elaboration of whatever of what was really going on in Lawrence's life. He focused back on Madyson and Paul.

She was speaking: "It's nothing like film; the benefits and cash don't compare, but the work is more fulfilling. It may be cliché but being in front of an audience, there's nothing like it."

"Yeah, yeah, yeah," mocked Paul. "The art of it... but what do you charge? I know it isn't the West End but you must be up there for what they pay." Paul could see Madyson shaking her head. "What?"

"You say this each time," said Madyson. "It's all about the money with you."

Paul shrugged as if he didn't understand what she meant. He looked over to Michael to explain.

"You know, those movies," said Madyson, "they didn't pay what you think they would. Especially as I'm getting older, my bargaining power isn't that strong. I never had any leading roles..."

Michael piped up. "What about *Revenge of the Killers*? You were all over that..."

She smiled. "Are you both trying to wind me up? Well, it's working..."

Lawrence felt his mouth drying up with the lack of a beverage. "Didn't you get 50 grand for the *The Angel Above*?"

"No, I didn't," she said without turning her head. "I wish that was true. Films and filming is ruthless. There's barely any royalties for actors of my level, even with these collection agencies. So I usually sign a lump sum deal upfront to secure any possibility of getting paid. Seriously, it's a harsh business, but for some reason I love it."

The bustle of a growing crowd dominated pub's acoustics as a silent pause rose between them. No one looked at each other, each searching for their own stories of relevance. Lawrence nodded, but its meaning was unknown. Paul wondered about Lawrence's new agency, and if Madyson was being modest about what she earned. He had read otherwise. Michael wanted to see if Rebecca had left a message but didn't want to be rude to Madyson's story.

A dark cloud shadowed them. A similar monotony of thought echoed between them and it only broke when they heard the voice of Allen, and realised the dark cloud hovering over them was *actually* a human shadow.

"Hey, hey," said Allen, hands occupied by drinks. "What's up with the sad faces, boss?! Look who I found at the bar?"

They looked up at Allen. Hedging behind was a medium-sized man, with an uncombed beard, trendy glasses and an Afro that needed a barber. He had an inviting smile, and raised his eyebrows. He lifted his arms to the direction of the ceiling, nearly spilling the beer in his hand.

"Whaddup, my niggas?!"

Madyson and Paul frowned, but Michael laughed and stood up.

"Daniel! What's going on?" They hugged and held tightly for an uncomfortable duration. Allen placed the drinks on the table. Madyson and Lawrence swiped at them and drank quickly.

Michael let go first. "You good?"

Daniel held eye contact. "Yep. Nothing but the usual. Other than that, I'm good. Life is crazy but I'm here, ain't I?"

"You sure are, you crazy fucker." Michael patted his friend's shoulder as he said it.

Daniel was sure he'd spill the drink before he could drink it. With the six of them and one small table, Daniel sensed a economical fit taking place. He nodded and hinted at sitting down so the others could scoot over. Lawrence looked at Madyson and she stared at Paul, who grinned at Michael. There was only room to add one extra chair from the side. Allen stepped back and waited for Daniel to take space among the others. A smile dwindled from Daniel as logistics of the table's seating arrangement were being worked out.

"Come on, dudes. Move over."

Following his instructions, they responded. Daniel edged himself next to Madyson, although it seemed more logical to sit next to Michael, who had the most space. *Maybe he has a thing for Madyson?* She welcomed Daniel next to her, putting her arm around his shoulders as he squeezed up closer.

Allen moved to another table and took up a free chair. "So, what's good?"

Michael took the initiative to answer. "We're just living, boss. You know that? How's tricks at work?"

"Man, sod work. I think I'm going to leave..." said Allen.

Perking up, Paul decided to speak: "You say this all the time."

"Yeah, I know. I need to do something about it. I don't know..."

Daniel chirped in. "Seems I didn't miss anything."

"No, you didn't," said Madyson, quietly. Only Paul and Daniel heard what she said, and this created a suble division within the group.

"Allen was telling me about your show. You excited?" said Daniel. He saw Lawrence looking his way. He could hear Paul saying something, too.

"You still playing ball this weekend?"

Michael turned from Allen to Paul. "Yep, you know I am. Gotta keep it up. This desktop life is not good on the body. Look at this, man."

Michael held an inch of superfluous body poundage from under his shirt. "I'm not even 40 yet and already feeling the pinch."

"I thought you were going to the gym," said Allen, watching Michael checking his phone.

Michael returned his eyes back to Allen. "I was. I am. You know, just gotta go on a regular basis, that's all."

"If you're lacking motivation," said Paul. "The team at work is starting a boot camp by Clapham Common. It should be good. I'm thinking of joining."

Michael wondered if Paul was serious, and analysed his friend. *What did he do? What was his kid's name? Why did he wear that cashmere blazer with ripped jeans? Why did he pick the cheap shirt but have an expensive jumper? And why have a Rolex, which didn't look like a Rolex?*

Michael noticed Paul's face seemed to extend when a gesture was made, and appeared circular when it wasn't. He wasn't sure what Helen saw in Paul, but he didn't understand women, period. He thought his phone vibrated but he realised it was imagined because he *wanted* it to ring.

"I prefer hooping to all those extreme exercise things you do," said Michael.

"Yeah, but isn't that the problem?" Paul said. "You've been playing *too much* basketball."

"I could never play too much basketball."

"Err, mate, what did your doctor say about it? You got that knee injury through repetitive movement only acquired from making lay-ups and jump shots," said Paul, smug.

Basketball had served as more than a exercise for getting fit, it had changed Michael's life, opened his eyes to a bigger world around him. He played recreationally as a way of giving back to the sport. To him, it beat coaching kids for a pittance salary or spending money on season tickets at the local team, knowing deep down he was a better player than half of those he watched. He would keep continually playing the sport for as long as he could.

"But what do doctors really know? They can only know so much based on what their experience tells them."

Allen chipped in. "But that's why we have specialists, doctors in their particular field who can deal with any injury."

"Man, guys," said Michael. "All I know is these guys messed up my playing days, and I'm never letting that happen again. I can't *trust* 'em. I'm all for second opinions, but when they just do routine checks, diagnose you in two minutes without really listening to what you're telling them, cos they're the doctor, it makes me think there's no point in even consulting them to begin with."

Michael smiled at Madyson, who was smiling at him. Lawrence was listening to something Daniel was saying, although Daniel appeared focused on Madyson. *She is looking good*, he thought.

"You been on Mindsite lately?" asked Allen. "There's a video I saw on there where a guy's being told by a doctor he can't play football anymore. He's crying uncontrollably and then starts to jump up and down..."

"I've seen this one..." said Madyson.

"Is it staged?" asked Michael.

"It's shown from CCTV so it looks real," said Allen. "...the doctor is just sitting there like he's used to giving bad news. Then you see the guy walking out of the office, and then come back in, with a gun and he shoots the doctor... "

"What?!" said Michael.

"Yeah, and the irony of it, the man jets out of the surgery quicker than anything, limping."

"Ha ha," laughed Michael. "That's hilarious."

Paul smirked.

"It looks real," said Allen.

The whole group redirected themselves to Allen speaking.

Daniel stopped referring about a lady at his office who had taken up a part-time role in a West End theatre show. Madyson saw through his efforts to connect her job with his life, but politely ignored him.

When she looked over at Michael, he caught her eyes and she half-wished Michael would tell everyone to go home, so just the two of them could talk. Michael returned back to Allen, engrossed in a form of story-telling.

Allen was 36 years old but looked ten years older. He worked as a digital project manager for a publishing company, but was struggling at work. The climate shift from magazines and papers to online and apps was unnerving and reinventing himself to maintain an importance at his job felt tiresome. The constant learning about code, data, javascript and a million other programming languages was an effort he wasn't sure he was built for. He had two kids and a fiancée he rarely saw during the week as a result of working late, and regularly felt out of tune with what was going on in their lives.

He'd lost a bit of weight as a result of work-related stress. The only plus point was he'd booked himself into a cookery class recently to start eating better and to limit his daily lunches, which consisted of fancy restaurants that charged obscene prices for their fancy sandwiches. His slim, tall look was appearing gaunt, and it was a path he didn't want to continue on. He'd known Michael from sixth form college in Battersea with Paul and Daniel, from which he and Michael went onto the University of Greenwich after taking A-Levels. They played on the university basketball team and he saw firsthand how competitive Michael was, so hearing Michael speak about basketball didn't surprise him.

Allen looked at the others, digested his view before picking up his drink. He often forgot how he'd been when he was young, how confident he felt around others. A calm demeanour generally, he was still very communicative as each word came across loud and clear, nuances where applicable and relevant assertions in each phrase.

"But most of the stuff on Mindsite is fake, isn't it?" said Daniel. "Everyone knows that. People add videos like that just to get more views and so they can dupe their friends that they have personality."

Allen didn't take the comment personally. He knew Daniel loved attention — and seeked it at any given situation. *This is one of those situations.* A moment's silence expected Allen to respond.

"Fake or not. It was funny as shit. Seriously. Have you seen it?" said Allen.

Daniel paused but sensed the group knew he hadn't seen it based on his reaction.

"Yeah, I've seen it. It's not that funny," said Daniel. He picked up his drink and took a sip.

Madyson turned to Daniel. "Have you really?"

Daniel leaned back, accidentally rubbing Madyson's arm. "Of course. Why would I say I have when I haven't? That doesn't make sense..."

His subconscious pushed at his temple and it spectulated where this was going.

"Err, maybe it's because of something you said last time we met up," said Lawrence. The dulcet tone of Lawrence's voice alerted Madyson, finding it attractive and sweet-sounding.

"What are you talking about?" said Daniel, leaning forward, getting his body in line with Lawrence. Being an ex-con meant Lawrence was always at the bottom of the group's invisible hierarchy pyramid of friends. An awkward stance, off-putting demeanour meant he was already on the back foot. As if aware of this, Lawrence coughed before he spoke.

"Yeah, last time you said you had moved to Dulwich, and when we looked it up it was Lewisham."

Daniel ignored the muffled laughter from the others. "As I explained then, I had just moved so I didn't realise the postcode came up Lewisham, okay?!"

Lawrence smirked. Madyson, stuck in the middle, watched them both as if she was at a tennis match. A tension was building and she had no idea if it'd go any further.

"How about when said you'd given up fast food?" said Lawrence. He looked at Michael. "You remember?" He extended to Paul and Allen. "... the wrapper of a FKC chicken burger fell out of your bag when you went to the toilets."

Daniel felt a surge of embarrassment, unsure where to look. They were laughing. He bit his tongue, and saw Lawrence, who was enjoying the moment, looking over at Michael, who was wiping a loose tear.

Catching Madyson smiling, too, made Daniel envious. *Should I respond?* But he wasn't sure if Lawrence could handle any personal comments. Michael was checking his phone and Daniel had a thought.

"Okay, okay," Daniel said. "I saw it but I didn't watch it completely."

"I knew it." said Lawrence.

More quiet laughter ensued.

"You're funny," said Paul.

"Yeah, well. Did anyone see that video about coltan in mobile phones?"

Michael put down his phone and held his gaze with Daniel. It was clear Rebecca wasn't coming.

"Cole what?" said Madyson.

Daniel had them back: "Coltan — the mineral they use in mobile phones. There's this American preacher talking about it. I saw it on Mind-site this morning..." Blank faces. "I'll share it later so you can see but basically he says how coltan mining has been linked to finance serious conflict in places like the Democratic Republic of Congo, where thousands of people are killed so they can export the mineral for the highest price."

"What?" said Madyson.

Daniel took his phone out and waved it at them. Michael grimaced, knowing about the video.

"I need to find it on my feed, but..."

"It's not just used for mobile phones," said Paul, staring at Daniel. "It's for most electronic devices. Coltan is used for tantalum capacitors in the production of phones and things like that."

"You seen it?" asked Daniel.

"No, but I read about it once."

"So, this preacher goes on and says almost 50 percent of those being killed are children."

Madyson held her breath to prevent gasping. Daniel felt her body stiffen.

"Yep," said Paul.

"Hold on," said Michael. "Kids are being killed for the production of mobile phones...?"

"Among other things," said Paul. "It's called the 'resource curse' because these countries that are rich in resources have poorer economic development than countries that have fewer resources."

"So, you're saying the distribution of wealth is worst in these countries despite the fact mobile phones are so popular?" asked Allen, chipping in.

"That's right," said Paul.

"Because of the corruption," added Daniel. Another small pause, empty in thought. Daniel had to exploit it. "The preacher goes on to say the politics and their dodgy leaders of these countries have created militias, who have no restrictions on who they kill and force families into slave labour, just so they can maintain their wealth and continue exporting coltan. Let me find the video now...."

"What, on your mobile phone?" said Madyson.

"Yeah, where else?"

Everyone shook their heads. Lawrence moaned softly.

"What?" barked Daniel.

"You're..." started Lawrence. But Michael raised hand flagged him down.

Daniel tapped at his phone, searching his Mindsite page to find the video. "It was here somewhere..."

"You guys getting anything to eat?" asked Madyson.

"You didn't eat? It's still early, I suppose," said Allen.

"I'm actually quite famished. They don't give you much to eat at rehearsals."

Paul wondered about the acting profession and the sacrifice of the art-form. *Was it worth being hungry over?*

"Um, Michael," said Madyson. "You eating? Or just getting drunk tonight?"

Michael didn't answer, his mind elsewhere. He'd been to Ghana a couple of years earlier, noted the disparity between rich and poor, something he couldn't understand at first. The African country, clearly rich in culture, and economically, he could see the money but the system set-up made it harder to keep a track of it all. And this meant corruption, he assumed.

He accepted Ghana was *not* the Democratic Republic of Congo, but he wondered about the parallels in government corruption that probably existed across Africa, and whether the continent would ever truly excel to world prominence. Ghana equalled a rich, influential position and was culturally rewarding. Neighbouring countries like Nigeria were even richer, a stronger GDP, but the inclusion in world politics, he felt, seemed limited. *Kids getting killed for mobile phones?* That would *never* happen in Europe or North America. Something wrong there. His Tema experience in Ghana opened his eyes to the country's development across the financial, oil and gas, and farming industries, but most business was still done with cash transactions, highlighting the lack of sophistication he was used to in England.

Madyson looked at the other guys when Michael didn't respond. *It's Rebecca*, and hunched her shoulders. Daniel was saying something about his phone and a buffering icon flashed onto its screen.

"Ah, come on," said Daniel.

Back to Michael, who had picked up his drink but didn't look at anyone.

"Hey, Mike," said Paul. "You okay? Madyson asked if you were eating..."

Michael: "Sorry, zoned out for a minute." He turned to Daniel. "You found that video?"

"Must be the Wi-Fi," said Daniel. "Maybe outside I'll get a better signal."

Lawrence grinned. He hadn't heard the term "signal" for about ten years. He was in prison, the other inmates snuck their phones in, complaining how crap they were as they couldn't connect properly from their remote location.

"Don't worry about it," said Allen. "Share it later."

Allen's words reminded him of the website's editor where he worked.

"Just share it later," Nuno had said after he told him about a potential breaking celebrity story. Daniel was concerned by his editor's lack of concern. The story of a leaked sex tape was the difference between millions of page views or a legal case, involving millions of pounds if not handled correctly. But he shared it anyway. And then the lawyers told them to take it down straight away.

"Okay," said Daniel, putting his phone in his coat pocket. Madyson looked his way and smiled at him. He couldn't read what she was thinking.

Michael sighed. He wasn't focused on the group, instead taking in the pub's surroundings and the people in it. Their colours, sizes, sexes and heights and the way they dressed. They bothered him, but he couldn't think why. They were comfortable; maybe they didn't have the problems of the poor families being killed thousands of miles away, just for being in the wrong place. Maybe.

Paul sensed something was up and decided to change the subject. "You guys hear about Alfie?" Paul asked. The table, except Michael, looked over to him. "Alfie. You know Alfie from college. Dark skin, heavy acne. Lived by that train station. Um..."

"What? Alfie, Alfie," said Allen. "He was with Maria for a bit, wasn't he?"

"Yeah, him."

"Why? What happened?"

"He got shot at some party in Hackney the other day. Dead and gone."

"What?" said Madsyon. She didn't know Alfie — she didn't go to the same college as them — but a tragedy *was* a tragedy.

"I saw a dedication on Mindsite yesterday and was puzzled by it all," said Paul. "You know when people are making incoherent comments. I had to scroll for five minutes before someone actually said it. Supposedly it was a random shooting."

"Those shootings are never random," said Lawrence quietly.

Michael heard Lawrence's voice. "What?"

Paul spoke: "Alfie, from college, bro. He was shot. At some club in Hackney."

"What club?"

"Didn't you like his sister?" Allen asked Michael.

"Huh?" blurted Michael.

"Never mind."

"His funeral is tomorrow," said Paul. "I'm not sure where but maybe we turn up? I need to book the day off work."

"When did you last see him? It's not like you were good friends," said Allen.

"Shut up, Allen," said Paul.

"No, you shut up, Paul. You weren't even friends with him at college. And come to think of it, you *were* trying it on with his sister — and she was butters!"

Lawrence and Daniel started laughing. Madyson restrained herself.

"Fuck you, you dick. The guy has just been killed and you want to make jokes," said Paul.

Lawrence and Daniel hushed.

"He's right," said Michael. "I *remember* Alfie — and I didn't like him that much. His sister wasn't a looker, but the guy just got popped and you still want to be funny with it. Not clever."

"Fuck you both," said Allen, sternly. Their views on Alfie were invalid. Both trying to make a point. He stood up. "I'm going to get something to eat. Or are we staying here or moving on?"

Nobody said anything.

"I'm getting some tacos, sod you lot," said Allen.

Madyson nudged Daniel and he smiled back at her. She nudged him again. "I'm getting. I'm getting out, going with Allen," she said.

Daniel moved his legs to the side so she could squeeze out, ignoring how to make it more easier, and courteous, if he stood up first. Madyson shook her head and took Allen's arm as he guided her through the busy pub on the way to the bar.

He'll calm down, thought Michael. *Allen loves to start drama*. He watched them drift from his eyesight until unrecognisable figures appeared before him.

The sound of glasses clinking, being lifted from the table and alcohol slipping down the throats of his friends and brother. He gazed at their faces, determining if they were real, their sentiments similar to his own, did they acknowledge an affinity to his rationale? He couldn't see their eyes, although seated next to and opposite him. He'd been taken to another planet and returned within another body. Finally inhaling, appreciated their patience, settled his thoughts before he said anything.

"Do you know anything else about the shooting?" he asked.

"For an place that's had shootings in the past, you'd think it would have been shut down by now." said Paul. "The third time in three years, someone said."

"No one knows who did it?"

Paul shrugged.

"You know, it was some hood fella," said Lawrence. "Probably beefing about a girl that didn't want him no more, and shot the first nigga in sight." He caught Michael looking at his mouth, not his eyes.

"These black folks gotta learn how to behave," said Paul, as if in agreement. "Every day, I switch on the TV to hear about this stabbing and this shooting — and nothing surprises me when I find out it's some fuckries black yout who ain't learned to control himself yet. Drives me bonkers."

Lawrence put his head down.

"I mean, I don't know if Alfie deserved it, but he *was* an idiot," said Paul. "He shouldn't have been in the club in the first place. It was that *type* of club. A place where dudes and chicks who ain't grown up yet go to..."

Lawrence bit his tongue. He had been to a similar establishment not so long ago and *had* a great time. The clientele wasn't business class but they knew how to get down.

"Those places, man..." said Daniel.

Michael stared at Daniel. "It's not the places, it's the people. There's a stupid acceptance among black people that it's cool to be negative, but ultimately someone like Alfie pays the price." He felt his phone vibrate. He saw Rebecca's name. She'd sent a message. *I can't make it. See you later.* Michael reverted. "It's silly, man. There's something fundamentally wrong with these shootings. It's not a political statement, or any religious fanatic clowning up the place. These guys *really* think they're gangsters. But don't make any money from it. They just shoot each other and have to live with it on their conscience forever, and haven't got any money to distract themselves from going insane about it. Think about it. You *kill* someone — and it's in the news, whatever, whatever, but you have earned *nothing* from it, so you're in the same spot, mentally and financially, as you were before but you know you took someone's life. You get older and you have to carry that around with you all day. It just makes you angry."

Lawrence looked at Michael. His brother wasn't speaking about him but the tone resembled talks they'd had when he was released from prison.

"Every day, I think about my life and experiences and wonder if I can change myself to make things better, but what if I had *shot* and *killed* someone?" said Michael. "Man, that must last a lifetime to get over. But I guess people don't really get over these things, do they?"

Paul took his last bit of drink. "I think if these guys don't get reprimanded on their crimes, then they *don't* care about living with dead people on their consciences. They think they've gotten away with it, or they think the system doesn't care, so they just justify it any way they can in their heads to make their day-to-day existence liveable, you know what I mean?"

Michael nodded. *Right*, he thought. Alfie was probably one of those characters that was just as bad as his killer. The sad thing about the shooting, the victim or the killer *weren't* going to be heralded anytime soon. *Especially in this society.* Not like The Krays. And not for having a story that meant both parties remained poor and the cycle of deprivation continued. *It's a cold-arse world.*

Michael thought about the coltan mineral story, wondering if there was any parallels between the gun crime in London and the civil unrest in Africa that cost plenty of lives. An unsettling and disproportionate number of black lives were being killed and though not proven, it made him think whether the economic plight of trying to achieve Western ideals and quick financial gain was actually working for black people. He hated labelling people into a monolithic group but the overriding experiences of poverty and death he'd seen or heard about from his travels across the world made him contemplate if anything could be done to reverse the negative fate. Whilst many African countries thrived on their own soil, their global positions were ubiquitous, possibly due to colonial imperialism and slave-ridden pasts, the overarching identity of black people across the world was frail. Self-esteem notoriously low and civil war (or cheap gun crime) impeccably high. Michael's own British existence, and the laws the nation held to uphold political unrest, provided a form of protection for him. Not everyone saw this, but the law gave confidence in people to be strong, and it was no coincidence that black people didn't trust the law and those who made legislations. In return, however, this created a worthless mindstate, a mindstate of powerlessness and one that disallowed someone to achieve what they really wanted to achieve. Michael saw Daniel, Lawrence and Paul watching his mind ticking. It was as if they had seen this before. They knew him well and suspected him thinking of a masterplan, perhaps. And they weren't far from the truth. It suddenly hit him. The idea. The thing that was going to alleviate all his worries with society here and abroad. Going to make a change.

"Okay, boys. Gonna do it."

Bemusement riddled their faces.

"Do what?" said Daniel.

"I'm going to make a difference in this world. A real difference. Something where people come together and can believe in."

"What are you talking about?" asked Lawrence, reaching for his phone.

"I'm going back home..."

With tacos and pints of alcohol in hand, Allen and Madyson's gleeful return to the table seemed misplaced. They sensed the mood hadn't changed much since they left, but were puzzled by the smile on Michael's face, and the concern from the others.

"Going home? We *just* got here..." said Allen.

"No, mate. I'm going *back* to Africa..."

Chapter 2

1996

There were no lights on, which meant nobody was home or everybody had gone to sleep. Boy A waited on his thought of a secret surprise party held especially for him to disappear. He could feel the breath of Boy B behind him, a little too close. He sensed a nervousness, and it caused a strange feeling. He didn't want to turn around, fearing Boy B's previous hard stance had turned slightly wimpish. That wasn't the leadership that broke into other people's houses, and it definitely wasn't the leadership he needed for his first major crime.

The petty robbings of chewy confectionary and out-of-date crisps from his local sweet shop seemed like a distant memory. The Asian shopkeeper always sceptical of his size, age and colour, but had a weakness for black women. The shopkeeper's wide grin would emerge when Boy A's mother smiled at the Asian man whilst requesting her daily top-up of cigarettes. It meant Boy A never had to worry about starving on junk food, as a blind eye had taken over the shopkeeper's vision. Thankfully, his mum had *only* participated in banter with the man. His mind interrupted by a whisper from Boy B.

"Ssh. Ssh. Someone is in there."

An extent of realisation to the situation, Boy A paused, looking round him, observing the scene. The property bigger than he had first thought from the front and hadn't predicted its pluralism in size. Usual terrace homes in the area were squashed-up places, with rows of nuclear families swapping rooms to accommodate the lack of space or growth in their size. This gaff appeared to be a four-bedroom wonder. To Boy A it was a peaceful palace, where adequate storage meant adequate spacing and no one complained about bathroom usage or stood shoulder-to-shoulder in any room.

The back of the terrace cottage had strong periodic features, with neat window and door trims, ornate door accents, simple privet hedges and shingle surrounding the garden.

He faced Boy B as if to indicate confusion. Boy B was sweating, perspiration evident on his forehead. Boy A stared for too long, knowing Boy B was bricking it and that tough talk meant nothing.

The air had turned bitter, too.

"We still doing this?" asked Boy A.

Boy B paused. "Yeah, yeah. Of course."

"Sure?"

"Yeah, but we may need to change strategy a bit."

"What do you mean?"

"I mean, instead of us both of us going in straight away, we need to go in one at a time. I'll look out for anything and you give me the all clear once you're in."

Boy A waited before answering. "You not setting me up, blud?"

"Wha? Don't be silly? We *need* to be smart now. Don't want the feds coming in because we didn't think about it. Just in case. Just give me the sign once you're in — and I'll join you."

Boy A sighed. It made sense but, *couldn't he be the lookout?*

"Listen," said Boy B. "It's the best way, truss me. Pop the door window and let us in. Then you can tell me if it's all clear."

Boy B's sweat had evaporated, his nervous stance disappeared. He was the leader again. Boy A's experience faltered, no counter argument to challenge Boy B. They locked eyes, and Boy B raised his eyebrows to indicate seriousness.

"Let's do this," said Boy B.

Boy A looked at the terrace cottage. His throat felt dry.

"The quicker we get this done, we sell the stuff and get paid, fam." It was Boy B. "You with that, blud?"

Boy A knew a cheap motivational speech when he heard one, but there was a point — they were there to get rich. With neighbouring roads and houses brimming in dead silence, the reason why they stood there in the middle of the night waiting to commit an act of breaking and entering on private property was bloody obvious.

Boy A stared back. "Okay, let's do this!"

2018

The new office room was still pretty bland. A recent promotion for Michael meant a new space. But for a cool PR company, and with a name like FirstThing.com, known for its innovative interior design and unique meeting spaces, the segmented office resembled a blank page on a notepad, waiting for a splash of creativity to emerge.

Michael leaned in his chair towards the back of the room, and still had last night's drinks on his mind. He searched on Huddle earlier the coltan video Daniel spoke about and it made for powerful viewing. The irony of it — it had been shot on a mobile phone, too, so its grainy effect worked appropriately with the preacher's rant. The preacher shouted about the killings in West Africa over the urgency to extract the mineral so local tradespeople could make a cheap profit at the expense of others' misfortune.

Michael looked down at his tie, and touched its soft silk fabric. He turned it over to read the labelling and to see where it had been made. No surprise to him that it wasn't from UK soil. Probably a dim sweatshop filled with minimum wage workers. His whole suit probably cost more than their average monthly wages. *But what could he do?* Give three pounds a week through a charity that *also* had to pay its staff twice or three times the amount its recipients received in a year? Or maybe donate a percentage of his earnings to sponsoring a child who lived in a less fortunate environment than he did? But he remained weary that the money would ever reach the intended destination.

Although not growing up rich, he'd seen extreme wealth close up and how those that had it were extremely protective over it. His basketball days had exposed him to businesspeople who had revenue streams beyond what many at that time could attest to. He dreamt of earning such amounts, but it just hadn't been his calling. He believed some people were destined to make obscene amount of cash and the only way the rest of the world could function — was to scramble over whatever amount of money that was left. That is what made the millions of people return to work each day, and it was why he sat in his chair, questioning the origin of his silk tie. *Love it or hate it, the system of wealth isn't going away anytime soon*, and he had to jump on or get left behind. He tapped his laptop screen in front of him, and incoming messages popped up as notifications. He pulled off the convertible screen and reclined further in the chair, admiring the product's metal chassis and 2-in-1 capability. *Pretty soon, they'd invent a computer that attaches to the skin, so they can constantly track your every move.* And while Mindsite showed outrageous video clips of what maybe possible, Michael realised the source of such development was usually not mentioned in such posts. This frustrated him. He touched the screen and opened a message sent to his personal email address. *Madyson*. An email from a friend he'd seen the night before felt odd. The subject was blank and maybe it was a virus, but how could he tell? His years playing basketball meant a lack of computer science knowledge. His browsing history would be cleared when he could, or to remove cookies, but sporting apparel brands still appeared on his searches and as small advert banners. Did he care about it all, maybe not, but he just didn't want his personal information sold to the nearest bidder.

The message from Madyson said she said she wanted to talk, but was vague in description. It bothered him for a moment. She and the guys were in good spirits at the pub, even after his random "Africa" declaration. He admittedly didn't follow up on his Africa thoughts as the tone of the night was borderline depressing. He waivered his sentiments, offering a change of subject, mentioning other holiday plans for the year and if anybody else was interested in tagging along. Cuba to Thailand, and other destinations, did wonders for the evening's vibe, although Lawrence remained low-key all night. Discussion soon turned to the latest movies, and Lawrence didn't contribute. Michael knew when some stories required a complete rewrite and others just had typos. Lawrence needed a complete rewrite. It was the way he described Lawrence to anyone who didn't know his brother. He didn't want to be negative, especially as Lawrence was coming around slowly. Michael used to believe that playing basketball, with trips up and down the country and international games, took him away from his brother and fragmented their close bond. But he realised Lawrence simply hadn't adjusted well to this phase in their lives, and had to stop accepting any blame for his brother's wayward behaviour.

It seemed that jail had taught Lawrence the consequence of his old ways, and to get back on the right track, but he had missed the real world and the changes in it while he was locked up.

Michael read the message from Madyson and was puzzled by it. She said it was good to catch up yesterday and wanted to speak with him. She had something important to share. *Dramatic or serious? Why she couldn't talk about it at the pub?* He half hoped it'd be a declaration of her love for him, but that'd be more of boost to his ego than anything else. The semi-celebrity status Madyson had acquired over the years added to the fantasy. He didn't fancy her like that. He knew some of her track record and knew it was something probably he'd never be able to get over. *She felt the same, so what could be bothering her?* His phone vibrated on his desk. He saw Madyson's name on the small screen. Confusion expanded, and he hoped she had some answers.

"Hey, Mad. What's going on?"

A small pause. "Er, hi Mike."

"Hey, hey. Yeah, it's me. Everything good?"

"I just called to see if you've seen my email?" she said. Michael noticed the quietness of his own office. She sounded alone in a wide, but empty, space.

"Yeah, I saw it, and I'm not sure what is going on."

"Well, I've been thinking about it for a while, and I thought about it a lot last night after we left the pub."

Michael couldn't tell where she was heading or what she was talking about. He checked the time on his laptop. He had a meeting in 20 minutes. "Okay."

"You remember when I talked about being in America and what that experience was like."

"You talk about America all the time."

"I know, but I mean," her voice sounded strained. "When I talk about America and how it big and lonely it was for me when I was out there, and how I thought it would have been more unified."

"Uh-huh."

"I thought about you a lot when I was shooting out there..."

Time wasn't on his side, and he needed her to cut to the chase. "What's up, Madyson? Everything good? I'm not sure..."

"Sorry, if I'm not being clear," she mumbled. "I'm trying to say.. "

He could barely make her voice out. Sounded like she had walked into a coffee shop. "Can't hear you..."

"Michael, I think what you said yesterday was interesting but I wanted to know what you are you going to do?"

"About what?"

"About 'Africa'. About going back. What you said."

Okay. That.

"Yeah, when I was in America and we talked that time about the economy in Africa and how undervalued it is. You remember? I was on a $100 million film set and you were in Ghana telling me about what you saw. It seemed like two different worlds. I sensed you were there yesterday. Am I wrong?"

He caught most of what she said.

"Yeah, I remember that call. Probably most expensive conversation I've had to date..."

She laughed.

"About yesterday, maybe I was drifting again, being a romantic dreamer or whatever, I don't know..."

Something inaudible. She had moved outside the coffee shop. "Do it, Michael. Do..."

His attention switched to his office door, a soft tapping. "Come in," he shouted, when he really should have ended the call with Madyson first. "Sorry, Mad..." he said. Bryan Maddox, the company's managing director poked his head through. "I'll call you later."

"Sure, you better..."

Michael raised his eyebrows to Bryan, indicating his availability. He placed the phone by his laptop and tried to switch his focus from Madyson to Bryan. She had realised the problem the Western world had with Africa, its inability to communicate with the continent on a humane level, not a resource level. During that long phone call, where Michael remembered it as being the longest time he'd spoken with a woman for on an asexual basis, Madyson told him of the constant racial differing she experienced during casting. The naivety that surrounded the poor people, the belief of their predicament disappointing. In comparison to where she and Michael had come from, they had let racism swarm their identity, being everything to their every move. Whereas a diverse city like London meant their lives shared common ground with other races, who simply wanted to get by without persecution or ridicule of their tradition and culture.

"Hello, you there?"

Fuck. He had to move on. He had bills to pay. Saving the world came next. Michael looked at Bryan and smiled.

"Yeah, I'm here. Just a personal call, that's all."

"All good?"

"Yeah."

"Good. We need you ready to tackle Balstec this morning. It's a big deal. Their marketing director is coming as well." Bryan stared at the dull decor in the office, shrugging before sitting down opposite Michael.

"You really can make this room your own, you know?"

Michael nodded with little expression. "I'm ready. Don't worry. Finan has done the deck and I approved it."

"I haven't seen it," said Bryan.

"You don't need to," assured Michael. "I included all the research and our discussion, plus what we'll deliver, and it's really impressive. Finan done a great job with design."

"You sure? She's still... young."

Michael weighed up Bryan's statement, but revoked any meaning from it. Bryan's style hadn't changed since he had first joined the company over three years ago, and still resembled a persona of being a married father of two children.

"New glasses?" Michael asked.

"Yes, you like? The wife actually got them. Just gave her the prescription and boom. Montify. Nice."

Bryan took off his glasses to highlight the quality, but realised he had bigger issues.

"I believe in you, Michael, always have. Let's get that money, please. They'll be here in ten minutes."

Bryan headed to the door. Well groomed as always, he wore smart shirts and trousers. Today being no different. He stepped out into the open plan office, closing Michael's door behind him.

Rubbing his forehead, Michael didn't want the stress to accumulate. He snatched at his laptop and downloaded the meeting's presentation, preparing for Balstec, and £500k that came with winning them over. He had worked with them two years earlier on a TV-led campaign but this time, it was a partnership with Mudderdeep, the obstacle course specialist, which everyone seemed to be talking about these days. The link for Balstec with Mudderdeep was tenuous but the opportunity to spread awareness of its new fitness range was evident and aimed to reach the new bodycentric generation, who gazed at their screens too often instead of being active and moving around. Finan's design was sharp, impeccably detailed and she followed instructions to the tee but Bryan was right — she was young. *Her skin is soft,* he could tell. *An over usage of lotion or something. But she is very pretty, too, and stylish. Straight outta some beauty mag. But damn, she is young... Balstec,* his mind interrupted. *I'm gonna nail this meeting. Balstec. Balstec.*

"What?!" he said aloud as his phone started to ring. Caught between indecision and proaction, he stared at the screen. He answered it, hearing the squeaky tone of Rebecca's voice upon his ear. She was apologising for not turning up at the pub, and wanted to see him after work. The apology came with no explanation of where she'd been instead, and whether he'd seen her text at one in the morning, which said she wasn't coming over. Her timing left Michael neither anger nor disappointed, and because Balstec was waiting, he couldn't divulge his feelings at that time. She felt guilty or thought he was asleep when she texted, as he didn't reply, and by calling him now it would clear her conscience.

"Yeah, baby, that'd be good. See you then." He said goodbye and hung up, smiling to himself and lifted his long frame out of the chair. Bases covered so far this morning. He had a meeting now to attend to.

Something about playing basketball that relaxed Michael like nothing else. Maybe due to the many years he'd given to the sport or the ability he found to simultaneously excel at the craft, whilst eliminating all the cares in his world, albeit on a temporary basis. He picked up a loose ball at his local sports centre in Deptford and bounced it on the floor a few times. He had never truly understood how such things as running, passing and shooting could remove other experiences from his mind. Perhaps concentration of being a good teammate and a better defender meant the daily occupations of his mind took a backseat. The meeting with Balstec had gone really well and they appeared to be happy with the presentation and the minimum level of guaranteed video and page views, and other tracking metrics they could report on. He remembered watching Finan walk past the boardroom while he was presenting and she stared at her design. She directed her smile at him and placed her eyes down, continuing through the office. Bryan sat in the corner of the room, smug, knowing another six-figure deal was coming in shortly. It was all easy for him.

"Haven't seen you in a while, son?"

Michael recognised the voice but his vision appeared to take a while to catch up.

"Yeah, been busy with work and other things," he said, aiming to use his reply as a way to build more time. "My knee was playing up a bit..." *It's Yemi. Bloody Yemi. Crikey, he's put on some pounds.*

Yemi stood a couple of inches shorter than Michael but a little wider around the middle area. He'd known Yemi for a few years through scrimmages and after-hoops drinks. Yemi was nowhere near as skilled as Michael on the court but he was more vocal, and used the chance to compete with like-minded individuals where his daytime job didn't allow. He worked in the IT department for a private equity company in the city somewhere. To Michael it sounded boring, yet Yemi was cool and well-travelled. He had plenty of stories and made Michael laugh. However, when Michael didn't play basketball, Yemi's invites were hardly accepted, as they normally clashed with Paul, Allen or even Daniel's arrangements, and Michael wasn't sure if Yemi's humour would translate to his group of friends. It wasn't intentional, just a feeling.

"I hear you," said Yemi. "I've just come back from Nigeria and haven't played in a while. Need to get rid of some of this excess."

Michael withdrew any comment. He grabbed a nearby ball and started dribbling. Michael could tell Yemi's handling skills were a direct result of being away from the court. It amused Michael how basketball often held a parrallel outcome with life, proving that mastering the basics were necessary to achieving your ultimate success. So thankful he had learned the game early, as the experiences that followed immediately won him plaudits from all basketball people he came in touch with. Other players, coaches and teams he wasn't familiar with, all applauded Michael when they saw him play, and for teammates, it felt easier to be part of his team and allowed him to take a leadership role. When he retired from playing, he knew office life would be another challenge. It required similar mastering — and the number one challenge: *communication*. In basketball, he could dribble, shoot and pass very well without verbally directing his thoughts. However, the office, a sharp grasp of the English language was more than essential. Eighty percent of everything was comms with technical skills taking the other twenty percent. The corporation set up of FirstThing.com followed most businesses with its hierarchical structure, and reporting to your boss, and that boss reporting to another boss. Not far removed from a feudal system and the media influence, communication and skills that came with it were more common and niche at the same time.

Michael watched Yemi try a jumpshot and the ball swished through the net. *Maybe he's a better player than I give him credit for.* Michael looked at the ball in his hands and shot it from 30 feet, watched it clank off the rim. More practice needed. The scrimmage with the other fourteen guys didn't relieve his mind like he thought it would. Sporadic thoughts of Rebecca and what was going on her; his daughter and her adolescence and how she was giving her mother constant headaches and wouldn't listen to him as he rarely saw her. Then, Lawrence, and the stress their parents seemed to have about his brother and how it usually involved money. Michael missed a lay-up, and thought about the Balstec deal and what it meant to the firm. He threw back his head in disgust as he used to finish lay-ups with complete ease. Age and lack of regard was catching up to his passion for the game. Outside influences coming to the forefront of his attention, his concentration slipping. He saw Yemi looking over and Michael felt worse than he did before. He was letting his team down.

Michael sat on his sofa later that evening with a bruised ego and stared at the news channel on the TV. They'd lost the scrimmage and he was responsible. They would get over it, he knew, but he wouldn't get to sleep any faster than usual. He was tired and had a busy day in the office the following day. His eyelids threatened to close as he heard his mobile vibrate. Daniel sent him a message. He would read it later, but the thought of Daniel reminded him of the coltan video. He searched across the site on his phone to watch it again and couldn't find it. He found another video that had been shared from one of his old school friends, who hadn't grown old gracefully. The video was supposed to be a funny, and called *'How Jamaicans celebrate the good news of a new job offer'*. A mish-mash of different situations where Jamaicans were acting outlandish, or downright silly, the point of it to show the difference in social behaviour from the normal. Michael didn't find it funny. Something about the 400k views the video had attained, the numerous comments that said, "That's hilarious!" or the 200k likes it amassed. Maybe seeing a young girl in tight spandex in a club dancing provocatively, or watching the man run into a convenience store and shoot randomly at people inside it, or maybe lastly, the cool elderly man who sat on the beach smoking a joint blowing smoke into the air, which made Michael angry. Casual and perpetual stereotypes for cheap laughs was one thing, but the cultural acceptance of what it compared itself to that concerned Michael. If British people were doing the same thing, the same type of video would not have attracted these numbers of views. And they surely wouldn't like being the butt of the joke, too. This *wasn't* an isolated case, of course. The Jamaican video was only funny to people because they were used to seeing such stereotypes everywhere, be it media or their immediate surroundings. It was often a manifestation of what the mind wanted to believe was true. Michael felt sure people didn't have the opportunity to view Jamaicans as anything else than what was portrayed through their own mediums of choice or limited interactions, so what else could they think even if they knew the truth was stereotypical, it was the *only truth* they knew?

He sighed heavily. Something had to be done. He hated being a passive consumer. Remembering how an ex-colleague had mentioned about starting a petition for a youth curfew in her local constituency of Orpington after her local council had not acted on her requests. Michael marvelled at her tenacity to eliminate the frustration she had with not being able to get a good night's sleep due to kids hosting regular freestyle rap battles outside her house until early in the morning. She left the company so he never found whether her petition was successful or not.

He typed 'petition' and 'Parliament' into Huddle's search engine and found a page: a website that requested signatures to take to Downing Street and make a difference on a long list of concerns. Michael realised his 'issue' belonged here as well, but he had to see if anybody else, apart from Madyson, felt like he was feeling, and this meant building up some awareness of it.

He paused, then crawled Huddle for a decent hosting platform that could accommodate his requirements. He found one. It looked perfect, and included multiple modules that offered personisation and data capture in its package. He decided quickly on a domain name and signed up.

For the next few hours, his tiredness passed and he developed the website to where its basic function could be easily understood, from the

Home, About Us to its Contact Us pages. Michael had worked on the FirstThing.com site before, but ensured the navigation on his own site was more simple. He yawned, realising he would need to go back to work soon. He couldn't manage an early start, so he'd finish the site first and then worry about work second. He sat up from his laptop and smiled. While it didn't have everything he would like from a website, it had what he wanted. He stood up, walked to his kitchen, pulled open his fridge door, staring at his orange juice and wondered if creating a petition-led site asking for the movement of black people to go back to Africa was the right thing to do. He took a quick sip, nodding to himself. It needed to be done. He just needed to promote it, but where? His phone on the living room table vibrated, and it gave him an idea. Logging back into Mindsite, Michael wrote a quick message and added the hyperlink that would connect directly to his petition website. He would wait and see whether people agreed with him or not. He also did similar messages on Postya and Javaload, limited characters and photo social media channels. He slumped back onto his sofa, finally accepting he had to sleep, but there was tapping at his door. Michael sighed softly and stretched his body towards the door.

"Hello," he said.

"It's me," Rebecca said.

Michael opened the door to see his girlfriend wearing her favourite coat. He duly observed the fact she wasn't wearing any clothes under it. Rebecca smiled at him, dropping the coat on the floor as she entered the flat, and Michael accepted to himself that he wasn't going to make his morning meeting.

Chapter 3

1996

The garden path neatly decorated and cobbled. Boy A tried to imagine the type of person who spent hours worrying about the pebble arrangements that would only be stepped on time and time again. Nobody. His vision subdued, and it came up empty. He opened the garden gate, surprised there was no lock on it, but Boy B had told him not all of these places would be locked, and the probability served them right. Boy A, however, put two and two together, and said it meant a higher chance of somebody being at home.

"Don't worry," said Boy B. "You worry too much."

Boy A nodded, but not in agreement. *Let's get it over with.* He pushed the gate softly, worried his trainers would make noise against the cobbled path. No indication of movement from inside the cottage. The well-groomed, yet small, garden that occupied adjacent sides of the path caught his attention. The gnomes felt too common but added some humour. Raked free of weeds, he saw the early sprouting of daffodils and tulips. A loose stone hitting the door just ahead of him made Boy A take note of where he was. The garden blurred in his peripheral and the darkness of the early hours provided the reality check. Walking to the door, he saw his breath steam up the glass pane as he approached it. The inside of the house still not visible, and he wondered how he would get in. He gripped the door handle, and smiled.

Locked. He dug into his pocket, pulling out a large stone. Large enough to cover his palm but small enough not to cause a messy infringement to the property. Or so. Only one way. Closing his eyes as he did it wasn't the best idea but the given effect worked. The door's glass smashed loudly against the empty silence of the night. He turned to look for Boy B, but he couldn't see anything. *Run back and ask what was happening?* But it had started: a crime being committed and it made little sense to leave the scene. *He wasn't a pussy.* The glass besides his feet seemed thick, the stone that cracked it sat next to the shattered solid. He bent down, a drip of blood on his hand as he picked up the stone. He put the stone back into his pocket. The door's damage wasn't vast, allowing Boy A's hand to slip through and grab the handle from the inside. He jerked at the handle twice, adjoined by the key below it, and smirked when the door unlocked. Looking back, he saw Boy B smiling, but his inaccuracy of the teeth reflection was actually an approaching light. Boy A dived on the garden surface, as the light drifted past. He inhaled when the noise that accompanied the light stopped, too, turning the light off. A door slammed, and he listened as footsteps trickled off into the opposite direction. He stood up and looked around, wondering when his time was up. *I'm making a mistake.* The unforgiving stance of his mum jumped to the front of his mind, and she told him it was wrong. He studied the damage and realised the serious trouble he'd be in if he was caught. But he had a weight of adrenalin running through him, which he loved, and he wanted to go inside the cottage and take what could be his. His face reflected off the glass door and it marginally made out his dark skin. He froze as a body approached him. It slid through the gate and moved quickly. *Shit, I'm done.* He couldn't make out the face to this body fast enough, and his reaction too slow. A hand rested on his shoulder.

"Bruv, nice job," said Boy B. "We're in. Let's do this!"

2018

There was something about Mindsite that bugged Allen. Addictive in its premise, finding his family and friends, seeing what the heck they were up to when he wasn't speaking to them. But the flipside, where *all* their intimate details were shared, you had no real control over censoring them. Just the other day, he found himself ogling his own cousin's party dress cleavage, zooming in on her unmistakably large breasts. He felt dirty staring, but kept checking her profile to see if she'd uploaded any similar posts. Any phone call or family gathering with his cousin wouldn't result in such sexual atonement, but that was the power of the web, and the power it had over him.

Early in the morning and he scrolled through his Mindsite feed at the office. He left home earlier than usual, to be ahead of the office noise that would filter through in an hour's time. It was also so he didn't have to speak with his fiancée. Whether the fault was his that their relationship was faltering he hadn't fully acknowledged. He just knew something was missing. The lack of date nights, perhaps, since the youngest child had been born, or maybe, the changing landscape of the publishing industry where he worked — and he *had* to change his skills without accepting a higher wage.

Or because he worked at a women's magazine and the daily sight of young, sprightly women confused the heck out of him and the choices he made with his fiancée. It had to be fixed, he sighed, even if just for the children's sake. He stopped scrolling. *Michael.* Michael's early morning post caught his attention. As with most Mindsite posts, the vague nature was common, but it was more than the normal update, shared video or selfie photo. It was a call to arms. A request to join Michael in something. Allen smiled, knowing Michael's character would do something like this. He liked the link that was added as it showed the website's homepage image — a silhouetted image of a group of men and women walking somewhere, anywhere. Symbolic of the site's name, goingbackhomesoon.org — and he clicked the link. Impressed by the effort put into the site, and its objective dawned on him, and what Michael was asking people to do. Michael wanted people, *black people*, to go to Africa and reinvest their lives there, so they could escape the judgment and prejudice and anxiety of being black, and focus on developing a nation of independence, freedom and self worth. The tagline under the site's name made Allen nod. The effectiveness of its simplicity. *'Making the change today because our history depends on it... Sign up now!'*

A form, a petition of some sort, requesting the names, email addresses and opt-in check boxes, so the user could be affiliated with the program and align with Michael's website and its requirements.

Allen wondered if Michael really knew the extent of what he was asking. He clicked back to Michael's post and noticed a few likes and comments under it. The likes were minimal and probably close relatives, who liked everything their family posted. The comments, though, made Allen sit up straight. Five comments in total and he didn't recognise who had sent them. One person was clearly in favour of Michael's appeal and had been thinking of something similar. Allen read it a couple of times to fully understand its sentiment, but the level of agreement rang loud.

"Gwan, bro. You out there. Been meaning to rep the manor with something like this for awhile. Believe we need it. Our people need this, playa. Truss. I'mma sign up, spread the word cos ain't nobody gonna help us but us, for real, fam. I can't believe you started it, though. In school, you were way off the Africa tip. Glad that you came round. Blessed..."

It frustrated Allen slightly because he still didn't recognise the person who made the comment. He jumped onto the next ones.

"I'm in," said one.

"Sorry, this is a mistake," said the other.

"I agree!" mentioned a professional basketball player, and the last comment simply had weird emoticons. Allen felt confusion. As a friend, should he click the like button each time a good friend posted something or should he pretend he hadn't seen it? The important social media question: *do you act as the voyeur or the participant even if you're not sure of how to behave?* He tapped the like button and felt better for doing so, and wondered what next Michael had in store. A group of young women walked into the office and Allen closed the page, and trawled through his email.

"Someone's in early, ladies," said Carrie Anderton, as she passed his desk. "Must be up to something!"

The other women, Bridget and Katherine, and both worked on the beauty team of the magazine, laughed in chorus, raising their pitches simultaneously and stopping at the same moment. Carrie flicked her hair back and caught Allen's eye as she reached her desk. They locked eyes for a small spell, Allen not knowing its significance. Carrie flirted with the best of them, but was also fiercely intelligent, which she clearly demonstrated, especially when wearing the tightest of outfits. Being one of two men on a floor of solely women meant Allen would dissect everything twice before responding and this left him vulnerable for pranks they often liked to pull. Down for the cause he was, but the ladies overtly didn't give a shit about it — they were just enjoying themselves, and even though he tried, he wasn't a natural fit with the magazine. Was it years believing stereotypes that he knew little of than to morally licence his thoughts, but deeply believe something else? He wanted at first to have sex with half of the women on the floor but this interest deflated once he got to know them, and it appeared they were becoming more interested in him. Allen's subconscious rattled, knowing he should have been able to adapt internally to whatever he appeared to be displaying externally. It is hard being this cool, he often thought.

At that moment, the creative solutions director, advertising manager and senior sales executive of the magazine all strolled in, whispering about something they had seen. Allen took note of their superiority to one another and how their strides replicated that.

"Morning, Allen" said Lucy, the creative solutions director.

"Morning, Lucy," he said, avoiding eye contact.

Lucy was around the same age as Allen but had worked at the magazine for a longer period. She commanded an astute level of respect whenever she had a conversation, and despite her petite frame, sad eyes and long blonde hair, she was always immaculately dressed, and keen to make a strong first impression. Allen didn't fancy her one bit, but genuinely liked her, and as she'd hired him in the first place, but more so, because her aura was still inviting. The advertising manager and sales executive departed ways and headed off to their desks without saying hello, as if Lucy's greeting had spoken for all of them.

Allen paced through his ascending list of emails, tackling the context within them and responding where applicable. One message had him leaving the email via a link and opening up his browser onto a Squareview page. He recognised the corporate branding of the site and remembered its early days before it became the internet's baby for viewing short-form video from. *The lack of advertising, lack of video description and lack of thumbnails that didn't resemble any part of the video footage.* He smiled as the video auto-played, showcasing a recent project he was working on. He couldn't see the error the video editor had addressed on the email, and he wondered if anyone else would. Allen sensed it could be a niggly issue that wouldn't disappear if he didn't confront it. Such were the perks of his role. A quick gust of air blew past him and a familiar lavender scent hindered his senses. It was her. *Maya.* He knew before he even raised his head. She just smelled fantastic. *Shit,* he realised, and he looked up — and yep, there she was. Tall, slim, and great legs emphasised whenever she had the opportunity; the prettiest face in the office; and dyed hair that matched her complexion and attitude. They had made small talk in the nearby kitchen and he knew her name, and he had now turned this conversation into a full-blown fantasy he was struggling to contain.

He watched her head to the kitchen as she did each morning, but her stride differed from normal. Casual blue jeans, a smart jacket, which covered a loose blouse, he knew the cause was something he'd probably said. That stupid email he shouldn't have sent her. The one where he said she was beautiful and definitely worthy of such complimentary attention, and how she had "won the most dazzling and stylish award of the week", but really was a fictionious award he had created. He listened as Maya spoke with Bridget and Katherine in the kitchen, and sensed it wrong for doing so, as the commonality of their personal lives became a talking point. Allen tuned out when girlie laugh swamped the conversation, and he couldn't figure out *why* they were laughing. He turned back to the computer in front of him. A wry smile flew from Lucy from her desk and he wondered its meaning. An account manager at an agency he disliked with a passion popped up on his inbox and he wanted to ignore her message.

"Hey, bro," she said. "You okay?"

Could have been anybody, but the warmth of her tone reminded him of who it was, and how she had approached him in a similarly surprised fashion. Allen turned to face her and Maya's smiling expression gazed directly at him. *Gosh, she's pretty, no question.* But he played it cool and returned the smile, nodding before he spoke.

"I'm good. How's you?"

She sat down on the vacant chair beside him that his freelance designer would be sitting in. Her body language relaxed and open, inviting. Allen swirled round to face her directly. He heard Lucy coughing in the background but ignored it. He glared at Maya's face, examining its detail, her nose, soft lips, light makeup around her eyes and minimal foundation on her skin. He wanted to reach over right there and then. She touched his knee. He didn't look down and kept eye contact with her.

"Allen, I've been thinking about you, and then I got your email. It was funny. Thank you for sending it."

"No worries. I meant every word."

"But you shouldn't have."

"Why not?"

She stopped herself before answering. She stood up and looked at him. "I gotta go. See you later."

"But..." She was gone. Allen watched her disappear and returned back to his computer, trying to take Maya off his mind, which felt impossible, and not appropriate as he checked a new text message from his fiancée asking whether all was fine when he dropped the kids off at school.

The difference between his and Bryan's office was noticeable. The decor, for one, showed an akin sense of meticulousness and personality, whilst the space was almost twice the size of Michael's. A new poster, highlighting the company's new mantra, 'We get stuff done... properly', on the largest wall. The sentiment lost and ironic to the recent campaigns several ad executives had trouble executing, and consequently, the clients hadn't requested their continued services. *The font on the poster is wrong*, too large in places, and the company logo too small. He assumed Finan had designed it, but the quality was beneath her talents. A voice spoke to him.

"So, Michael. Good news on Balstec. Partnership with Mudderdeep has been signed, and they're sending us the purchase order details today. It seems you still have the magic touch."

Bryan profusely smiled, cheekbones stretching in length. From behind the desk and laptop, Bryan could hardly be seen but it didn't matter. Michael liked the compliment, appreciating the reason why he got paid in the first place. He had a way with clients who required respect and a level of guaranteed leadership for their projects. It helped that the campaign's vision, and benchmark results offered, would win over the high profile clients every time. Michael touched the armrest of his chair, a quiet confidence surrounding him.

"One thing, though, Mike," said Bryan.

The change in tone made Michael sit up straight. He saw Bryan avoiding his stare, and tried to think where this was heading.

"The *Mindsite post* you made last night..."

A quizzical stare from Michael suggested he didn't understand.

"... 'The African one'. About joining the site you put together."

Michael nodded.

"I got the intention of it, to rally people to help out Africa. It's admirable, but you know you have to be careful with posts like that."

"I'm not sure if I know what you mean. "Be careful...""

"Well, what if someone from Balstec saw it, and thought you had an hidden agenda..." said Bryan.

"Agenda against what?" Michael simmered any anger in his voice.

"It doesn't matter 'what', does it?" Bryan moved from behind his desk and walked to the free chair adjacent to Michael's. "We've discussed this in the pub plenty of times about social media and its possible implications. I'm just trying to make sure that the purchase order has no disclaimers or conditions against us, which ultimately jeopardises the value of the deal."

Michael looked down at the floor. The carpet was cleaner than the one in his office, and he sensed a theme of discrimination.

"Bryan, the post was personal and the website is personal. Has nothing to do with FirstThing.com, you can see that. It's my thing, anyone can see that."

Michael felt his phone vibrate in his pocket as he spoke.

"I'm just saying, this isn't good for *business*," said Bryan. "That's what I mean. You know what I mean, right?"

It is something about having conversations with the person who hired you where they feel like they're responsible for your actions, made Michael laugh internally. Was Bryan putting him on this foray of interest to ensure the bigger picture was addressed? Michael knew FirstThing.com had nothing to worry about. And he *wasn't* stupid.

"Okay, cool. I trust you," said Bryan, "and the site looks really good..."

Michael shook his head, disappointed by Bryan's stance. "Can I go? I've got *business* to attend to..."

"Michael. Hey, don't be like that!"

Michael left the room, feeling the anger wash over him. Sure, Bryan had a point but there had to be a cut-off point between work and personal life, and he wished he'd never accepted Bryan's friend request in the first place, and then Bryan wouldn't have seen the post. *But I shouldn't fear the outcome of the post as this was the reason I set up the site: to gain attention to my cause.* He just had to get the right people to sign up first.

Reaching his office room, he checked his phone and saw a few Mindsite notifications, more than he usually received. There was also a text message from his daughter, Shanice. He tapped at his phone and opened her message.

"Dad, please call me. I need to talk."

Stress lines formed on his forehead, and this message could mean anything. Michael knew being a parent before actually becoming a parent would leave him vulnerable to the child's demands, but the unpredictability of their requests was something that only experience could explain. The years of Shanice's growth had flown by and he was lucky her mother appeared content with their situation, despite living in separate cities. Distracted, he tapped open Mindsite and saw people responding to his post about returning back to Africa. He smiled as he saw 'a like' from Allen and other old friends he hadn't seen since school. Most comments that accompanied the likes were positive, and there were more than he expected. Sitting down by his desk, Michael remembered Shanice and dialled her number.

A long pause filled the air after the ringing stopped and Michael waited for Shanice to speak. When she answered, she sounded winded and distant.

"Hi Dad," she said.

"Shan, you okay?" Michael said. "What's up? Everything okay?"

Hearing her call him Dad still gave him chills. Something great and grotesque about it. Probably the separation with her mother meant it felt strange than perhaps if he heard it every day and was around her regularly, it wouldn't be a thing, but it was. *A small one though*, he registered, before returning to the phone call.

"It's the school, Dad. The school..."

"What about the school, honey?"

"*They're* picking on me. All of them."

Michael leaned back in his chair. "What? All of them. Don't be silly. You love that school. You've been there for years..." But his rationale was frail, and she could have been going through anything at the school — and he wouldn't have a clue. Very rare was the moment when his ex-girlfriend shared information about their daughter, and in turn, it had rubbed off on Shanice. She never told him anything...

"Did you hear me, Dad?"

"Yes, but why am I only hearing about it now?"

"It's never been this bad... A new girl has joined our class and she started it, and now they all think it's funny. I don't know what to do."

"You told Mum?"

"Of course, I have but I couldn't worry her anymore than I have."

She was 14, smart and pretty. He was sure she had friends at school.

"When you say, 'picking on you,'" said Michael. "What exactly are they doing and saying?"

Shanice hesitated. "They call me 'white girl.'"

Michael paused, inclined to laugh. But stopped himself. Shanice had a darker skin complexion than his own, and this meant the bullies were being sarcastic. *Why*, he didn't get it, but given the way she had been raised, it kinda made sense. Polite, well-spoken, articulate, an excellent student and most of all, attractive to the eye. Michael was lucky to have such a daughter but clearly not everything could be as perfect.

"They what?" he said.

"They see me by the cloakroom every morning and crowd and shout, "White girl, white girl, ooh, how's the white girl?" And I hate it, Daddy. I hate it."

He could sense the tears building up from her voice. He had to do something.

"Should I speak to your headteacher?"

"No."

"Well, what's the solution?"

"I don't know," she said.

Michael sighed. "I think you do. You wouldn't have come to me unless you needed me to do something."

A short pause. "Can you please talk to this girl's parents? That's the only way I can get through to her..."

It's a good idea, he admitted, but the distance she lived meant missing a day or so from work. He would have to call them.

"Have you got their number?" he asked, assuming she hadn't.

"Yeah, it's...."

Michael laughed quietly as she relayed the numbers to him. She had it all planned out for him. More notifications on his phone from Mindsite and Postya. Bryan walked past his office, grinned, but a recurring feeling of cynicism took shape. Michael hung up the phone and wondered if Shanice's mother really knew what was going on. He doubted it.

It was a strange location for Daniel to be meeting Paul, and paying for his cappuccino at a well-known coffee shop in central London was inconspicuous and weirdly discreet. Paul raised his cup as they made eye contact and headed over to the quiet section in the corner.

"So, what do you think about Michael's post and website?" asked Paul.

"It is what it is," said Daniel, "but sounds like he was inspired by our linkage the other day. Is that why you said we meet here?"

"Yes, and no."

Daniel took a sip of his coffee and questioned the loyalty of Paul to Michael, contemplating if a hidden agenda was reality or fiction.

"What I mean by that is, I see why he thinks this is the best idea for inspiring black people to rise up and take a hold of their lives and reinvent themselves, blah blah, but I don't..."

"What?" said Daniel.

"I don't think he's thought it through properly. The ramifications of these posts could be devastating."

Daniel watched Paul's mouth and caught a glimpse of a sharply yellow-coloured tooth among the relatively white others. As usual, Paul was wrapped in a tight-fitting suit that made the veins in his neck more noticeable. Daniel thought he was overreacting, even if there seemed to be relevant point.

"How's Helen and Jamie?" asked Daniel.

Paul caught Daniel's eyes, puzzled by the move. He had known Daniel for close to twenty years, but admittedly hadn't gotten as close as he did with Michael. Daniel was *always there*, but the input to Paul's life wasn't substantial and because of that, they only linked up when the group was doing something. Michael introduced Daniel to him back in college, and although Paul accepted Daniel, they'd never naturally bonded.

"Why are you asking?" Paul said.

"Why not?" Daniel said.

Paul rolled his eyes. "I didn't invite you to Jamie's birthday party for a reason."

"What does that mean?"

"You know what that means. Let's not pretend we're tight," said Paul, looking directly at Daniel.

Daniel coughed quietly at the statement, the frankness of it, but also the reality of it. He disliked Paul for this very reason. He didn't respect the guy for it, either.

"I just want to make sure this doesn't get out of hand. You know what type of environment Michael works in and I don't want any publicity for his cause to blow up and we're in the press defending his actions, especially when it's something as silly as this."

Daniel ignored his personal feelings for Paul and thought about it. He nodded.

"Yeah, I agree. I won't be encouraging it. You seen how many likes the post has got?"

"No, but I suspect it's measly cos most of his posts are basketball related and his circles are tightly matched to his interests." said Paul, "but you never know in this day and age."

Daniel nodded again. He watched the cashier argue with a customer about the change she'd given him.

"We are people with influence so what he says can affect our professions and that's the last thing either of us needs."

Daniel thought about it and again, *Paul is right.* It would be a nightmare if his personal life was exposed in the tabloids or on some dutty website. To be on a quick headline or in some badly-written gossip-fuelled blog wouldn't be ideal, especially as he couldn't picture his big body being a part of anyone's trending topics.

"I hear you," said Daniel, thinking about his kids and their mothers, thinking he had more cash now that his face was in the media, and not as a whimsical journalist who wrote quick-fix stories for a poor salary.

Paul held out his palm for an understanding of their potential situation and that they were in it together. Daniel shook his head before allowing their hands to clasp with each other's. This was the reason why they were in a coffee shop during lunch and going behind their friend's back.

Chapter 4

1996

He could feel the draught of squeezed air touching his neck from the broken door glass. He realised he couldn't reverse the situation now. *We're criminals and we'll get locked up for this.* He made eye contact with Boy B, and it came back to him. They were there for a reason: a reason that should have never left his conscience — to get paid... *by any means.* He'd been dealt life's unfortunate hand and only had one way to rectify that. That was to take it. Take whatever he could.

Boy B nodded. They were in it now, and all previous and future hanging-outs would be defined by this point.

Boy A felt Boy B looking right through him. A stance he didn't recognise, or his level of inexperience was somehow overwhelming him.

In his zone, Boy B oozed readiness to take whatever he could. He pointed to something. Boy A turned towards the kitchen floor and followed the direction of Boy B's fingers. There, in the corner of the room, were shopping bags. Boy A's eyebrows raised, apprehensive. Boy B pointed furiously at the bags, then shrugged when Boy A displayed ignorance to his request.

The kitchen itself sparse, yet huge in size. The usual hob, sink, and white goods surrounded the boys. The fridge held dominance in the room. Awkwardly placed next to the washing machine, and at a 30 degree angle instead of alignment with the rest of the kitchen, the fridge stood out like an afterthought.

He couldn't wait so Boy B moved past Boy A and approached his target. He headed to the corner of the room where the bags were. Stopping next to the bags, he faced Boy A. Then pointed down and huffed quietly to emphasise.

Boy A stared profusely, acknowledging any recognition also meant admitted ignorance. He continued to stare at Boy B.

Boy B was unsure of what Boy A was doing, but didn't have to time to dissect its meaning. *We have to grab the goods and get out.* Bending down, he picked up one of the bags, and threw it over to Boy A. Boy A stumbly caught it, making a ruffled noise in the process. Boy B could feel a sense of aggravation building but determined to not let it come through. He picked up another bag, and grimaced. Heavy and he slipped his hand inside it. A bottle of something lay inside the bag. Boy A watched, puzzled, and held the bag that Boy B had thrown, pending instructions from his accomplice. Boy B held up the product, a bottle of bleach. He dropped it hastily on the floor as if with disgust.

"Come on," he muttered, to no one. The bleach had a small leak and liquid ran passively along the wooden floor.

Boy B avoided Boy A's eyes and grabbed an expensive-looking ashtray on the cooking surface next to the sink. He presumed it was made of marble and worth a decent penny. He dropped it into the bag, unaware of its slightly bleach-soaked interior.

Boy A waited and continued to watch, noting Boy B wasn't the leader he'd hoped for. The whole strategy of "just get something" felt too loose. What is "something" exactly? He scanned the large kitchen, wishful his eyes connected with something valuable, but beyond the dried dishes and other pieces of cutlery, it remained unclear what was worth attaining. Boy B, however, grabbed a couple of knives and forks from the drawers, and then a crystallised drinking glass from the dishrack. The glass didn't shatter when inserted into the bag but its presence seemed noisy.

"Hello, is anyone there?"

Boy B flinched, dropping the bag and appropriately made more noise. Boy A froze. They looked over at each other, trying to read their minds, and scanning the kitchen for a hiding place. The kitchen was pretty much the worst part of the house they could have been in if they were trying to be discreet. Alongside the whistling breeze of wind that continued to blow loudly through the door's cracked window.

"Shit," mouthed Boy B. He was panicking. He searched for the closest weapon.

The voice said again... "Hello."

It came from upstairs, near the landing. Distant, yet close enough to be audible. The boys recognised a man's tone, meaning they were in for it, and there were only two ways out of the situation: fight or make a run for it. Boy B now held a knife in his hand and nodded to Boy A. Still wanting to fulfil their midnight activity, and if that meant blood on his hands, then so be it, thought Boy B. His face grew menacing, like a caricature was overtaking his body. His stance firm, a fist clenched, with a sharp butter knife, pointed with directness and an assigned meaning.

Boy A stood confused. His mother kept entering his thoughts. She was shaking her head. She hadn't raised him this way. *It isn't going to end like this.*

"Hello, is anyone th...?"

Funnily enough, and while it wasn't a funny situation, it was one that didn't end in a death or one where anybody got seriously hurt. The voice belonged to the man of the house; a tall and skinny barrister, who that day had assisted in sending a group of young black men to life in prison. The evidence of them killing a young boy made it clear and easy to identify the crime, but the irony of his new predicament wasn't lost on him. He mumbled and murmured his innocence, but he wasn't innocent. He wasn't even relevant. He was just in the wrong place at the wrong time. It was that simple. As he entered the kitchen, he saw Boy B standing directly at him, and wished he had a chance to defend himself. He wished he brought his cricket bat up off the hallway floor, as he initially thought. The noises in the kitchen he heard, though, weren't real. Every night noises occurred. But here he stood — the noise had faces... dark ones. Scary ones. One had a knife, the other had a bleeding hand. *Shit.* He tried to talk money, tried to explain why it wasn't worth throwing their lives away for, and that there, of course, was nothing expensive in the house. *Everything is in the bank.* They didn't listen. They saw him trembling. They heard him stammering. And somehow within the next five minutes, the two boys forced him to stop talking, to stop moving away from them, to keep his hands high and get on his knees like a dog. But he didn't have a chance to bark, as Boy A presumed was coming next, because Boy B had already lifted the man's leg and kicked the man in the face. The man dropped to the floor with an ungratifying thud, body slouched uncomfortably, unexpecting the blow.

Boy A sensed his initiative forming and when he moved to a drawer and spotted the duct tape and string, his purpose was at last unveiled. The enjoyment of tying up the old fella as he remained unconscious was something he didn't expect. Boy B blinked with approval and Boy A half-smiled. He felt good. They had taken out the main obstacle to prevent them getting their immediate riches, meaning the rest of the night would be easier.

So they continued. The boys were expecting the man's wife or somebody else to follow up, and to see what had happened to the man. But there was nothing. Not a peep. Maybe he lived alone. The boys grinned, picked up the bags and began filling them up as quickly as they could with hand towels, napkins, bowls, knives, platter dishes, mortar and pestle, an immersion blender and a hand mixer. The man won't stay tied up for long, they knew that much.

Boy A headed out of kitchen and saw the size of the living room and quietly gasped. He'd never been in one so large. Its size reminded him of his school classroom without the 30 pupils in it. Boy B followed behind, registering a lethargic gaze, knowing the man had taken some of their energy. Boy B opened up a bag and grabbed at the nearest object; a picture of the barrister and his young family.

2018

Simon Thomas, the Balstec CEO, sat in his velvet sofa, rubbing its fabric tenderly. He looked at Michael in admiration but his expression didn't show it. Since the meeting at FirstThing.com, they had spoken a few times on the phone, and Michael hadn't displayed any intimidation towards his position, and as someone who had the power to sign off a £500k deal in one afternoon. Simon had researched and analysed FirstThing.com, but Michael's quiet assurance it would deliver the campaign's targeted reach offered him more confidence in the organisation. And why wouldn't it? The presentation was just the initial phase of the partnership and as the year progressed, more developments and activity confirmation would mean further revenue and holistic opportunities.

"So, Michael, how do you anticipate the year blooming out for our campaign? The problem we have is that we need to coordinate the operation of Mudderdeep so it's in-line with our bigger plans. Then we have to check with the proposed media owner to confirm their brands are onboard. I need the circulation and digital figures."

Michael smiled confidently. The media owner, Subject Publishing, which he'd secured for the campaign, was a reputed UK publisher that had seen massive spikes in its digital business since selling off its print titles. Subject was known for its search page ranking as well as its unique high-impact ad formats. The insightful pieces of fitness content that spurred on its quality SEO was bound to resonate with Balstec's target market.

"Simon, we're more than on it. I recently sent over the benchmarks and guaranteed figures from Subject, and from other projects we've done with them, they're on it, too. Their retargeting, dark social, first and third data plans are all solid. They respond quickly to optimise change and their delivery is precise and professional. I believe we're pushing at the millions side of things here, so your investment will definitely reap its return."

"Yes," said Simon. "That's good. But do you have the reach of each brand involved?"

Michael was prepared for this question. His phone vibrated against chest as he reached for his bag to grab documents he'd printed out the night before. He assumed Rebecca was calling, or maybe Finan, who randomly texted him on his drive to the farmhouse. It was unclear if her "I can't wait until you get home, big daddy" message was for him. He didn't respond and brushed off the temptation to follow up on it. The distraction would have been too great; the timing off.

Michael handed over the documents, which outlined the digital and media consumption of Subject's audience, along with the influence of its brands. He watched Simon scan the papers quickly, soaking up the information, aligning the benefits to Balstec's business goals. Simon nodded, impressed. Michael had predicted this reaction and glad the meeting was going as planned.

"Thanks for sharing this, Michael," said Simon. "I'll hold on to this. It's just the thing our shareholders like to see and to understand our investments. Can you email me the soft copy version?"

"Sure," said Michael, pulling out his phone and saw the missed call from Shanice's mother. He disguised his concern. He tapped at his phone and then placed it back in his pocket.

"It's on its way to you now," said Michael.

Simon stood up from his chair and inhaled loudly, stretching his arms at the same time.

"Come, let me show this place. We can walk and talk."

Michael followed his host from the large front room into an immaculately kept kitchen. It appeared tidier than any kitchen he'd ever seen. Strangely, too large as well, with the cooking surface too far from the stove. Plus the fridge, dishwasher, all neatly positioned on one side, but not practically placed if moving back and forth between cooking. Michael wondered if the logic and common sense of rich people were inherited. They entered a separate downstairs living room area when Simon spoke.

"So, Mudderdeep... we have regular meetings you should attend... "

Michael nodded.

"...Mainly because I don't trust their director of operations, Jack. You remember him?"

"Yes, of course," said Michael, slightly puzzled.

"Well, believe it or not, my close sources say that he's been known to rip off clients with extortionate rates for their advertising."

"You're sure?" asked Michael.

Simon gave Michael a quick glance. "This is actually a well-known fact. The industry rates for these fitness events are hard to determine so basing them on the number of attending participants is how they charge clients. It's unlike outdoor advertising, because it involves sponsorship as well. And using a formula of say, £100 per thousand means the customer gets a poor percentage of the takings, and Mudderdeep's cut is always twice the amount of the client's initial investment."

Michael was bemused, uncertainty lingering around Simon's calculation. He wouldn't question it at that moment, but he hadn't heard anything like this before. Jack is a sound guy. *Why is Balstec doing business with Mudderdeep if there's a question around finances?*

Simon held his gaze a while longer waiting for Michael to digest the information. Michael could only throw up a wry smile in attempt to change the subject and to move from this small dinghy room that served no purpose other than as a boredom cavern. A room of zero distraction, where whoever in that big house could run to when they had no place to go. Shanice's mother crossed Michael's mind, and he sensed a long drive home.

"Er, okay," Simon finally said. "Shall we check out the bedrooms... or tour the garden, stroke the farm? Oink, oink."

Michael admired Simon's humour, yet an air of undiagnosed sexuality wafted uncomfortably around him.

"Think the garden will be just fine. Need a bit of fresh air," said Michael.

The rest of the morning involved talk around FirstThing.com and its position for year-on-year growth, and it'd manage to monetise any opportunity without dismantling the premise of its core business and what it was good at. Michael sensed client retention when these types of conversations arose. He was sure Bryan would enjoy the feedback of the meeting. Although talking yields and turnover, with the sound of snorting pigs behind him, gave the discussion a sense of surrealism.

As expected, Simon waffled on about himself, how he came to be CEO of

Balstec (sticking to his "instincts" supposedly, and climbing over whoever "to achieve success", noted Michael.) The company's technological proposition of fitness apparel and monitors were impressive, and used each and every strand of metaphysics possible, but problem was, so were all the other big tech giants. Although the fitness market was still specialist, according to Simon, they were aware of the competition and how getting in front of right audience offered guaranteed returns, but did limit its offering to the general public. Mudderdeep helped with alleviating this predicament and working with FirstThing.com, there were avenues upon avenues to be explored and strands of cash to be taken from it all.

The garden's muddy surface held steady for Simon's Wellington boots. Michael accepted Simon's offer to wear spare boots, even though they were two sizes too small. The childish exuberance of Simon reminded Michael of Natalie, Shanice's mother. How she'd know (or strongly presumed) the outcome of everything. Michael wondered again what her call was about, but it could only be two things: dates and times when visiting Shanice, and has the maintenance money increased? Raising a child alone wasn't easy.

Simon extended his arm to Michael. "Come on, let's go inside and grab something to eat."

They walked through the muddy grass and then kicked off the excess on the concrete patio by the kitchen's back entrance. Simon stepped into the house, and turned to Michael with a big smile, both puzzling and easy to read. *That Natalie smile.*

"Oh, I didn't say earlier, but I hope the website goes well. It sounds like a good, ah, idea."

Michael responded automatically, nodding without speaking. As Simon dimmed in his view, he grimaced and thought of Bryan standing in his office, smug, with a 'told-you-so' expression.

Driving back to London was painfully long, and meant returning home in the late hours. The 50 miles per hour limit, governed by speed cameras and continous roadworks, made him tired quicker than usual. Michael pulled over for a bite, and looked at his responsive website, admiring the way it fitted on his mobile as well as his laptop. The sign-ups were stagnant, only a couple more names and email addresses from his last view. A slight feeling of dejection and anxiety made him think if his moment of intervention may have been wrongly timed. Would he be judged by it forever, too? Would he be that clown who had a great idea but watched it die through weak execution and no real delivery plan? He'd seen many ideas disappear into thin air and his website was on the horizon to follow suit. He was agitated by the prosperity of his situation. *It's going to be success, isn't it?*

Michael snatched at his phone on the table next to his coffee and digressed a little. As he dialled the number, he sunk into remembrance, picking parts of his daughter's conversation and what was important. He tried not to focus on anything except her fragile state of mind and to find a resolution to her problem. This was hard to do as the dial tone rung in his ear. The ringing stopped and in the space of two seconds, a mixture of pain, concern and relief flooded his sensibilities.

"Hello, Mike. What?"

"Hey, Natalie," he said. "How you doing?"

She wasn't doing great.

"What do you want?"

"Shanice called and sounded upset." Thinking Natalie *had* called him.

"She's always upset, Michael. Part of being a teenager."

"No, I mean, she was *really* upset..."

He heard a noise and wasn't sure to address it. Natalie ignored it, so he did the same thing.

"What do you mean? Is it the school?"

"Yes, of course, it is. She's not happy there. She says she's being bullied..."

He waited, sure there would be a negative reply. The same noise, a shuddering large object perhaps, interrupted the silence and made him pause before continuing.

"They're picking on her for being clever. "

"Well, yes, Mike. As you know, some of these kids aren't as smart as Shanice, but she's got to stand up to it."

"Stand up to it?"

"Yeah, that's what I said. She is smart. Smart enough to deal with these schoolgirls. She likes to... Um, never mind."

Michael heard the hesitation.

"'Never mind', what?"

"It's not important, Mike. If you were here on a frequent basis than you'd know what was what. I've been dealing with this and Shanice is more than capable of fighting her own battles. I can't believe she called you..."

"Clearly something needs to done if she's not happy and calling me, right?"

"Maybe."

"Maybe? Natalie, do you know the name of the girl who's bullying her?"

"Yes, but..."

"Can you get me her parents' details, please? I just want to call them and make them aware of what's going on, and let them deal with it, and then we'll see if there's a change in behaviour from Shanice." Knowing he'd asked his daughter for the number already.

"Okay."

"You see, by Shanice calling me, she knew what she was doing and she probably understands the ramifications along with that, but whether she can cope with the consequences of it, and if things change in her school, there's only one way to find out. "

"Hmm, I guess you're right, but you need to see her more, Michael. Perhaps it's a call for that, and the bully thing isn't really real."

Michael paused, not wanting to get into a discussion about parental responsibility because he discussed it a million times with Natalie. S*he's probably the most difficult, yet prettiest, woman I've ever known.* And as the muscles of his loins often took over when he saw her, she tried to use his deflating masculinity to gain a favourable sense of reality. They were separated and weren't together for a reason. When one of them tried to ignore the fact, and rekindle the good times and that their daughter was a symptom of that goodness, the blurred lines only delayed the inevitable arguments that would arise from the other's frustrations. There was a reason he should increase his maintenance payments because it was all good between them, and she hadn't taken him to court or called up the CSA. The old days when she rallied behind him as he slam dunked and actually made lay-ups, and he'd looked into the crowd to see if she was smiling at his performance, meant something. But ongoing injuries caused more bench time and his eyes trickled from the stands to the bubbly cheerleader that seemed to be waving her pom-poms just for him. He didn't mean to make it so obvious, and when Natalie found it hard to understand his diverted interest, she assumed he was having an affair instead of realising he was suffering from depression. The reality of his fading career, without a solid plan B to fall back on, with a young family to support, he was at a loss for how to boost his self esteem. The cheerleader was a one-time mistake he didn't regret but in hindsight, he should have been more sophisticated about his feelings and reached a better conclusion for his failed relationship with Natalie. In truth, she tried her best to salvage what they had, but Michael wasn't interested — and played basketball until his injuries took him into an early retirement, and until he knew he'd made their relationship irreparable. The immediate result was that he rarely saw his daughter. Especially since she started school. He hadn't pushed himself enough to be the role model she needed, but he had made sure she knew of him, and what he did. She didn't have a stepfather to replace him, and Natalie's boyfriends hadn't the gull to stick around, either. And this made Michael understand the problem further, a problem in Natalie where she couldn't move on beyond her fantasy relationship with him, and putting her own daughter before everything meant her life with men was always destined to be flawed and filled with pain.

It was a long pause, and it was a silence that had no conclusion.

"You going to Africa, Mike?"

"No, why?" he said, before thinking about the question. He hadn't spoken with her in a month, he couldn't understand where it was coming from.

"You forget we're still friends on Mindsite?"

"Yeah, but. What you talking about?"

"Here's the number of the girl's mum. You got a pen?... It's 07769 100976. I've spoken with her already but a few months ago. Give her a call. She's nice."

"Thanks, and yes, re, Africa."

"Why?" asked Natalie. "Ain't nothing there but bushes and trees."

"I will let you know what she says," said Michael, ignoring the last comment. "Oh, what's the mum's name?"

"Annabelle."

It played on his mind for a few hours. That name. For whatever reason, it was, he owed an Annabelle an apology for being abrupt, for not giving her full explanation why he didn't want to see her again, why he left her crying after having an argument he'd insinuated to get her worked up and say the wrong things so he didn't have to. He thought it was comical for a few months afterwards but soon acknowledged his cowardice and why he shouldn't do it again. But he had.

He looked up Annabelle online but came up with no recognition of the woman he'd known. He feared his daughter's bully was the result of his earlier actions. He believed in déjà vu but this would have been ridiculous. Bullying didn't favour anyone, especially the bully, as they always found the reason for their mistreatment to others was more indicative than the bullying itself.

Before calling Annabelle's number, he realised he had no plans to meet up with Daniel or Paul, or even Lawrence for that matter. He was ticked off by this. Usually something was in the diary, usually there was a reason to meet. *Is the website the cause of the lack of contact? Did they really detest his objectives and point of view about his Africa post?* Becoming a bit paranoid, he was sure of that, and thought the respect he'd earned from his friends and peers over the years was due to his forward-thinking, his ability to bring them together and his resilience to work beyond the status quo. He had been excited by his site's possibilities, the response he had so far and the response it was going to generate. Even the Balstec CEO had mentioned it.

A week later, and the sign-ups to his website had stalled. He sent out another post but didn't want to overdo it, and didn't want to seem desperate. The link-up with his friends had been cancelled for no real reason other than to be lazy and cancel it. Rebecca was irritating him with her irregularities — infrequent calls, cryptic messages, stayovers, occasional goings out — and was seemingly distracted. She kept talking about her colleague, Jason, and how her mother was annoying her. He didn't know whether he should be interested in her issues, especially when he was trying to get his website petitions off the ground.

He sighed when he saw Natalie's number appearing on his phone, knowing he hadn't spoken with Annabelle, or sorted out his daughter's bully. He rejected the call, disappointed by his action, and aware he only had a few moments to rectify it. He watched as Finan walked by his office, and appeared prettier than usual. He shrugged it off and couldn't allow her to enter his mindstate. He had a race of people to help while he still cared about it.

He logged onto his Mindsite feed to see if there were any developments and was attracted to a post shared by someone he didn't know but had tagged Madyson on it. He watched for a few moments before feeling the desire to get back to his Balstec paperwork, but then saw Madyson in the video clip. She looked thinner and healthier in it, and more attractive. Their last call entered his mind and what did she really wanted to say. The video was old footage from a TV show she had been in whilst she was in the States. Her double denim outfit clearly was something she'd refuse to wear these days, but her acting hadn't improved greatly. The same mannerisms seemed to follow all her shows and productions, and as if she had the same director for all her features. Michael smiled at the screen, not absorbing the point of why it was shared on Mindsite. But took note he had to give Madyson a call to catch up, and he'd do it after work.

He looked over some of the comments on his latest Africa post and realised he didn't know that much of what he was asking people to do, and what the consequences would duly be. His trip to Ghana had been one of enlightenment, yet this request of his required thorough planning and management and further education. There were questions around who'd lead the movement, questions around accommodation, jobs, money, hospitality and general fear of acceptance. He had expected these questions, it was standard with any move — of job or place, but this would be the biggest project he'd ever work on if it did go ahead. A sense of doubt about the scale of his ambition and whether this optimistic effort for further attention on the common, yet negative, media reporting about black existence and plights could work. *What is the real benefit of shifting from country to country, continent to continent?*

Michael inhaled softly, knowing the scale was probably unachievable but something triggered inside him. Something beyond his own feelings, his own reality, this was bigger than life itself. He smirked at how silly it sounded. *What the fuck am I doing?* He looked at his social feed and its virtual, semi-real existence. It just needed a bit more of a push. But a big push...

The scale of research needed for his objective was going to be huge. *It's not unfathomable*, but like everything else it would be time consuming. He had to remember it would be worth it. The freedom would be unheralded but the feeling would be second to none.

He paused, looking at the Huddle homepage, and unsure of where to begin, bit guessing of what could help him. Thinking it was crazy as he was unsure of how to conduct research prior the invention of the Internet. Was it CD encyclopedias, going to the library, reading endless books, or asking friends and family for advice? As he scrolled, he realised not much had changed — just the method of finding the answers, just the way he communicated, but it was just the same: the same feelings and thoughts of those he trusted the most. And nothing was more important than that. He jumped on a BCB News link shared via Mindsite. The link posted by a old friend and it read how Africa had the world's fastest-growing labour force but still needed a jobs growth to catch up with the rest of world. Michael grinned, this was exactly what his mission was about. A few more people with Western knowledge would ably create the right type of work and develop a new infrastructure to create new job opportunities. But his smile disappeared as the article continued, stating a major bank was leaving the continent, and how this could have a terrible effect on African business.

Michael's eyes scanned the copy in front of him. Supposedly, the bank was pulling out because of internal bureaucracy, finding itself in a struggling merger with another prominent bank, and realising it needed to cut its loose ties to be a stronger force in the corporate world. The bank was overly dependant on the economy of South Africa to cover for the investment of the rest of the continent. Listed on the Johannesburg stock exchange, and employing over 45,000 people, it was strange reading to Michael. *Why would such a business leave Africa?* The bank was part of a bigger group, which owned banks in ten countries, and had been in the continent for over a century. But the bank was still removing its 63% stake in the group to make better usage of its capital. With growing unemployment, the depreciation of countries in the continent, and the slowing of China helping out its development, Africa was no longer the hot spot the bank once thought it would be. It wasn't only Africa where its interest moved away from. The bank was also downsizing in other countries, such as Brazil, Russia and Sri Lanka.

Michael shook his head. It didn't make sense. Africa had the most potential in the world. His eyes glistened as he came to the end of the article, noting the bank's chief executive was "making these bold moves, and is under pressure from shareholders", but had experienced a big fall in the South African Rand by 40 percent, reducing their equity value. The article ended with a question Michael was asking himself throughout the read, *Who will buy the bank?* At a $60bn cost, there weren't many suitors, although speculation floated around a pension fund organisation, who was thinking of taking the cost on. Depositors funds were safe, and only share certificates would be changing hands.

Michael spluttered, realising what he always knew: there was serious money going around. It just required the right idea, the right business plan, the right market to make it all happen — and then, take the money. That's what Africa needed: money. And the means to generate it. His website idea had the potential to cultivate it all together, and to sync all the capital needed to make Africa investable, prominent and a business paradise. He just needed to put it into action to show it wasn't just another social media post.

Picking up his phone, Michael scrawled through his contacts until he came to the letter Y. Yemi. His basketball brethren. It was an instinctive move, but when Yemi answered and sounded genuinely happy to hear from him, he knew it was right thing to do.

"You've been to Africa, Mike?"

"Yeah, you know that?"

"Well, then. You know what it's like. It's our home. But its history is fragmented and its past is only celebrated on the continent. You can't expect the world to feel as you feel. It's primitive in places but this is a good thing."

"But do you think we can make a real change there and here?" asked Michael. "It's too much of a coincidence that we're suffering across the globe and our motherland isn't in a fit state to help or assist its people worldwide."

"My brother," said Yemi. "There's a lot of Africans out there. Millions. I mean, millions. Your petition can reach a few of them and you really need to think what will happen if everyone took this seriously. How would that affect the global scale, the balance of power and this is just the African people, not the European or American-Africans. You need help, brother. You cannot do this alone."

Maybe so. "Thanks, Yemi. I appreciate you talking about this. I have quite a few sign-ups and need to notify them soon on any plans I need to make. There's a lot of stuff to think about."

"You need some fante fante and jollof rice, my friend. My girlfriend serves up a wicked dish, bro."

"Haha. Thanks, Yemi."

Michael swore he could smell the food cooking as he hung up the line. But Yemi was right; this was an ambitious project and he had millions of people to convince his idea was the right thing to do.

He tapped into his laptop and looked for something on Huddle but couldn't clarify his thoughts and ended up on the same sports website he visited daily to check his favourite basketball teams scores. While it took him away from the bigger task at hand, it was a soothing experience. It reminded him of yesteryear when he too was playing professionally and would analyse his box score stats to see how well he, and his opponents, played. He was surprised by the lack of efficiency the pro players were performing at, whilst getting mega-sized contracts to play the game. *Amazing*, he thought. He acknowledged the multiple levels of competition on one hand, which meant playing as hard as you could was the name of the game, but couldn't get his head around the efficiency ratings. It was unclear how hard these guys were playing based on the stats in front of him. He stared at the screen, bemused, and upon feeling a sense of jealously creeping up on him, his phone rang.

It was a number he didn't recognise.

"Hello."

"Err, hello. Is that Mr. Featherstone?" The voice had an American accent.

Michael straightened up. "Yes, it is. Who is this?"

"Sorry, to disturb you Mr. Featherstone. My name is Renaldo Paul. I'm calling from *The Choice* newspaper. Here in London."

"Okay."

"Erm, I'm calling you because my editor would like to run a story on you about your 'Return to Africa' campaign."

It wasn't really a campaign, but then again, it was. Michael hadn't put it on that scale. He wondered quickly if the press would give his "campaign" a negative spin, but he needed the publicity as his numbers were low. *If I tell the truth, then what could go wrong?*

"Hey, Renaldo. What kind of story did you have in mind?"

"We saw your posts and your site and wanted to know how serious this is, and if we should paint you as a crusader or not."

Or not. Hmm. "All right. Fire away, I can only tell you what I'm doing and hopefully it's interesting enough for a story," said Michael.

"Don't worry," said Renaldo. "We're sure it will be."

"Can I ask you how you got my number?" asked Michael.

"We're journalists, Michael," said Renaldo. "It's our job to know such things."

Whether this painted *The Choice* as a legitimate paper, Michael held his thoughts close to his chest, and just hoped the interview gave his idea more publicity and sign-ups. “Okay, let”s do it.”

The interview barely lasted twenty minutes and it was refreshing to relay his plan to an outsider. It meant it had potential resonance and was something that could be taken seriously. He told the reporter of why he decided to start the project and how he felt it would end. Michael focused on the positive side of each area, aware his claims, promises and overall vision may not come true. It didn’t make sense to dwell in the possibility of it being nothing more than a fancy idea. He explained his research and how the benefits of social media meant he could promote the plan at a relatively cheap cost. Admittedly, more work needed to done, but it wasn’t impossible, and with any secured investment, he’d ultimately put all capital into this mission of his.

Renaldo sounded genuinely impressed and said he’d follow up if there was a requirement to do so, either from his editor or from the readers. But the story would appear in the paper and its website the following week. The reporter asked Michael if there were any images in circulation he could use for the article.

Mindsite is probably the best place to look and download, said Michael, as there were already selfies out in public domain, and essentially copyright-free. Michael relaxed as he pressed the end call button. He agreed to doing the story and had been as honest as he could, but whether the article came out that way was beyond his control. He thought of Rebecca. She’d been acting strangely, working late, and had no real justification behind it, claiming the pressures of work were getting to her. He squashed his mouth onto his nose, making a childish expression, partly in disbelief. He scrolled through his phone, jumping from app to app, but came back to his phone call icon, and noted there was somebody he hadn't spoken with in a while. He picked up his bag and headed home. On his tube journey back, he remained undecided on the reason why he hadn't seen the guys lately, and thought about his position within the group. *God, I need a drink,* his larynx feeling dry, but he ignored his thirst for the moment — he had a call to make.

"Hey, Lawrence. Everything okay with you, bro?" asked Michael.

Seated in his battered Vauxhall Astra, Lawrence heard his brother's voice on the phone and wondered how he could answer such a question. He thought briefly of Paul, Michael's 'bro'. *Funny guy.*

"Yeah, I'm grand. Just chilling," Lawrence said.

"What you up to?" continued Michael, sitting on his couch. "It's been a minute."

"I know, I know," said Lawrence. "I'm just busy at the agency."

Michael frowned, and waited for some elaboration.

Lawrence looked outside of the car and blinked his eyes. He was no longer at the agency. It had been just a temp position and he needed to find work really soon. The car was parked not far from the Annual Drupal Conference for web designers and developers. He couldn't afford the ticket to attend and the agency said temp workers weren't allowed such perks. It would have been a great opportunity to network and to get his foot back on the ladder. He'd get a permanent role at reputed firm and hone his Drupal platform knowledge. The stint inside had messed up his progression, and he hated it. Hated everyone who was now doing well because they hadn't gone down, and hadn't dealt with the shit of the system.

"Yo, Law. You there?"

"I'm here, bro. Just thinking a bit."

"Anything I can help you with?" said Michael.

A million things flashed through Lawrence head, but he couldn't say any of them.

"There is one thing…" Lawrence remembered.

"Okay, what it is?" *A parting with money*?

"Your site, Africa.com..." said Lawrence.

Michael resisted commenting.

"...it needs work, bro. People are going to visit and leave when they see the design. Your bounce rate must be high." There was a tapping at his car window.

"I haven't checked in fairness," said Michael. "You're probably right, and I did it quickly. You like the messaging?"

"Yeah, what you want?" asked Lawrence to the lady at his car as he rolled down the window.

Michael listened intently, but didn't speak. He heard a woman's voice.

"You know you can't park here?"

"Yeah, I know," said Lawrence.

"Maybe you take it somewhere a bit more quiet."

Michael couldn't figure what was going on as the volume on the phone had gone lower.

"Are you going to do this or what?"

"£20 quid, right?"

"Only head for that. Can't get inside me with £20. Gotta double that."

Michael tried to listen in on the conversation further but it was clear the phone wasn't near his brother's face and the car was moving. He wanted to know if Lawrence had spoken with their parents lately, as they'd recently asked about Lawrence's wellbeing.

"It'll be £20 or nothing…" he faintly heard his brother say.

The phone switched off, and Michael tried to call back. He was told that "the person you are calling is unavailable". He shook his head in anger.

He placed his phone on the table in front of him, and realised he hadn't opened his letters. He checked the bank statements and the outstanding gas bill, knowing he needed to pay it, despite the principle of its inflated estimate for that quarter. The shock of the increase made him not want to pay it, but as he scanned another letter he accepted he had to ensure all his bills were paid, especially if he was soon to appear in a newspaper article. The letter was from Companies House, questioning the status of his old registered business. He'd set up a PR consultancy firm called Forward Thinking after two previous clients were keen to work independently from FirstThing.com but to have the same level of expertise. They were good paying jobs, Michael remembered, but their promises of retention dwindled and he had to stay with the nine to five. He hadn't declared whether the limited business was active or not in a few months, and knew this would affect the annual records he had to report.

If the big plan was to move back to Africa, then the business would need to adapt to this notion as well. He had to establish funding, capital and build financial investments worthy of taking the cause seriously. And without a company, he wouldn't achieve the scale of money needed to make his idea come to fruition. Michael read the letter and filled it in. His business was active, he'd declare it as so. He would add a pledge button to the site, *goingbackhomesoon.org*, to help get the money in and acknowledge that his plight wasn't just an emotional one, it was fundamentally a business one as well.

The doorbell rang shortly afterwards and there stood Rebecca. Her long hair flowed to her neck and her face blushed red from the day's cold weather, rinsing her cheeks. Michael watched as a sense of angst disappeared when she entered his flat and took off her shoes before slumping into his couch.

"You okay, babes?" he asked.

"I'm fine. I think."

He sat next to her. "What do you mean?"

"I'm not sure what's going on at work. Whether it's the right company for me."

"Is that Jason guy being a nuisance?" said Michael.

Rebecca stressed how Jason had called her out at meetings recently when she wasn't prepared, and Michael remembered from the office party that the guy clearly fancied her, and probably wanted to alienate her the only way Jason's bullying tactics knew best.

Rebecca looked at Michael to see if he was being serious. "No."

"Spoken to your sisters?"

"No," she said.

He wrapped his arm around her shoulders. "What's going on, babes?" Sounding as if he was thinking of something else when he said it.

"I heard from my dad, says he thinks Mum is going to marry Charlie."

Oh crap.

"I can't believe she would think about doing such a thing."

"Well, they have been together for ten years…"

"That doesn't matter, does it?" Rebecca was welling up. "It's the bloody principle."

Michael waited for the tears to come and they drizzled out. When he met Rebecca, her vulnerability was attractive, but it now felt dated as she had to, someway, get over her mother issues. But looking at her, he suspected any mother marrying a child's ex-partner would be gutting.

"I can't believe they're doing this, Michael. And Mum will want me to be there, I bet."

"Has she said anything to you yet?"

"No, but she may…"

Michael squeezed her tighter. "Don't let it stress you out until you speak to her. Okay? You know how your dad can be."

"Yeah," she said. "He loves a bit of drama. But…"

"Don't think about it. Give your mum a call tomorrow and deal with it then."

"Why not now?"

He kissed her lips, allowing further bemusement. "Well, because I was just interviewed about my website and campaign and I'm going to be in a national newspaper."

Checking if he was serious. "What?"

"Yep, I think it could really happen."

She didn't say what she was thinking but thought it was amazing. She couldn't believe how her mother was really thinking of marrying her ex-boyfriend. *That's beyond gross.* She couldn't understand why Michael was smiling at her and playing at her clothing. She grinned but he looked like Charlie to her, and she smiled back, suddenly getting excited.

Chapter 5

1996

With the dad tied up in the kitchen and unconscious, Boy B continued to grab whatever would fit in the bags. He signalled to Boy A there was no turning back and this was it — *this is what was going to make them rich*. He held up his bag, indicating the plan and not to worry about the old man in the kitchen.

"Come on," Boy B whispered. "There's serious money to be made here if we get this stuff and get out of here."

Boy A breathed louder than normal and thought of his mum. *Why is she still clogging my memory at a time like this?* He nodded back to Boy B, picking up a loose bag, and put a VCR player in it. He saw a few videos he hadn't watched, but heard about, and wanted to put them in the bag. He caught Boy B waving that idea away. He frowned, but agreed when Boy B pointed to a watch left besides the sofa. His eyes lit up as he rushed over to the corner of the room and dropped it in his bag. Boy A wondered if somebody would come downstairs to check on the man, but there wasn't any noise. Maybe they were alone in the house.

They scurried around the front room but were disappointed by the search. Anything of value was too big to drop into their bags. Boy A suggested the television, the polished hi-fi music system and the desktop computer, but

Boy B signalled they were bad ideas. Boy A was confused by the experience and tried to understand why they were even there if they weren't going to steal anything significant. *How much money were they really going to make?* And there was a battered man in the kitchen. *Shit*, thought Boy A, *this is going to end badly, isn't it?* The silent, yet animated, movement meant he couldn't linger on his thoughts for too long. He saw a ring on the table and held it up to show to Boy B, proud of his discovery. Boy B nodded and waved him on. Boy A studied the gold-plated ring for a moment, before dropping it into the bag.

The circumference of the living room area had a diameter the boys were getting familiar with, and it became clear they weren't going to discover anything else of value there. Boy B stood at the door's threshold, signalling Boy A to come and explore the rest of the house. But Boy A sensed money. Boy A began to move the furniture around, looking behind each large item vehemently, and not putting them back. Boy B stood flustered, but waited before saying anything. The single chair sat oddly in the room, in front of a vase with dying flowers in it and a dracena pot plant that appeared devoid of soil. Boy A held the single chair and swung it around, so the back now faced him. The reason why he was doing this sat dislodged in his memory without explanation. The material of the chair loose and its fabric softer at the back of it. Boy A kicked at it, unintentionally knocking over the vase but kept going. He remained determined, seeeing his mother appear in his thoughts. She'd hide personal valuables at the back of one of the sofa chairs. A long shot, sure, but this random house may just do the same thing. Boy B breathed in deeply, feeling the urge to shout at Boy A.

Boy A lifted his leg, placing as much force behind the exertion as he could and winced as his leg shifted through the material. The move made him topple to his left side and he held the chair for balance, awkwardly stumbling over. He removed his leg, which rubbed against the steel strings and the foam and fibre inside the chair. He stared at the now gaping hole he'd caused. There was something there. Something. He put his arm back into the chair. A silky material entered his hands, and it had further objects inside it. Boy A gripped the silky material as firmly as he could, believing it to be a pouch or a string bag or similar. He pulled it from the chair and allowed it to drop into his hands, in full view. The shadow of Boy B darkened his space and stood above him. The eyes of Boy B sought clarity and full development of the situation in front of them. Boy A put a hand inside the pouch and pulled out an item. They stared at the diamond necklace in his hand. *Jackpot.* Their search had taken an interesting turn. Boy B glanced over to the kitchen and then back to Boy A. They didn't have much time before the man came back to consciousness, and before somebody suspected something unusual. Boy B opened the bag and hinted for Boy A to throw the jewellery towards it. Boy A chucked over the necklace at quick speed and watched Boy B catch and analyse it fondly. A small suspended silence trickled the air. It was time to move on to see what else they could get.

2018

Travelling to his parents' home always made Michael think of the worst. The small suburban terrace house in the leafy part of Surbition was a step too remote from what he envisaged from his life. Getting out of the car, he remembered how he felt about where he lived in Deptford. What if this 'Africa thing' took off and a fleet of cameramen started loitering outside his flat, examining his ends with a documentary about nothing. The crushed bottles; cigarette butts; overweight ladies talking about the night before; children with coats too small and living in homes too small with absent dads worrying about money; oblivious adults harbouring yesteryear with their large headphones on listening to Leon Bridges and Will Young, and thinking of which summer festival they can attend without appearing too old. This was Deptford, not Surbition. Real problems for people who probably wouldn't find a solution anytime soon. Michael reached the door of his parents' home, aware his sullen mood had to disappear in order not to worry them any further about the lives of him and his brother. He tapped on the door out of respect, the spare key in his pocket rubbing against his thigh. His phone vibrated, a message from Daniel popped up.

"Great idea, bro. Whatever help you need with this Africa plan, I've got you."

Michael smiled as his mum opened the door, looking at him up and down. She momentarily frowned when she couldn't decide if he was eating properly or not; grabbed his hand and ushered him into the hallway, baffled as to why he hadn't called to say he was coming by to see them beforehand.

Michael sat in the living room's leather armchair of the matching three piece. It was nice to know his friends were supportive of his idea, and to know he could talk to someone about it without preconceived notions of its likelihood to fail.

"Mike, you want some tea?"

He took a proper glance at his mother, Glenda — and noticed her age immediately. She was ageing well, though the small lines on her face and stretched skin on her neck symbolised her time on Earth. She'd always used moisture from a young age so her skin was still smooth, yet the grey in her thinning hair was dominant and he imagined she fought the urge to don a wig like her own mother did.

Glenda watched her son curiously, and hadn't yet said anything, about anything. Despite retirement, and having a good pension fund saved from her time as a nurse, Glenda frequently helped out at a local residential home, using the money earned for the cost of holidays and trips. She sighed and stood up, realising her son wasn't going to answer her.

Michael watched her graceful movements and could feel a wrench tugging at his heart. He observed the room and wondered if it was the same for every British migrant, who tried to replicate the houses they'd seen at a distance but were now ones they owned. The family home to Michael still felt very West Indian with the furnishing improving slightly from the family home they'd lived in for 35 years in Streatham.

"Where's Dad?" Michael yelled, loud enough to be heard in the kitchen. Silence. Lawrence mentioned that her hearing was going, but Michael hadn't believed it. *Maybe Lawrence is right.* Michael's smile grew into a sombre grin, illustrating his emptying mind at that moment. Being at his parents' home instantly relaxed him and made the visit beyond worthwhile.

Glenda re-entered the room with a shaking tray of tea mugs, milk, sugar cubes and a couple of custard creams. She knew how he liked his tea, but the host in her couldn't help it. Once Michael saw her, he leaped out of the chair to assist her, but it was too late. She shook her head as she placed the tray on the small coffee table, and muttered a brush-off that was purposely inaudible. A little disappointed but Michael quickly resigned to her 'mum's know best' stance.

Glenda smiled at him. "You say something to me?"

"Yeah, Dad. Where is he? At the tennis club?"

"He upstairs. Usual afternoon nap. Love a sleep, that one."

"Someone say somethin' bout me?"

They both looked in the direction of the voice coming from the doorway. Michael's dad, Franklin, stood there, smirking, slippers and dressing gown apparent and probably naked underneath. Michael stood up, partly in embarrassment.

"Pops!" Michael embraced his father and inhaled a whiff of his freshly-showered scent. Being the middle of the day confused him.

"Come, finish your tea," Glenda said.

Michael returned to his seat, and poured in his milk. As he drank his tea, his parents eyed him, absorbing each sip as if he hadn't had a drink in ages.

"How's that brother of yours?" said Franklin.

"He's all right, I think. A bit here and there. Still looking for that golden opportunity."

"At least he's working," said Glenda.

"Hmm," responded Franklin.

Michael sipped further on his tea and pondered on eating a biscuit or to wait for another question. He reached down towards the tray but was too slow.

"That white girlfriend of yours, Rachel. How she?"

"Rebecca, Dad. You know her name."

Glenda smiled. She knew her husband loved to tease Michael, especially when discussing relationships.

"So, what's this about you and voyage to Africa?" said Franklin.

Michael moved his attention away from the tray and the custard creams. "I've been interviewed by a newspaper about it," he said proudly.

Glenda piped up. "What paper? Not one of dem red tops. Be careful, son. They'll…"

Michael scurried his eyes around the room and found the object of affection. He couldn't reach it without standing so he pointed instead.

"It was *The Choice*, Mum. You read that."

His dad smiled. "All the papers are the same, Michael."

"*The Choice* is a good paper, Frankie. What you know?" said Glenda.

"I know, m'lady, that everyone has to sell a story and this is just fodder for them," said Franklin.

Michael took offence of the word 'fodder'. "It was a good interview, Dad. It should help the website and the cause."

Franklin chuffed. "Not everyone in Africa will like other black people coming to their country."

"But that's our home, Dad. Black is black, right?" said Michael.

Franklin stared at Glenda for a second and shifted his attention back to Michael. "I know your job doesn't pay you four thousand a month to chat foolishness, so why do it here?"

"Leave the boy alone," said Glenda.

Michael knew his dad was sensitive to the issue of Caribbean blacks versus African blacks, and knew a one-size-fits-all black logic didn't address that. "What I meant to say was, it's the place where we came from. It's the place where all of this started. For us to take control of our lives and fully understand the extent of our offerings to this world, and most importantly, ourselves that we need to go back."

Franklin huffed. He didn't know Michael meant that. And the kid had a point. But...

"Lots of paperwork to sort out," said Franklin.

"Don't start, Frankie," said Glenda.

"And money. What about money? How are you going to raise the money for all this?"

"Have you been on my site? There's a crowdfunding button on there where people can contribute to the cause."

"How much you made so far?"

"Not enough yet, Dad."

"Going to need millions…"

"Yeah, I know. But look at everything in this room. How you think it got there? What made you buy it? It's the same thing with my site. It's an idea, a concept that will make people want to do it and then subscribe and then want to be a part of it."

Franklin looked at Glenda again, unsure of their child's ideology and what scheme he was really planning. Franklin reflected to when Michael sat in front of the TV watching basketball and said he was going to be a professional player. Franklin didn't believe it at the same, but watching his son play for the international team in front of thousands of people years later made him realise his son had a strength of belief. But, Franklin questioned himself, he wasn't worried about his son, it was the other people that Michael wanted to join him that was the problem.

"Be careful, son. You know the world out there is tough to change. Especially for the best of things."

"We'll see what happens, I guess."

His phone vibrated and he checked his parents' clock, assuming it was a message from Rebecca. He saw Finan's name on his phone, and kept a straight face, but immediate arousal swamed his thoughts and he imagined her message to be sexual. It was, in fact, work-related and despondency took place in him, disappointed but relieved as his face remained expressionless.

"Everything all right, Michael?" asked Glenda.

He wearily smiled. "Yes, Mum. Business as usual."

In his car on the way back home that evening he thought it'd be a good moment to allow his mind to roam, and to imagine the unimaginable. The drive itself, though, seemed restrictive, with frequent traffic jams, bad motorists or unruly pedestrians stepping out into the road at any given time with their eyes on their phones. Michael huffed, but at nothing, really. People were just doing what people do. He could feel himself delving into retrospect, but the vibration of his phone against the material of the passenger seat caught his attention. He tried to reach for it while focusing on the road, but he couldn't do it. He pulled over in a free space, and answered before the caller hung up.

"Hey up, Paul. What's going on?"

"You, my man. That's what."

It was a strange reply, even by Paul's standards.

"I'm good. Just come back from my folks' house."

"Ah, Sir Franklin and Glenda. How are they both?"

"They're doing well, thanks. Bit unsure of my campaign."

"*Campaign*," said Paul.

"Well, that's what…"

"You make it sound as if you're running for Parliament…"

"You mocking me?"

"No, no. Don't be silly. You just need to be careful where you're going with this all."

"What you talking about?"

A short quietness emerged.

"Well," said Michael.

"I don't want old stuff to come up as a result of this. The media is not a playground, you hear me."

"What old stuff?"

"Don't play dumb, Mike… That stuff."

Michael sighed. He hadn't recalled the hinted reference, but he finally understood Paul's point. "Ah, don't worry about that. That's all in the past."

"Yeah," Paul uttered quietly.

A beep of another message echoed in his ear, and he moved the phone away to see it was from *The Choice* reporter.

"How's Rebecca, anyway?" Paul added, noting the silence.

"Oh, she's all right. A bit worried about her mum marrying some dude who's already too close to the family. Wild stuff, believe me."

"Things between you, good?"

"Of course, mate," Michael said with confidence. "That office ting is just my mind playing games when I'm stressed."

"As long as it stays in your mind, then you're good."

"Thanks for the advice, Paul but I'm parked illegally."

"Ah, is that a metaphor?"

"Nope."

"Oh, yes, course. We'll speak later, okay?"

Michael hung up without saying goodbye, but figured Paul wouldn't mind, or wouldn't have noticed.

He scrambled through his phone's applications and dug out his messages. The first name on his message list was Renaldo Paul. The message made Michael beam. *The Choice* were going to publish his story on page 5 the following Monday. Renaldo asked Michael to share the article online as it would appear on *The Choice*'s website as well, and it'd hopefully help his 'campaign'. Renaldo asked him if 2025 was a realistic date for his Africa proposal as it was very close. Michael had itchy fingers and replied, "Yes, the sooner the better. The more we push back on the this date, the more likely we revert back to the status quo. And that's the opposite aim of this campaign."

He thought of Paul as he typed the last word and pressed send. He wanted to get home, and dropped the phone back onto the passenger seat. His hands graced the steering wheel, but the phone began vibrating again. A voice call from Daniel. Michael didn't hesitate, and answered it immediately.

"Wasss good, fam?!"

"Haha, Michael," replied Daniel. "You're all right, I take it."

"Yes, of course, never better," said Michael.

Another message on his phone from Renaldo. He agreed with Michael's view, and added he should touch base with the Society of Black Politicians, as this would definitely interest them.

"When we linking up again, bro?" asked Daniel.

"Whenever you want, Dan. I'm always free…"

"Not with your African plight kicking off on social like crazy."

"What you talking about?"

"That's all I'm seeing, bro. Goingbackhomesoon.org — *"Making the change today because our history depends on it"*."

Genuinely surprised for a moment, Michael then acknowledged the money he had added onto Mindsite to boost each post so they would get greater amplification. "Okay, I see it's doing well, but not enough. I need more sign-ups. I need to take it into a business."

"You sure, Mike? This could take over your life."

"I think so, but it's not enough yet to where I can consider it too seriously. A few questions here, a few interviews, but it's not popping. There's no dynamic. There's no money."

"You're right, Mike — but what movement ever started from zero to hero overnight? None. When did you have this idea? Like two weeks ago."

"Haha, yeah."

"But I'm calling cos, err, I've got a problem…"

Michael got comfortable in his seat. "Um, okay?"

"A real problem. I think…"

"Come on, bro. Spit."

"I think I've got a crush on Madyson… don't say anything…"

"Err, what." Michael playfully shivered, wondering where this was coming from. *Had Madyson linked up with Daniel? Is this what she was calling about the other day, trying to say?*

"Yeah, I know she's part of the crew, but…"

"Dan, let it go. You know she has history."

"What you mean? Nobody in the group has…"

"Not with us, dude. Her life isn't straightforward. You remember back in college when she was trying to make it to Hollywood, and left to go to Mississippi. She had problems from there, dude. She's looking good, but you don't want to spoil the dynamic."

"Sssh. Come on, Mike. You holding out on something?"

"Nah, Dan, I swear. I was talking to her the other day, about her show, and I swear she was going say something about her love life, but I don't know…"

"What?"

"No, that's it. She's complicated, man. She has an interesting past. She's not young, and you're managing your business, too."

Michael sensed Daniel would push back on the subject, but it didn't happen.

"I know, I'm not the fittest guy in the world, and I've not been good with women, but bro, she was looking good that day in the pub. I could sense she wanted me…"

"Dan, you've got to take care of your kids, and those crazy mothers you decided to sleep with, before you mess with the crew's only down-ass chick. You feel me? If you're horny, I'll get you some women who'll like someone like you." Michael looked out the window and saw a beautiful Asian woman, and admired her stance, recognising she was probably too good for Daniel.

"Hey man, I look after my kids."

"I know you do."

"So?"

"So what? Why you calling me?" asked Michael, in the politest way possible. "Talking about Mads wasn't it, was it? Or you want to discuss your missus, Karen?"

"No," sighed Daniel. "I won't entertain these thoughts of females in front of you. Okay. I just called to check on you, brother. This thing you're doing is big, and I'm not sure where it's going with you. It may turn into…"

There was a pause and Michael held out his phone to check whether he'd lost reception.

"Dan, you there?"

A voice came back. "Yeah, I'm here."

But then another pause.

"Everything okay, man?"

Dan spoke: "Yes, of course. I've been thinking. I want to help you promote this."

Michael listened intently. "Go on."

"I'm thinking of putting this thing of yours as one of my stories in the 'Who's Doing Dirt' section."

"What?"

"I know, I know. It's not the best section to put your appeal onto, but we get millions of users a month, way more than your Mindsite or Postya could reach, and some of those millions may have the right connections you're after to build it as a business, like you were saying."

Michael looked to see where the Asian lady had disappeared to, and noticed a young black woman, who reminded him of Finan. He thought about Daniel's suggestion, and whether it could take his project to the next level. *The Choice* was a good start, but Daniel worked on *Dodgy*, a website that poked fun at the lifestyles of celebrities it quietly idolised. The 'Who's Doing Dirt' section was negative and not the right vein for his petition, but people visited the site in droves and these were the people who voted, travelled to work, had kids, and did what normal people do. These were the people he was after, but he hoped they were black, too.

"Whatever you can do, bro. Really appreciate the support."

"Alright, if I can get it, done. I'll send you the URL so you can see what you think. Let's do this for the motherland."

"Err, no you didn't."

"Yes, I did."

"Dan, I'm going but let me know, please. It's important."

"Yeah, Madyson is important to me, too…"

"Bro, I'm gone…"

Moving the car, he headed for home. The car park below his flat was busy, and looking at the expensive vehicles parked near his, showed him where people's values really lie. Could he convince people to stop spending on their A to B lives and focus on regenerating a shattered community to its proper strength and wellness? His body felt sluggish as he opened his front door, and sat on his couch. His laptop stared at him, and it hadn't fully charged since he'd left it in the morning. With 20 percent to go, he jumped on the site's analytics page to view its numbers of visitors, where there'd been a small upward spike. The sign-ups were increasing, too. He had to send this petition to Parliament soon or people would start demanding action or their interest would dwindle and his reputation would sink along with it.

He rubbed his chin furtively. Relying on *The Choice* and Daniel to produce more followers to his cause was small minded. Big organisations used trade distribution and mass marketing to achieve a simple objective, and he couldn't be any different. He looked over the design of the site, its user journey and experience, and knew if this project was to become bigger than he ever expected, he'd need a site to reflect that. Lawrence could help him. He had developer experience, and he was *his* brother — he would be free. *But what was Lawrence talking about during their call?* Why wasn't anything free?

Only one way to find out. He called his brother's number and startled at how quickly and loudly his brother responded.

"Hey, hey, Mike. You okay?"

"Turn down the music, Lawrence. I can barely hear you."

"Sorry, what?"

"The music. Turn it down. Please."

"Haha, of course. You don't like dem gangsta tunes anymore since you work with *these* people. What happened after your b-balling days, man? You changed."

"Lawrence, where are you? Are you high?"

"Of course, *I'm fucking high.* This is the best feeling ever… "

It was at that moment he knew... getting Lawrence to upgrade his site could be a bad idea.

A bit of food and drink seemed to calm Michael's senses that evening, and even the quick call to Rebecca worked wonders for his soul. She wasn't coming over that night, but she'd see him tomorrow as she needed to talk about her mother, work and "other stuff"— and wanted his rationale to make it seem logical and practical for her life. She repeatedly said, "I love you" and wondered if he did, too — as his search for something bigger may not have involved her. He wanted to get married, but was she really the one he saw walking down the aisle? He didn't ponder, or speculate, on it. He was just chilling at home, no real pressure for him to deliver anything he didn't want to. Allen sent him a message on HeyBrow to check if all was fine, but ended talking about Allen — and Allen's problems with matrimony. *It's not looking good for people,* Allen concluded on a 4389-character analysis of why adults have too much choice, but little in common, which creates higher rates of divorce and dysfunctional families.

Michael joined in the rant for a moment, but the mention of families meant he had to call Shanice and ensure she wasn't still suffering from adolescent angst and bullies at her school. Unable to get through to her mother's phone built a space of bewilderment, but as he relaxed on his bed looking at his phone, he knew it was partly due to change in society and partly, his parental anxiety. The phone in his hand ruining his life instead of maximising it. The phone bill was a day overdue, and his calendar reminder hadn't popped up like usual. Maybe the overnight upgrade had reverted its settings. Michael threw the phone down on the bed, closed his eyes. *The smartphone is probably the dumbest invention ever created.*

Chapter 6

1996

Boy A grinned. He'd found the most expensive item this house contained, but the burglary wasn't over yet. Boy B was a true criminal — and true criminals kept on going, believing the potential for a greater discovery lay ahead. They moved from the living room and were now in the hallway with only a downstairs toilet yet to be searched. Boy A pressed on toilet door handle, and opened it, uncertain if another surprise would jump out, but an empty quietness of air stood before him, a calmness exuded. He pushed the door wide enough to show Boy B it wasn't worth exploring. Of course, Boy B knew differently. Slouching his shoulders, Boy A entered the toilet space. He saw a shower area in the corner, revealing the room to be much larger than he thought. Tidy, porcelain tiles covered the floor and walls, and wide mirrors were hosts covering the wall cabinets. The shower appear untouched and newly built, with no residue or discoloured grout. Boy A leaned forward but stopped as a sound interrupted his movements.

"Dad!" A girl's voice.

Boy A looked at Boy B, who tried to move back so he wouldn't be seen, although this was impossible. They waited for another cry from the girl, but it didn't come. Boy B stared over at Boy A, then indicating their search had to continue. Boy A could hear the rustle of Boy B's bags and knew this would give them away.

"Put the bags down," he whispered.

Boy B reluctantly did so. A bit of common sense from Boy A, and he walked over to the toilet and pulled off its tank lid. He rolled up his sleeves and placed his hands into the tank, lifting the float arm and float ball. He dropped his left arm further into the tank, reaching for something. Boy A waited, not understanding what valuable item would be put in a toilet tank, and would be beneficial to anybody if it was wet.

Boy B moaned, and then released his arm. He was empty-handed. He grabbed the towel nearby and uttered, "Let's go… upstairs."

2018

Michael was on his laptop when the video call request came through on his phone. He didn't recognise the number and was surprised by the approach for somebody he didn't know. He answered nonetheless, blanking out his real face with a default image.

"Hello, can I help?"

"Is that Mr. Featherstone? Forgive me for calling you this way." On the screen, he saw an attractive woman with painted eyebrows and braided hair. He paid closer attention.

"Sorry, I can't share my screen with you. I'm a little unprepared," Michael said.

"I do apologise, Mr. Featherstone," said the woman, "but it's come to my attention that you're running an experience for the advancement of black people. Is that correct?"

"I wouldn't call it that exactly..."

"No, then what it is?"

"I'm not too sure right now. Err, sorry, but who are you?" asked Michael.

"Forgive me, Mr. Featherstone. My name is Melissa Grant. I work for the Society of Black Politicians and from your social platforms and *goinghome* website, you are involved in running an experience that is similar to our stance within Britain."

Michael pondered the call and her delivery. She was way too posh to be doing any cold-calling, and way too pretty to be randomly video-calling people. Confusion reigned, but an opportunity to make money was possibly the only reason she'd called him.

"Sorry, Melissa, it's not a good time. I'll check out your webpage and get back to you. Is that okay?"

"Oh, yes, that'll be fine." She seemed offended. "Please do, Mr. Featherstone."

"I will. Society of Black People. I'll check it out."

"Politicians, Mr. Featherstone. Not, People."

"Yes, of course. That's what I meant. Gotta go. Thanks for the call, Melissa."

He ended the call before she could reply. It wasn't rude, he argued to himself. It was balance. He had to gain control before she whittled her reasons for her untimely call. He just didn't need it at that point.

He studied the design of his mobile phone, the aurora specs trembling at its sensors and turning it from blue to purple when it caught reflective light. *Impressive.* But his attention wavered to the messages he'd just received, probably delayed due to the video call with Melissa and her Society nonsense. One message was from Renaldo at *The Choice. It's out,* he texted, *please put it on your site, Mindsite, wherever,* and the others were from Natalie, and Madyson. Natalie wanted to talk and Madyson was coming round if he was in. He closed the message app and clicked on his sports channel news page to see which basketball player was in a worse predicament with women than he was. It looked like he topped that list for the day.

The call with Natalie wasn't good. Shanice was barely speaking with her, and her school marks were dropping as well. A concern Shanice may not even be able to take her end of year exams if she continued in this fashion entered the conversation. Natalie wasn't exaggerating, either. She had that tinge in her throat that made her voice hoarse and meant her pride was on the line. Michael used to revel in this sound when they were younger, but recognised the issue was different now. Her personal pride as a mother at stake. And she was asking for help. He couldn't make fun of it, although the thought filled his mind.

"We'll work something out," he said, earnestly. And he meant it. Shanice yearned for structure that appealed to her talents, and the school refused to offer it at the minute. He wished he hadn't started his site, and could concentrate totally on his daughter, but with children, he reconsidered, *something is always going to happen.*

He hung up the phone, saying he'd give Shanice a call later, but he'd also come by to see Natalie and discuss it face-to-face, as it'd been a few months since they'd seen each other in-person.

Not sure if his day would get any better, and hearing Madyson's voice at his door, his doubts resurfaced. He opened the door and beamed. She looked amazing, and it was a delight to see her smile as she entered. Daniel flashed into his head, but vanished quickly when Madyson took off her jacket and threw it on a chair. Her radiance disappeared and she flopped onto his couch, eyeing his laptop, nearly sitting on it.

"You okay, babe?" he said, unconsciously.

Madyson looked over at him, and pondered on her response.

"I'm okay," she said. "Just need to get away from it all for the minute."

"From where? The show? You got a couple of months to go, right?"

She leaned over and took off her shoes. Michael noticed a darned sock but held back his opinion on it. Madyson closed her eyes, tiredness overcoming her. The comfort of the sofa connected with her bones, and she disallowed the strength to fight it off.

"Wow, Mike. These chairs are something else."

She disintegrated right in front of his eyes. Her glow refracted, looking like she hadn't had a good night's sleep in ages. He waited to see if she would open her eyes again, and engage in a conversation. He walked over and grabbed his laptop. As he did, Madyson looked his way.

"You working?" she asked.

"Not really, but got a few ideas, you know."

"Is it this Africa thing?"

"Yeah."

"You gotta do it, Mike. Or you'll never know what will be."

Michael sat down in the free chair opposite her. "I know. And you know we spoke about it when you were in America. This is maybe the time to do it. We're older, we know from people's experiences whether we can achieve this or not. We just need somebody to push it forward..."

"Somebody like you?"

"Maybe..."

Madyson brushed her hair away from her eyes and wondered if she could be honest with Michael. She'd always been a close friend since college, and even after her mother died, she preferred hanging out with him than her relatives at that time.

"I've got something to tell you," she said.

Michael looked at her carefully and waited for her to continue.

"I've been thinking about it for a while, and I don't know how to say it out loud. I just think it's time I get it out there and..."

"Ah, hold on, hold on. Sorry," interrupted Michael. He jumped up from his seat and rushed to the dining table where he'd left his phone. "Hello..."

Madyson moved uncomfortably in her seat. Her confession had been halted, and she knew it'd be a life-changing moment if she confessed everything to Michael at that time. Could he handle it? Could she? She could hear Michael talking.

"Okay, bro... Yeah, sounds good. I'll be there. I need something to clear my head."

He pressed at his phone and put it down again on the table.

"Everything okay, Mike?" asked Madyson.

"Yeah, of course. We've just been invited to a barbecue from a friend, Yemi. And yes, you're coming. It'll get you out of this mood."

A worthless smile crowded Madyson's face. She'd tell Michael her confession another time, and try to enjoy the moment with strange people who didn't know anything about her. She shook her head as Michael threw her jacket at her and seemed to forget what she was about to say prior to taking the call.

Madyson stared nonchalantly at Michael as he drove to Yemi's house, only 35 minutes from Deptford to Thornton Heath. He was playing his R&B music a bit too loudly by her standards, assuming it was a way to avoid serious discussion with her. Maybe using the barbecue to lift her spirits, even though he remained unsure of her 'issue'. They reached Yemi's home, which resembled a bed and breakfast in Earl's Court, and he broached the subject.

"Oh, you were saying... before," he asked, as they glided through the narrow hallway of the two-storey house. Music hit them as soon as they entered the property, while the majority of people were huddled in the garden. He held her hand like a school child and guided past random looks and occasional head nods. She wanted to let go, but appreciated his form of attention.

"It was…" she started.

A sea of youthful dark skin and white teeth swarmed them upon entering the garden's terrain. Bright colours, hearty conversations and good vibes were being shared and they'd emerged into a party unlike one they had been to in ages. It easily beat the smoke-filled pubs where they usually met.

"...Nothing."

Michael let go of her hand, and saw the DJ in the corner of the paved garden, not too far from where the burning food and drinks were being served.

"There's Yemi," he said. "Let me introduce you…" But something weird occurred at that moment. A beautiful young woman crossed his path, smiling, softly moving her body to the vibrating rhythm, clearly having fun. Michael stalled his steps towards Yemi and pretended he hadn't noticed the woman, occupying his eyes with other people in the vicinity.

"Mike, what are you doing?"

He caught eyes with Madyson, but it was no use. He had to tell her, he believed. But as he turned around towards Yemi, the woman had disappeared from his view.

"Did you see someone?" asked Madyson.

"Oh, it's nothing. I thought I had cramps."

"Really?"

"Yeah, yeah."

They moved over to Yemi and Michael introduced Madyson. It was a good move, as Yemi had seen her in a couple of films and shows and was overwhelmed by her presence at the party. Yemi winked a few times at Michael, impressed. Yemi's ability to mix songs and speak with Madyson at the same time was no easy feat, and Michael bopped his head to one of the songs, but became distracted by that woman again. On the opposite side of the garden she sat, and was talking to a guy.

Finan. Michael wanted to discuss work as an icebreaker, but he could see she was in a different mind space, and so was he. Striking in a floral summer dress, her golden arms were on display, perfect body and hair neatly tied back, showing her full face. He put his head down and sipped at his drink. It wasn't the place to do what he really wanted to, and not with Madyson with him. Finan looked over and smiled gently. The guy she was with headed towards the kitchen. This was Michael's chance to go and speak with her about everything. But her eyes blinked as the guy's hand clasped on hers, taking her along through the small crowd. Michael turned back to Yemi and Madyson. *I'm too old to be feeling like this.* It was going to be a long afternoon.

Rebecca sat there, quiet, trying not to imagine what people would be saying about her at the wedding. What they would be thinking about her family at the wedding. Beyond the opened blinds in the living room, she caught the beach and coast not too far from the home where she'd lived part of her childhood in. Her mother was making a cup of tea in the kitchen, but she had declined the offer. She had spoken with Marie, and it was her idea to visit mum, especially with the wedding only two months away.

Her mother, Amelia, entered the room, exuding a newfound confidence. In her 50s, her mother's body shape hadn't changed too much over the years. Her dress style in the recent years had progressed massively, and Rebecca sensed a spate of jealousy emerging. *It's silly,* she knew, but since the announcement of her mother and Charlie intent to marry, she found it hard to fathom their relationship as serious. The white blouse, red waist belt and black pencil skirt made her mother look like a CEO of a FTSE 500 company, and her light make-up made her prettier than Rebecca remembered her last.

"So Becky, what brings you home? I thought you loved London a bit too much," said Amelia.

She ignored any sarcasm. The zest from her mother made her question the anxiety against her relationship with Charlie and their wedding plans. She thought back to being 16 when Charlie was her boyfriend. How he made her laugh. How he made her feel sexy. How he was the one guy she'd ever been with. And thought the only one she would ever be with. Forever.

"You sure you don't want any tea, love?"

"No, thanks."

Amelia sat down on the sofa next to her, no regard in her proximity. Rebecca moved away, slightly.

"Don't be like that, honey."

"Dad told me, Mum — and when I tried to talk to you about it, you acted like it was nothing, so that's why I'm here."

Amelia was taken aback and placed her cup on the small table in front of them both.

"Mum, please don't marry him. This isn't right and you know it. I don't want to be mad at you forever, but I need this not to happen."

"I'm sorry, baby. But for once in her life, your mother is thinking of herself. You and your sisters are all adults, and Charlie wants to be with me forever."

The door creaked and for a moment, Rebecca thought Marie or Debbie would enter.

"What about Dad?"

"What about that... that philanderer?"

"Mum."

"The least you know about him is the better for all of us. I can't help it that me and Charlie are in a committed relationship and actually love each other, and are willing to take it to the next level. That's just what real relationships are about. They're about honesty and about trust. They're about…"

Rebecca looked out of the window again. No longer listening to her mother as her plea had not been heard, the rant of what a relationship should be like didn't appeal to her senses. She saw the tides rising and a young family rushing back onto the beach. She had to leave Bournemouth now, and the remnants of why she thought she could talk like an adult to her mother. She would never get the final word. That wouldn't change in a million years.

"Thanks, Mike. I needed that. We'll catch up soon okay."

Madyson closed the car door when they pulled up by her home after leaving Yemi's party. She had been smiling non-stop since meeting Michael's friend. Yemi's fandom about her career was a unique experience, and the detailing of her scenes made her wonder about what future she had in the business. To hear it first hand at how films could be impactful in people's lives made her believe her life path had been worth it. Michael, though, wasn't so pleased by attending the barbecue, and wished he hadn't. As a result of seeing Finan, he thought about Rebecca and whether she was the woman for him. *Why is she even with him?* Because he liked rap music like she did. She was a netball player in her youth, and he played basketball. Or their relationship was just the extension of that first meeting where they had found someone who wanted what they wanted… back then.

Michael muttered his goodbye to Madyson and he watched her enter her home, a modest two-bedroom flat in Hammersmith. He couldn't make her his sexual relief now and she could never be. Their friendship was more important than that. He switched the engine back on, and drove home, noticing a missed call and message on his phone. It spelled trouble. Late evening calls usually were. Stopping at a traffic lights, he saw it was Lawrence and tried to remember when they'd last spoken. He raised the phone to his ear and listened:

"Yo, bruv, man. It's Law. Need your help, but I can help you, too. I can do the site somethin'. I can develop it into something — like you want it. But.. but… shit… I need help on the…" It was too slowly delivered and caused Lawrence to not get his full message through. Michael sensed it was money. The only reason Lawrence would call him. To say, "Hi" — those days were a thing of the past.

Michael decided to wait before he called Lawrence back and to check out *The Choice* story, and share it onto his site and social channels. It was fun reading his name and his personal story mentioned in third person, something which hadn't happened since his basketball days. Would it truly relate with those from the Afro community, for which the publication was aimed at. The positioning of black people away from Africa was fragmented and his story would provide the possibility of unification and establishment he believed was highly needed, but generally unspoken about.

He posted the link of the story, so his followers would know the efforts to go back home was supported by a reputable business and newspaper. Only time would tell if it helped. He quickly checked the site's stats to see if he'd had any more page views or sign-ups, and there had been an increase. Up to 5,500 sign-ups. *Okay*, he thought. *We need a marketing plan. Something special to blow this number up. We'll get there… Maybe we'll get out a loan under Forward Thinking to do it. Maybe.*

Michael picked up his basketball in the hallway by his door and dribbled it, fully aware the next door neighbours would complain, but his adrenlin was rising. He did a shot and let the ball slide from his hand and saw it drift to the corner of the utility room, landing right in the middle of it all. His left arm arched high as if he was in a real game and he kept his arm there for five seconds before bringing it down again. There were some habits he couldn't get rid of.

As he looked around at the imaginary crowd, he heard his phone beep. A message from Daniel via HeyBrow. Daniel was saying he wasn't going to put the Africa story into 'Who's Doing Dirt' section as it wouldn't justify the worthy cause. Michael smiled at the sentiment and lifted his arm back to his basketball pose. *Perhaps it would all be worthy,* he thought.

Chapter 7

1996

You would have thought that the sound of a girl's voice in a strange house may have convinced the two boys that breaking and entering into an unknown property, and leaving a grown man unconscious, had been a bad idea. Boy B, however, seemed to have a spark in his eyes as they headed up the stairs to face whatever next their adventure entailed.

Boy B didn't even wait a few minutes after the girl's cry for her father had happened to consider going up the stairs. He appeared excited to confront the opportunity of more obstacles in his way of gaining somebody else's riches. His steps weren't subtle, almost unnecessarily loud, as if trying to provoke another cry from the girl. Boy A realised the situation heightened Boy B's assertion. The bags remained by the staircase and the jewellery and other stolen items still inside.

"Wait. You doing the right thing?" asked Boy A.

Boy B stopped halfway on the stairs, which were newly carpeted. He shook his head. "Hey, bro. We deep in this now. We can't let her see us. Gotta gag her or something."

Shit, thought Boy A. This night had become an experience he wildly underestimated.

"A few video tapes and ting." He remembered the activity being promised as. He turned towards the kitchen, positive he'd heard the man moaning in the kitchen. He pointed his arms to its direction, trying to hint to Boy B.

"He's not coming round yet. We got this. Come on, let's handle this, and then we get out of here."

Boy B moved upstairs, and Boy A duly followed. Boy A could have made a run for it, but he would have been a bigger pussyhole if he'd done so, and would have been called one for the rest of his life. *If I can get out of this predicament in one piece, then that will be it,* he rationalised. He felt incredibly powerless and powerful at the same time, although his acceptance to common sense was decreasing by the second.

Boy B stood on the first floor hallway, and scanned the surroundings. It was larger than the space on the ground floor and neatly decorated. A smartly-placed candlelit table under a wall mirror perched prominently near its centre. It leaned against the wall and had a women's magazine on it. Boy B couldn't make out the brand in the seminal darkness, and couldn't care less which mag it was. He walked by the table and stared at himself in the mirror. His disposition admirable, clothing attire sweet, reflection solid. The buzz of it all overwhelming, churning inside him and produced a befuddled reality that was taking hold of his mindstate. The rest of the hallway landing became a distant memory. Boy B wanted to know where the girl's voice may have come from.

Boy A watched Boy B, who appeared animal-like, and soaked in self-absorption. *It's creepy,* he thought. He knew Boy B was looking for the girl. There were four closed doors and she could have been behind any one of those. *And there may have been other people in the house, too.* At the far corner of the landing, Boy A saw a small flight of stairs leading possibly to another room, or an attic. His school teacher often spoke of these "attic spaces" or "attic conversions" and the stairs appeared too small to lead to anywhere else. He trailed Boy B towards a door with child-like inscription on it, and read a name that was going to be Boy B's first port of call.

Boy B saw Boy A coming up to him via the mirror reflection. He knew which door to try first. They walked closer to it but heard a voice.

"Dad!"

It was coming from the door near them. They stood still, waiting, weighing the options.

"Dad! I want some water! Now!"

Boy A realised this wasn't sleeptalk and had no idea of how to resolve this young girl's thirst, and subsequent elimination. Boy B gave him a gentle nudge.

"Showtime, son. Showtime," he said, moving forward to the girl's room.

2018

I*t's quietly noisy*, thought Michael, as he looked through the glass panel in the door at the FirstThing.com office. He moved away when anyone he recognised approached it or walked past. People were discussing his going back to Africa mission, he believed and had shared their opinions with everyone but him. He spotted Finan by the kitchen and imagined she'd been part of these talks. She hadn't said anything to him, even after Yemi's party, about it or who she was with then. They had just come out of a meeting about the Balstec partnership and she kept her views to a minimum as Michael described how the owner Simon was happy with their plans, but had expressed several content marketing intentions he wanted FirstThing to fulfil. As usual, the meeting started with good energy with compliments and daily observations among the attendees. However, a strange ambiance darkened the room when Michael stood up and ran through his slides. The eyes on him weren't interested in Balstec, they were interested in Africa. *They didn't say it.* But he felt it. Bryan didn't utter a single word throughout the whole meeting.

Michael moved away from his door, sighing. He hoped his site didn't cause him to resign or be fired. He needed the *bloody* money. It wasn't something he could live without for now. He picked up his phone on the table and looked through his text messages, and tapped on Rebecca's recent one. He rubbed his head as he read it, attempting to stir up sympathy to her emotional position. He pressed the call icon and thought he'd show his worth as a boyfriend by taking an ear to her concerns.

"Hey, Becky."

"Err, hello stranger."

The jab felt unwarranted but he understood it. He'd been distant of late.

"Checking if you're all right? You know with your mum and everything."

"Mum is fine, if that's what you mean. But she's still doing the wrong thing. She just doesn't give a shit. Neither does he. Neither does Dad. Neither does my sis..."

"He who?"

"What?"

As soon as he asked the question, he was in trouble.

"Are you listening to me?"

"Of course, I am," said Michael.

"So why ask who then?"

"I just had a lapse, sorry."

It was more than that. It was inconsiderate, and he knew where it stemmed from.

"Yeah, well. It'd be good for you if..."

Here it comes. The bomb.

"If... never mind."

Fuck, she's holding back. It was unlike her. Their relationship was futile at best and needed a boost. He couldn't remember the last time he'd seen her naked, or what she felt like. It hadn't been that long, surely.

"How's work?" he asked.

"Fine, you know. Getting through it. Starting a new project with Jason next week."

Ahh, Jason. Always around. A twinge of jealously ran up his spine, and meant he wasn't ready to give her up to some work colleague just yet. He had to treat her like the queen she deserved to be treated. *Or did she?*

"Ahh, okay. Sounds good. You looking forward to it?" he said.

"Yeah, it should be good. Probably means late nights with Jason, though..."

Michael held the phone away from his face. He smiled, knowing she was winding him up. He returned the phone back to his ear to hear her still talking.

"...not sure if Jason has been lifting weights, but his body is looking stronger these days."

Michael wanted to argue but he could sense she was testing him. "That's nice, dear."

But she wasn't finished. "The girls at work say he's got serious VBL."

"VBL?"

"It doesn't matter..."

"Go on."

"Visible bulge line."

Okay, that's it. That's it. I get you're upset, but that's below the belt (literally).

"I gotta go." It was all he could say. Her goodbye didn't register. Fuming. Filled with obscenities to shout at her, he couldn't understand what just happened. *Was she serious?* No way. With Finan or work or his website, he was confused where Rebecca fit in. He didn't miss her when he thought he should. Suddenly a slow song by Boyz II Men clouded his mind, and maybe they had reached the '*End of the Road*'. He sighed and looked back at his laptop screen that had gone black. He tapped on the keyboard, hoping to revive it.

Somehow Michael made it through the day and sat at his dinner table alone that evening when he got home. He whipped up a quick spaghetti bolognese, knowing he should have sauteed the onions a bit longer, and added more vegetables to the mince, which also needed extra seasoning. He was famished as the day involved ensuring the Balstec partnership moved in the right direction, and it was aleady taking a toll. Bryan had shifted complete responsibility of it to him, primarily after the last time they'd had a heated discussion about his website. Michael accepted the work, believing he'd get some internal help on the project management side of things. He'd sort it out before it became too much of a burden, he told himself. He didn't see Finan in the office much either, and he did his best to forget the conversation he had with Rebecca.

Taking another bite of his dinner, he sifted through the news apps on his phone for any updates he thought he should know. He avoided his Mind-site and other social media pages, keen to educate his mind, and not to just reinforce his feelings. A message from Allen came through and he smiled. Michael understood what Allen was going through, but only at a distance. Allen had young kids and a fiancée to sort out, and his yearnings for a younger woman were reactive to his emotional struggle with his home life. The younger woman represented a pathway to the easier life, but when Michael reminded Allen, they both nervously laughed as if weary on how quickly they were growing up. How older they were becoming. Why the future didn't resemble their immediate ideals.

He texted Allen back, letting him know he'd get in touch later, which probably meant tomorrow. However, Allen sent him a quick reply, with an image attached.

"This is what she was wearing today". Michael had seen a picture of Allen's fantasy woman before, and she was cute enough. But when the image opened, Michael realised the issue Allen was having. The figure-hugging full-length dress was one thing, but the stripes and the slit for her left leg gave her an ominous stance, which could only be defined by the viewer. He found himself biting his bottom lip as he zoomed in closer, looking beyond her cute face, and amazed by her structure and confidence. *She's stunning,* he thought, closing the image, and replied again to Allen.

"Sorry, bro. I can't help you with this one. She looks hella good."

"She said, she 'wore it especially' for me."

"Damn." Michael tried to find a emoji that could encapsulate his feelings, but it took too long, so he didn't bother and replied anyway.

He spun his fork and whisked up a few more mouthfuls of his spaghetti before he heard the tapping noise at his front door. The knock wasn't forceful and knew he wasn't in trouble as a result. It couldn't have been Rebecca as they hadn't spoken since the morning. He reached the door, swiped the door's peephole to get an idea of who it was. He couldn't make out the person. He partly thought of Finan because of the person's dark skin and feminine-shaped face, and hair style. *But it hit him...*

The door opened quickly as he tried to eliminate confusion and understand why Shanice was looking at him with a sullen expression on her face. It took Michael a moment to digest the situation and he half-expected Natalie to pop out into the hallway and yell, "Surprise, nigga!". He ushered Shanice into the apartment and didn't say a word for another five minutes. He looked at his near empty spaghetti bowl and pictured the cold taste if he took another mouthful. Her young round face appeared happy, relieved by his presence, although slightly nervous by the silence. She had a bag with her. It was her mum's, he could tell, and he suspected Natalie either didn't know, didn't care or was fast asleep when Shanice made the journey to London.

The pieces of this puzzle weren't coming together quickly enough for him, and it would require some explanation. He sighed, closing and reopening his eyes within a split second, and gave his daughter a long stare. *What the fuck is she thinking? She bloody has school tomorrow, didn't she?*

"So, you going to tell me what's going on?" he said.

A tear shot from her face. "Sorry, Dad. I didn't mean to. I..."

His phone seemed to magically ring at that moment. It broke the dead air and offered comic relief with an unseen surge of energy. He walked towards it and guessed it was Natalie.

"Don't answer it, please."

Michael ignored her and continued on to the device, stretching down as he became close enough to reach it. As he held it in his hand and saw Natalie's name, the ringtone stopped and so did everything else in the room.

"Hello."

There was nothing. He moved the phone from his ear and realised she'd gone. He looked over at Shanice. She'd briefly dodged a bullet. He held the phone, wondering if he should call Natalie but became distracted by a Mindsite notification. He tapped the message, and read the post by Paul. It was a comment to his request for more sign-ups to his website petition, and it seemed negative. *It is negative.*

"Haven't we had enough already?"

The context was unnecessary. It was clear what Paul was implying.

Michael heard a chair moving.

"Dad."

Yes, of course. He turned and looked at his daughter. It was strange, him watching her. Beautiful in appearance but worldly youthful with so much to learn. She must have taken a forkful of his spaghetti as there was a red stain on her top he hadn't noticed before.

"Hey, you hungry?"

"Starved."

He reheated the spaghetti in the microwave, and asked her what she was doing and to tell him everything before her mother called back. Shanice had no problem telling her story and seemed happy to get it off her chest. As he put the food on the table, and as Shanice ate, she tried to explain why living with her mother wasn't working.

"She doesn't listen to anything I say, and says it's because I don't pay the bills that I have no reason to offer any opinions. It's so frustrating. And the bullying at school is still going on."

That hurt Michael. He shouldn't have left it to Natalie to resolve. He didn't follow up with the bully's parents like he said he would. *Why didn't he know more?*

"'White girl, this' and 'white girl, that'. I can't take it. Mum says, I should just stand up to it, but they do it in every lesson, when the teachers aren't looking. I don't want to go to that school anymore. I want to live here. Can I stay here, Dad?"

He paused, when he shouldn't have. He missed her eyes pleading towards his, begging for a positive, requesting parental understanding.

"Look. You know what you've done is wrong. And how did you pay for your train journey?"

Shanice stared down at the near empty dish in front of her. "I took one of my mum's credit cards."

Michael shook his head. It just got better. His phone started ringing and they both knew it was her mother. Natalie probably didn't suspect that Shanice would actually venture to London on her own but knew Shanice would have tried to get in contact with her dad.

"Don't answer it, please."

Michael let it ring out.

He scratched his head, feeling a layer of stress occupying him. He wasn't in the right frame of mind to deal with this, but needed to address it, resolve it and get it sorted asap.

"I gotta go to the toilet."

He sat on top of the seat and thought about it. He wasn't sure how long he'd been sitting there but there was a knock on the door.

"Dad."

She was still there.

"Yes."

"Your phone is ringing and it's not mum. A woman called Melissa..."

Melissa? Who? Grant. Ah, Melissa Grant. SBP. What did she want?

"Is she on the line?"

"No," said Shanice.

Michael opened the bathroom door and saw his daughter standing there with his phone in hand.

"Thanks." Michael took back his phone.

He saw the missed call, and noted a voice message had been left. He tapped open his voicemail and listened to what Melissa had to say. His face remained clueless, puzzled by Melissa's intention by calling in the first place. Her message was just to touch base again to see if he'd given any thought about the Society since they last spoke. Michael threw his phone on his sofa and held Shanice by the shoulders, looking into her eyes. He gave her a soft shake.

"Eurgh. What are we going to do, huh?"

Whether he was referring to Shanice or his Africa website, Michael wasn't so sure himself.

Chapter 8

1996

Boy B opened the door to the voice of the young girl. He assumed she must have been a teenager, barely. He wondered if she looked good, whether she looked older than her years. He found himself licking his lips, and knew he'd entered a new thought process. He wanted to just focus on the objects they could get and sell for cash. But the journey was more interesting. *Why can't I enjoy myself as well?*

Boy A watched Boy B curiously. The reservations about the burglary eliminated, but how long would this night continue for? They moved closer, the purpose of the girl's room unknown. *We have enough things by now, maybe.* No idea on what they were doing, really. Just following the moment. The man downstairs? Surely alive? Guess.

Boy B turned back at Boy A: "The fun has just started, my friend."

Boy A realised he didn't know Boy B that well, and realised Boy B was that guy who'd hang out with his friends, and then suddenly disappear at those odd moments, before they had to buy something or go talk to a group of girls. Boy B didn't live on the same estate, but Boy A's friends allowed Boy B to hang with them. To this day, Boy A had never seen the road where Boy B claimed he lived, or seen the brother Boy B said had come out of jail for murder. Or that girlfriend who was a model and earned £2k a show. Boy A remembered those stories. And it was crazy to think he could now trust his life with this guy, who wasn't even that close to him. But a sense of excitement trickled within him. Something right about doing something wrong. He couldn't put his finger on it.

Boy B pushed the door further until they could see the full extent of the bedroom. A girl's bed was placed in the far corner, next to a small bookcase and lamp. The obscene usage of pink exemplified the girliness. There were artistic posters taped to the walls and a matching rug that connected aesthetically with the bed's duvet. Boy A stood back in shock at the strength in colour. Boy B seemed drawn to it all, walking into the room smiling, and looking for his target. Boy A wondered if the plan to steal valuables was still on the agenda. Boy B walked up to the bed, grinning as his steps became softer. The floorboards creaked, but the sound was ignored. Boy A turned holding the door, positive the old man would soon come around. They were in it too deep to worry now. They'd fight their way out of anything.

Boy B stood by the bed and seemed to be flinching.

"What's up?" said Boy A, watching.

Boy B didn't respond. He leaned further over the bed and pulled at the duvet cover. Boy A waited before saying anything. Boy B turned around and faced Boy A. A "look at this" expression, and he raised his hand to emphasise.

Boy A curled his lips in confusion and then looked at the bed. It was empty.

2018

Simon Thomas emailed Michael in the morning and had Cc'd Bryan as well. Simon then emailed again, and again. The context of the messages was the same: we need to talk about Mudderdeep and how we can maximise our investment.

Michael held his phone as he read the emails, shaking his head in response. He was working at the office, while Shanice was at his home. He hadn't yet figured out what to do with Shanice and was waiting to see if Natalie would get on a train and follow suit of her daughter and end up on his doorstep as well. He imagined Shanice in his spare room, moving around and doing something, *god knows what though.* He returned back to his phone.

The Mudderdeep events were soon to start and Subject Publishing weren't playing ball with its key brands, and restricting the level of the client's exposure — and this isn't what FirstThing were being paid to do. Michael needed to think of solutions. *Solutions. Solutions.* This was becoming a theme in his life, but recognised this is why he was who he was, and why it would ultimately be okay. He just didn't like the fact that his boss was on all of Simon's emails. *Ahhh.*

He sat down at his desk and scribbled on his notepad. From previous campaigns, he could optimise any issues that were sure to arise. It just didn't make sense to exercise the worst case scenario just yet. Simon was a delicate being, despite his wealth, and just needed reassurance as all clients did. Michael drew a spider's web formation with Mudderdeep in the centre of the notepad and built the lines of the web as problems with extra lines for the solutions. It became clear what he needed to do, and it meant eating into FirstThing's profits, which Bryan wouldn't be happy with. Michael knew Balstec was more important to the business of FirstThing than any annual fluctuation that Bryan would point out as a result of further company spending. The first move was to hire a secondary agency to amplify the content of the media owner, but without anybody knowing. It was a trick he'd run before. The agency he'd choose would share links, feeds and pages with its list of paid subscribers and notify them when something needed promoting. These subscribers would be global, meaning their immediate locations or geo-positioning couldn't be found. Only complaints to advertising authorities would require all IP addresses from computers, but as the agency weren't directly linked to the client and was a third party, buying this type of traffic wasn't illegal. It just guaranteed exposure, and allowed firms like Michael's to legally keep working. Big clients wouldn't work with them unless they reached millions of users, and what would a few grand do to the economy if the staff lost their jobs because they couldn't pay them, and they walked out, and the business had to claim voluntary administration, thus pushing more unpaid taxes to the DWP offices.

Michael shrugged, he had no choice. This was the business he was involved in. He had to make it work. He dialled a number on his phone, and was happy to hear a familiar voice.

After the call, Michael concluded it was the best decision for the campaign. He'd get Finan to work up some slides, putting his thoughts into a easy-to-understand structure. He remembered what she looked like at Yemi's party and wondered if her date was satisfying her. They had spoken more over email than in person lately, and he imagined it was for reasons they needed to discuss, but probably wouldn't.

He snatched at his laptop and wrote his email, grabbing images from Huddle to highlight his point. It was professional, he acknowledged, reading it back before he sent it to her. The focus was Balstec, not his pathetic fantasy of an office romance destined to provide more headache. Michael looked up as his phone vibrated. He grabbed it and saw Rebecca's name on it.

"Hey you," Rebecca said.

"Hey."

"You okay, Mike? Can you talk?"

The vision of a pleasant conversation began to dwindle. Maybe he was wrong. He looked around his empty office.

"Yes, sure."

"Er, I know things have been a bit weird between us lately. But I don't want it to get worse, if you know what I mean. I really think we can work at this situation, or whatever it is that's going on. You know I know you're busy with work and the other stuff going on, but I want you to know I'm here for you. You don't have to feel alone. I'm here. I'm sorry if I haven't been as supportive as I could have been but my life has been busy, too. With mum getting married, I've been confused and trying to get a promotion at work, or even putting together my CV for another job, maybe. I'm not sure. I just believe what this is all about, we can rise above it and we've been through tougher times."

Michael raised his eyebrows and knew he wasn't in the mood for this.

The last call they had and how she tried to wind him up about Jason's body was a desparate ploy for attention, but she shouldn't have done it. He wasn't feeling Rebecca at the moment. Her demeanour was off-putting as if she was seeking freedom from their relationship but going about in the reverse way, so she didn't have to claim responsibility. He knew it was lame.

"Becky, I can't do this now. I've got work and Shanice to worry about..."

"Oh yeah, Shanice..."

"Yes, Shanice."

"When is she going home?"

"She is home... with me."

"But... what... never mind."

"Yeah, never mind."

"Mike..."

"I gotta go. "

It's time to put this chapter to rest, he thought. She wasn't exciting him and appeared concerned with only things that involved her life. He had bigger things to worry about.

He took another look at his phone before putting it on his desk. It was a text message from Lawrence, but didn't read it all. Something about HTML5. It was probably about the Africa website, and how to improve user engagement, but web development wasn't top of his list, and his interest in *going back home* were fading. He had to think positively and keep going with the momentum he'd built up already, but it wasn't paying his bills, and only adding more stress in his life than necessary. He then thought about Lawrence's interest in it, and it was the first time in years they'd had shared similar passion points. For that reason alone, he couldn't give up on it. Not just yet anyway.

Another text message from Lawrence came from his phone, but Michael didn't read it. He thought again to Rebecca, and if she was worth staying with. Although he knew the answer. He wondered why he hadn't linked up romantically with Madyson but understood life had a plan for all people and he couldn't force things to happen if they weren't a natural or an organic fit.

He checked his email on his laptop. There was one from Finan. Without fully explaining, she was too busy to work on his Balstec presentation. *Is she avoiding me?* Probably. He didn't really care, though but disappointed by her youth and how she didn't address their tension. Or maybe he was imagining the tension between them. *Shit, I hope not.*

The flashing notifications from his phone caught his attention. He tapped at the screen and saw his brother's messages.

"Bro, I need some cash. Got into a little trouble at the casino and they've got people looking for me." *What?* "I need that money. You know, a little advance. The website stuff I'm gonna do. Gotta pay child support, too."

Michael shook his head and thought of calling his dad, to let Franklin deal with Lawrence. But Michael could hear Franklin saying the same recurring phrases: "He'll come around", "He's not as smart as you", and "He'll learn from his mistakes."

This message didn't sound like a mistake, it sounded like another error of judgment. Another one. He thought, replying immediately would be a good idea, but ignored it for the moment. He had to. He got up, left his office room and headed to the kitchen to make a coffee.

"I was on his Mindsite page the other day, and it was all this... *black stuff*."

"Well, he *is* black."

"Yeah, but it's too much. Africa needs to sort out its own problems if you ask me. He shouldn't bring it here..."

"I agree. Africa is another continent, for Pete's sake. It's like... err, hello, Michael."

Michael entered the kitchen, which led in from the long hallway and extended beyond his room and the other office desks.

"Hey Martin, Fran. Everything good?"

Fran's blushing cheeks were changing colour, and Martin stirred his teaspoon about twenty times. He'd caught them, he suspected, either admittedly in a new office romance, or they were talking about him. Michael grabbed the milk, granules and added hot water from the boiled kettle and poured into a cup.

"Mike. All's good," said Martin. "How long have you been standing there?"

"Not long. Why?"

Fran looked at Martin and then put her head down. "No reason. We just haven't seen you in the office much lately."

"I've been busy. Got a few things going on all at once."

"So we heard," said Martin.

"What was that?"

"Oh, nothing."

"You okay, Martin?"

"Yeah, mate. All is grand. Why not?"

Just asking. Michael picked up his cup and walked out of the kitchen without saying a word. *They're stupid. They couldn't even lie.*

Back at his desk, Michael checked his phone, returning his thoughts back to Lawrence. He would answer back later, maybe. He thought of his bank balance and to how the site could be financially viable as well as fulfil his African pledge. But became distracted, and headed to his favourite sports site to check on the professional American basketball scores. Some of the performances were poor, and he believed he could have played for the top teams he followed and analysed. *It's all timing,* he told himself, but had to denounce the thought and accept he wasn't good enough. Maybe not physically, but probably mentally. At 20 years old, he wasn't as mature as he'd like to think he was. That was the real reason he didn't travel to the US to play in their pro leagues. His British career was brief, and he earned respect for his play, but it reminded him that the British stage was nowhere near as big as the American one. A few of his British friends had managed to gain small contracts during their stints there in the US, and despite their limited play, they were happy with their level of success. Michael wasn't. Maybe that was what made him do the Africa website and to do something bigger than anybody else had done. Maybe.

He decided to text Lawrence when Allen called him.

"Hey, mate. What's good?"

"Ahh, man. I'm having some problems, bro. My mind is everywhere."

Michael suspected this was a personal call.

"What's up?"

"Fine lady at work is driving me bananas."

"Okay."

"I think she wants the banana."

Michael started laughing.

"It's not funny. I don't know what to do. You've seen her. She's a dime, 100 percent and aggressive, too. I like it but..."

"You got a potential housewife, too. Can't let that go."

"I know. I know. You know what it's like..."

He sure did, but didn't want to divulge any more details about his crush on Finan. It was childish, and lust was prevailing everything. He didn't know her favourite film or clothing. He just liked her style, and her age.

"Allen, you'll do the right thing."

"Like Spike."

"Like Spike."

"Yeah, I guess," said Allen. "Anyway, how's the mission coming? You got any investors from those petitioners?"

Michael was happy for the change in conversation tone.

"Not yet. Only small donations."

"You need to get that sorted or this whole thing will crash before your very eyes. Try crowdfunding, that may work. You can do it, bro. We need this. Our reliance on the British economy doesn't favour us, or our history. It's time to move on..."

Michael paused in thought. *Allen is right.* Everything successful in this world needed a cash injection to support its cause, whether it was political, business or voluntary.

"Any thoughts?" he said.

"I'll give you a couple of links to some sites that I know of, and also I think you may want to see if any capital venturists, is that a word, could help. Although they always want their money back."

"Thanks, mate. Send over any links or ideas. I've got somebody in mind who could help, but I need to be careful as I don't want it to affect the day job."

"Hey, remember," said Allen. "That day job is probably the only thing that's holding you back from achieving what you need to."

Michael knew those final words would stay with him for the whole day.

But one thing was bothering him: the Mindsite comment from Paul. The negative tone. He revisited his page's feed and did a screenshot of the post and sent it to Paul, asking what it was about. He didn't expect an reply so when he checked the phone to ensure the message went through, he assumed Paul was digesting and over-thinking it on how to respond.

Knowing he had a meeting soon to attend, Michael sat at his desk and looked at his laptop. He wasn't sure if he was making the right decision but he knew the question had to be asked. He started writing an email to Simon Thomas, and to see if he wanted to be involved in his Africa website and its movement in making this dramatic change. As he typed, his phone vibrated again and notified him of a message from Daniel.

"Hey, mate. It's Daniel. I've done something that can help you, but, um. It may have cost me a job. Ahh. Call me when you get this..."

Chapter 9

1996

Boy B looked at Boy A with confusion. It didn't last for long, though. His befuddlement soon allowed a smirk to thrive on his face. Boy A had stopped, uncertain.

Boy A glimpsed over his shoulder, sure somebody would come in the room and see them or worse still, arrest them. The plastic bags of stolen items were still by the stairs and he couldn't understand why they weren't enough for Boy B. *The man is going to get up, maybe*. Or maybe not. But they couldn't waste time in this kid's room, which barely had anything worth taking. An expensive laptop caught his eye and he nodded to Boy B. Boy B looked over to the small desk.

"Okay," Boy B said. He didn't offer any suggestions to the idea of taking it. Instead he stood besides the bed, looking at the emptiness of it. His smile widen, and staring back at Boy A to see if his accomplice understood. He had to describe his thoughts more vividly. He grabbed at the bed sheets and threw them to the floor. A mattress, a pillow and a teddy bear remained on the bed. Boy B jumped onto the mattress and leaned back, closing his eyes, with his hands on his head, before sighing loudly.

Boy A looked on, puzzled by Boy B's actions. He held up his hands, waiting for an explanation. Anything. *Is this a trap*, he thought — and were they supposed to get caught? *Here. Now.* He waited for Boy B to respond, to take some responsibility. They had to get out of the house as quickly as possible. He didn't know what to do, but understood that entering the property with Boy B should mean that they left together also. Maybe Boy B had other ideas. Or...

Boy B opened his eyes and continued to smile. He caught contact with Boy A, and this settled the teen for a moment. He removed his hands from his head and placed his arms in the air. He waved them precariously, not indicating any meaning for the actions. Then he stopped. He rolled over to his side and allowed his arms to fall besides the bed, with his right hand touching the floor. His hand almost touched the sheets he'd thrown a few moments earlier. He touched the carpet in his fingers and observed the warmth it brought. The material reminded him of his aunt's house, when he'd stay over when he was younger and play fighting games with his cousins. The eagerness of his mother to drop him there each weekend was never questioned until he was a teenager. He understood they never bonded that well, especially as he had no recollection of going on day or weekend trips with her. His aunt explained the weekend absence as work-related but back home his mum never mentioned work or anything else for that moment. She just told him to be quiet. So eventually, he did.

The feeling of the carpet disappeared as the memory faded. The girl, Boy B remembered. He leaned his body further, and allowed himself to fall from the bed. Boy A stood still, tempted to panic at the behaviour of his strange partner in crime.

Boy B hit the floor and laid quietly as his body moved in reaction to the slight pain that ran up his legs and arms. Instead of acknowledging the discomfort, he caught the eyes of Boy A and smiled again. The plan was to be unveiled. He turned his head towards the base of the bed and maintained his smile.

"Hello," he said.

Boy A didn't know whether to answer and or to look around him.

"Hey," said Boy B, to the young girl under the bed. "It's okay." He noted she was shivering. Cold. Trying to be quiet and not scream. Boy B gave her a once over, horizontally. She had on light pink-coloured pyjamas, buttoned top and a cotton-stitched bracelet on her wrist.

"Come on out, we won't bite."

The girl didn't speak or move.

"Come on," said Boy B.

Again, the girl remained still. She stared at him motionless, blank in her gaze. It was as if she'd fallen asleep under her bed and was still in her dream.

Boy B looked at Boy A. Not a word spoken and both knew their time in the room was short. *What you doing, bredrin?*

Boy B couldn't coax the girl for any longer and appeared disappointed she wasn't a keen participant.

"Time to come to Daddy," he said, reaching under the bed to grab her. She tried to shuffle away but had limited room to manoeuvre. Her clothes were damp when he touched them. The collars were the first thing he held. He let go to touch her face, and liked the softness of her cheeks. She made no noise and this intrigued him further. But he had no time to play the friend. He used his strength to pull her from under the bed, feeling her resistance and nearly ripping her pyjama top in the process. He moved backwards as she was finally revealed to them. *She is a pretty, young thing,* Boy B thought. Boy A stood still, awaiting any orders.

Boy B lifted her from the floor and placed her on the bed.

"There you go." He marvelled at his find.

The girl quiet, her body shivering, though not expressing fear nor jubilance at being trapped in a room with two boys she didn't know. She absorbed their detail and differences.

"It's okay," said Boy B. "You won't remember us after we're done here."

He looked over at Boy A and nodded. It was an ambiguous gesture, but one that invited Boy A to be a part of the next thing they had to do.

Boy A turned to the closed door, thought a noise was coming from the hallway.

"Don! Are you okay down there?"

An older woman's voice.

Boy A turned back to Boy B. *It's the girl's mother.* Boy B put his finger to his lips to indicate quietness for the room's occupants, and crunched his fist in the other hand to prepare for whatever was going to happen next. They could hear the woman standing on the hallway, waiting. This lasted only a few seconds. She then walked quickly down the steps. Boy A scanned the bedroom to see where they could hide, but the plan changed when Boy B echoed their worst feelings. They had to get out of the room. They were now in the thick of it. Boy A opened the door without looking back and closed it when he stood on the landing.

"Don!" He heard the woman. "What's going on?!"

Boy A realised she'd seen her husband and the state of the furniture. He heard the footsteps increasing as she ran up the stairs. She wanted to check on her daughter, but almost fell back down the stairs when she saw Boy A at the top of them, waiting for her.

2018

A silence harboured over them all. As if the bartender had made the last call for orders. As if nobody wanted to go home, but they had no choice but to. Ironically, they'd just arrived only five minutes earlier. Drinks were ordered and placed, occasionally lifted, in front of the respective drinker. The white wine glass was Madyson's, but the dense gold liquid colour and olive-shaped glasses meant there was no distinguishing which beer was really who's. Michael snatched at his drink, picking it up too quickly, a splash pouncing onto his chin before he managed to get some into his mouth. He looked around to see if they noticed, or if they cared. Lost for words to make the situation more of what they were used to: a funnier, calmer atmosphere. Not this tense environment, careful of what to say and who would say the right or wrong thing. Michael invited them out so the onus of creating banter was his responsibility. Even with the beer touching his lips, his mouth still was dry and words struggled to come out.

"Um," he said.

The circle of friends turned to face him as he uttered nothing in particular. Allen, Madyson, Paul, and Daniel (no Lawrence) shifted their attention and looked over at Michael.

"Hey, I know it's been a minute since we last linked up, but thought it'd be good to see you all again…"

A terrible intro and he knew it. He thought of Shanice, still at his home. On her mobile phone, pretending to do school-level work, all day cooped up with no friends to see. Her HeyBrow message said she was fine, and could survive being by herself for another couple of hours, but the accompanying dancing emoji wasn't clear. Paul ruffled his jacket, Madyson moved awkwardly in her seat. It was a different pub from the last time they'd met. This one had a better designed interior and wasn't as crowded. Probably due to being situated, not far from Tottenham Court Road station in Bainbridge Street, and where after-workers would struggle to find its location.

"I know I've been doing this thing," said Michael, "but you know it's something that I need to do."

Paul looked at Daniel, unimpressed.

"I apologise if any of this affects your life, but you shouldn't be… affected. This is my cause and any issues will come back to me. I just wanted to say thanks for your support and for being my friends."

Paul sighed. The outcome of this gathering was still unclear. Michael hadn't been upfront about why they'd meet tonight and why Lawrence wasn't there, too. The 'Africa thing' is getting known, thought Paul, but it isn't likely to dent the radar of any serious newsrooms. Daniel had broken their code, taking their pact on his chin, dismissing it and not letting him know. Violation of brotherhood 101, but he half-suspected Daniel to do such a thing. It reinforced the pathetic nature Paul believed Daniel possessed, throwing away a career and lifestyle to help out a friend — it was a stupid move.

"Daniel," said Michael. "I mean, putting that post on the front page of *Dodgy* was a great help for sign-ups and spreading awareness for the site. I can't repay you now, but I will… and appreciate everything you've sacrificed for it. Means a lot, bro."

Michael reached across the table and extended his palm. Daniel looked at Paul first before accepting Michael's grip and clasped his hand in acknowledgment. Madyson and Allen, murmured in agreement.

Paul reached for his drink and hid his thoughts.

"Nice one, Dan," said Madyson.

"Yeah, big one there, mate. You got a screenshot of it," asked Allen.

Michael pulled out his phone, sharing his screen of the grab he'd taken of the 'Going Black Home' post Daniel had swapped in to replace a story about Ed Sheeran. It featured Michael's name and bold text of 'sign up today' under the headline. The holding image resembled a clip from the film, *Amistad*, with a black naked male standing on a ship behind the steering wheel. Definitely attention-grabbing.

"Holy shit," said Allen, as Michael put his phone back in his blazer pocket.

"Yep."

Daniel crumbled slightly in his seat. He'd been suspended by doing the post, and his line manager took it down two hours later after first being published. He knew it was enough time to help Michael's project as he'd put it on during peak time, scheduled for 8am, when users were checking their phones on their way to work. He thought about his kids and Karen when he tried to explain it was published by mistake, and whether he'd be evicted from his home if he couldn't pay the rent. The suspension was without pay and while he tried to anonymise his CMS entry for the post, his computer's identifier was easily traced by his manager. An air of disappointment from his team around the move, as he could have approached them first about it, but Daniel knew it never would have happened. So when he called Michael about it, and heard about the increase in website views, and the social spike Michael had in shared posts and followers, Daniel accepted the *Dodgy* readers had nothing better to do in their time than to find out what was trending and follow the bandwagon where possible. He had to do it.

"I respect you, Daniel," said Madyson. "That was a power move." She leaned over and put her hand up for a high-five. Daniel softly slapped her palm.

"Yes, respect," followed Michael, unnecessarily.

The touch of Madyson's skin and watching her face gave him a buzz he wasn't expecting. *She's bad*, he thought, but looked at Michael, sensing disapproval.

"Hmph," moaned Paul.

"What's up, mate?" said Michael.

"Nothing."

The table waited for Paul to address his non-thoughts.

"Come on, we're all men, and woman, here."

"Nothing, dude. Leave it."

"No, mate. I won't," said Michael. "You left a comment on Mindsite and still haven't explained it to me."

"And you want to do this now?" said Paul.

"No time like the present."

"Well, if you must know..." Paul stopped. The eyes and ears of the table followed his words, leaning on something dramatic and unforgettable. "Don't worry about it."

"Don't be scared…"

Paul held his breath, not caring who he offended, but didn't utter a word. He'd had enough of this group. Pretending to care about something that they had little knowledge of how to achieve it. Not understanding their premise in the society they lived in was to serve it, not to go against it. *It's a stupid idea*, and something he didn't want to be a part of. His life was just fine as it was. He looked at Michael.

"What?" said Michael.

"Can I get out, please?"

"Ahh, come on, Paul," said Allen.

"Yeah, Paul. What you doing?" said Madyson.

Michael moved over, allowing Paul to squeeze past him.

"This isn't for me, guys. Call me when it's over." He ruffled at his jacket before standing up, and headed to one of the exits.

"Paul…" said Michael. But Paul was gone, not looking back, the swing from the door exemplifying his missing presence.

"Don't worry about him, Mike," said Daniel.

Michael placed his hand on his head, unsure of Paul's anger and reason to leave.

"Yeah, I know. He's a big man. He'll come around."

"At least there's more room at this table for us," said Daniel, looking in Madyson's direction.

Allen noticed the unfinished drink of Paul's, wondering if he should finish it or if he, too, should go home and work things out with Michelle, his fiancée. He had sent her a text but didn't check if she'd replied or not. Their kids, Marcus and Jeanette, were probably keeping her busy, he thought.

"Hey, not to dampen the mood even more, guys, but we've postponed the wedding."

Madyson shrieked. "Allen. What?"

"Yeah, she is having cold feet. There's a lot of money still to be paid for it, which I'm not sure we can afford and it's driving us apart, not together." The monotone of Allen's voice dismissed any emotion he genuinely felt about it.

Understanding, Michael made a sullen expression. He raised his shoulders as Daniel looked his way, and tried to present a sense of ignorance, despite Allen mentioning it to him the previous day. The perils of Allen's colleague, Maya, were becoming obvious and Michelle made Allen confess about everything, and this caused the postponement of their marriage.

"Allen. I'm so sorry," said Madyson, putting an arm around him.

Allen nudged closer and rested his head on Madyson's shoulders. "It's just delayed, that's all."

Daniel watched Allen, and wondered if they fancied Madyson, too. He tried to remove the thought.

"At least, you're still in the same house, bro," said Michael. "It could be much, much worse. You know, that."

"Yeah, true dat," said Daniel, as if answering for Allen, and contemplating his own situation, whether he'd find another job, where he didn't have to explain everything about *Dodgy* to Karen, again.

Allen moved from Madyson's comforting arm, and exhaled. "I hope so. I think I may have crossed the line this time. There's this..."

"Okay, okay, okay..." said Michael. "No need for all the details, bro. We're not here to judge or condemn, you just handle yours, right?"

Surprised by Michael's reaction, Daniel wondered what the guy really knew. Madyson seemed to be thinking the same thing. He hesitated before speaking, keen for Allen to continue, but Allen was somewhere else, thinking of a resolution with his deferred spouse.

"Thanks again, Daniel, though..." said Michael. "The uptake in visitors and interest is definitely helping..."

Avoiding eye contact, Daniel said: "It's fine, bro. Seriously, no worries. I wasn't happy there and the rarity of black interest stories we posted was silly. I mean, they're probably going to thank me in the long run, but I'm not sure if I'd go back there."

"But what about... money?" said Michael.

"Something will come up. It better..."

A small laugh from Madyson made Daniel question his choice in fantasy. She worked as an actress, she should have known better than anyone about work gaps. *Man, she looks good, though.*

"You gonna check if Paul's all right, Mike?" asked Madyson.

"No, he'll be fine, or whatever happens, happens, yeah?" said Michael.

"What about you, this Africa site?" said Allen. "What's next? Is it going as you want it to?"

Michael had answered this question a few times lately as it's all people wanted to discuss. He only knew as much as he knew and couldn't predict the future. He could presume it, and plan for it, but he remained victim of it as much as anybody else.

"It's going… somewhere."

It wasn't an answer of confidence, but it helped skim the oblivion that surrounded the table guests and whether their friend was really making the right decision.

"You should do a video, Mike?" said Daniel. "It'll boost views and your message tenfold. It's all the kids are doing these days. Put it on Squareview, Mindsite and Postya – and you'll see. Every campaign is doing it."

Michael picked up his drink. His little boost posts with links weren't enough to gain a real following. All the videos he watched had millions of views and weren't necessary worth watching in the first place. Subjective, and there was his plight to get black people to Africa was ultimately subjective, too. He placed his glass back on the table.

"Good idea."

"Great idea, Daniel," said Madyson.

Awashed with pride, Daniel smiled. He ate some humble pie and waited for somebody else to speak.

"Nice," said Allen. Thinking of Michelle, he wondered if making a video about their relationship would quicken the process of their nupitals.

"Yeah, I might just do that," said Michael, remembering the retargeted video adverts on Mindsite that dominated his feed regularly. The pixel code used by the websites he visited meant their ads would appear whenever he scrolled on Mindsite as he was deemed a user of interest. The onboarding process and interactions he made on Mindsite allowed them to create a data profile and algorithm of his behaviour, along with millions of other users.

He would get Lawrence to copy the Mindsite pixel, place it on goingback-homesoon.org, so his advert would appear on other Mindsite users' feeds after visiting his website. "Let me get onto that."

Distracted, his phone vibrated against his chest. It was Renaldo from *The Choice*, who had been texting a lot lately. He ignored the call, knowing another interview was on the cards. He thought of Shanice. He had to get home and check on her first.

Michael made it home but panicked as he couldn't find Shanice. Had she left with Natalie? Had somebody kidnapped her? He rushed to her room, the spare room, and relaxed slightly as her clothes were still in the wardrobe. He dialled her mobile number and waited for her to answer.

"Hey, Dad"

"Where are you?!"

"I'm at the shop across the road, I'll be back in a minute…"

The speed of his heartbeat decreased and didn't extend into palpitations as a vision of fatherhood blurred in front of him. To give up on Shanice, just because she was getting older and more independent, would be the wrong thing to do. He had to be the parent she envisioned when she left Milton Keynes to be there with him. But her schooling hadn't been sorted, her supposed bullying or even understanding her elusive mother, who appeared happy at the arrangement in London, despite not seeing her daughter in-person. He threw down his phone on Shanice's bed, angry at the timing of it all, whether he could fulfil his daughter's needs as well as his own. She was falling behind at school and if he allowed it to continue, only he would be to blame. Shanice's old school called several times, said Natalie, but only concerned by the lack of attendance, not Shanice's wellbeing. Natalie would hold out as long as she could, but said social workers and the police may get involved if they didn't give the school a legitimate reason, with evidence, why Shanice wasn't at school.

Anxiety flustered Michael and realised he hadn't eaten since leaving the pub. *What's up with Paul?* Sure, his friends had reason for concern but only Paul appeared against his African project. Michael's stomach rumbled as he turned to leave the room, but found himself stopping when his phone rang again. He thought to Shanice, but didn't recognise the number. And he'd already stored Renaldo Paul's number. The curiosity bothered him and he reached for the phone.

"Hello."

"Is that Mr. Featherstone?"

"Yes, it is. Who is this?"

"Sorry, my name is Melanie Watson from *The Stardium* newspaper and wondered if you were available to answer some questions?"

"Errr..." he said. *The Stardium.* Jeez. This is major. "Sure, what can I do for you?"

"You are Michael Featherstone?"

"Yes, that's right."

"And you're promoting an effort for black people to go back to Africa?"

He paused. "You could say I am…"

"I've seen your Mindsite page and it's impressive. You have a good number of friends and followers and your posts are getting a good response," said

Melanie.

"Can I ask what this is about?"

"Yes, yes, of course. I'm a journalist at *The Stardium* and working on a feature about black British identity in politics and the trials, conflicts it has towards encouraging BAME people to vote."

"Okay. Why do you need me?"

"Well, your petition and website is just about that. It's about the advancement of black people in Britain and why you feel the need to leave the society."

"Okay. I get you now."

"Are you around tomorrow to answer some questions? It'll simply be to ask why you started your petition and who can get involved."

"Yes, sure. I'll be around anytime…" he said. "Can I ask how you got my number?"

Melanie laughed. "You put it on Mindsite and I found it on your profile page."

That simple, huh?

Shanice entered the room and gave him a look to imply he was in the wrong part of the flat. Michael said goodbye to the journalist, realising it was becoming serious. He'd soon be getting calls from all the national papers if it continued, and he'd needed to understand how to make the petition seem as professional as possible. They'd be looking for cracks in the business, and would try at any cost to question his character. He walked over and gave his daughter a hug, happy to see her. It was something they wouldn't be able to do easily.

Michael typed into his subscribed web hosting domain, and changed its service to premium. It meant his site could accept advertising, produce cookies, pixels and connect with bigger analytics platforms. The advertising units were standard but provided a scale of potential business where corporate messaging could be included and he could start logically thinking about company revenue and how to develop an annual turnover.

After dinner, Shanice headed to her room, content at being alone and not facing the third degree about school from her mother. Michael meant to bring up the subject of her going back home, but couldn't do it as he enjoyed her company.

He returned to the backend of his site, and opened a new tab on his computer. The formulation of a business plan was due. How Forward Thinking would be the company name, its site URL would be goingbackhomesoon.org and the petition and donation sections would be separate entities but belong partly to the cause. He'd already opened a business bank account, added Forward Thinking onto Companies House as a company limited by guarantee. He would need to register its accounts and complete an annual return each forecast year, and would have himself as the main director. Floating the business would come later if successful, so currently he didn't require any share capital or any shareholders, but could accept investment. He listed the services of a treasurer and accountant on his document, among sales people, PR and social media editors, to help spread the message and ultimately, collect the money he'd need for the first wave of transportation and accommodation to Africa. He breathed deeply, as if only aware of the magnitude of the operation. His phone vibrated next to him and he saw Rebecca's name on it. "Hey."

"That's all I get nowadays, 'Hey,'" said Rebecca.

"What else do you want? I got drums and skittles in the back if that helps."

"Oh sorry I called."

"Hmm."

"What's up with you? I just called to see if you were okay. Maybe we'd go out somewhere as we haven't done that in a bit."

"I need to sort out Shanice before I make plans, and I got other things going on."

"Sounds like you're avoiding me, Mike."

"I'm trying to do the right thing, sorry if that doesn't involve you."

"What does that mean?" Her voice upset.

"Nothing. I gotta go…"

"What…"

Silence followed and a text message made Michael move the phone from his ear. It was Renaldo again. He texted back: *I got an interview with The Stardium tomorrow.* Renaldo responded instantly. Michael replied: *Yes, really. Gonna take this where we can!* Again, *The Choice* reporter messaged back. Michael smiled: *Of course, brother. You can get another interview — and thanks for the support.*

"Err, hello. Mike, are you there?"

Crap.

Chapter 10

1996

For a split second, Boy A wondered what he'd been up to for most of the year so it'd feel that all prior experiences were nothing in comparison to the night he was having. He saw the woman flinch, doubting her movements and worried about approaching him. The vest and shorts she wore made her susceptible to being overanalysed and sexualised, but she didn't care about herself, she was concerned about her husband and daughter.

"Don!" she called out.

"No," said Boy A. Meaning Don won't respond anytime soon.

The woman observed Boy A's position and couldn't figure how to get around him to save her child.

"Just leave her alone. Take what you want, but leave her alone."

Talking to her wasn't on the agenda for Boy A, and he realised any conversation meant a recognition of who he was, and could be arrested for, if he made it out of there in one piece.

"Look, we don't have much," she continued. "Our money is in the house. There's nothing valuable here." Boy A knew she was lying. He looked around the landing to see if Boy B had heard her speaking. A glimmer from the mirror in the darkness. Only then he saw how he appeared to the woman at the bottom of the stairs. His dark skin hardly visible against the poor landing lighting. His tracksuit more prominent than his skin colour.

She walked up the stairs, confident in her stride. "I know you're a nice boy. You don't mean any harm, and if you go now, I won't call the police."

He wasn't listening. Her skin slightly tanned, with a beach body worthy of summer Ibiza tourists. Her steps exposed her feet. Calves and thighs were impeccably shaped. Boy A blinked to dismiss the quiet admiration.

The woman pulled out an unlit candle from behind her back and waved it at him. Boy A stumbled back, and tried to gain balance. He held onto the wall as she came closer. Her face crunched together, a rage evident. She ran at him with the candle, which was red, thick and shortly-stubbed, but could inflict damage if aimed correctly. Boy A leaned on the mirror and didn't know what to do. She swiped the candle at his face, and he moved to avoid its intention.

"Where is she?"

The cry was stretched, tugging at her throat to reveal her pain. Boy A found himself smiling. The woman's face was closer than before, and he knew she wasn't young enough to take him on. She unleashed another attempt of striking him with the candle, but instead of moving or ducking from her, Boy A caught her arm as it came around, and held it firmly. The woman paused and watched her arm lose control. Pushing her arm down with might, he punched her in the face with his free hand. The blow caught her off-guard. The candle rolled along the landing's carpet, the impact of Boy A's punch recoiled her back onto the banister by the stairs. He moved quickly to her and hit her again; this time with multiple punches. Her face ruined by the repeated nature, and his enjoyment of physical violence.

"What? You think you can *test* me."

"Oow." She became unconscious and fell onto the carpet. Her world black and her legs unable to respond. She crumbled into a human ball besides Boy A's legs.

"Katherine!" The voice of the man cried. It was a weak cry. He had to react fast and do something before she also came around, too. *Why am I doing this alone?* The storage room door on the landing opened at a five-degree angle, and Boy A was unsure why he hadn't seen it before. He looked towards the set of stairs that led to the attic. He *could* put 'Katherine' up there, but the storage space was more convenient. Once opened, towels and bed sheets of all colours stared at him. Room just below the shelves meant maybe enough room to put her in it.

Boy A grabbed at her shoulders, her weight instantly signalled she was out cold. He pulled her body across the carpet and dragged her into the storage room, not thinking about its temperature or its limited space. Her body barely fit inside and he leaned on the door as he closed it. He had to move on and get out of there. The old man was still tied up, but would get free at any given chance. Boy A wanted to see what Boy B was up to, before deciding to leave the property as soon as possible.

The observation wasn't pretty, as it'd sunk in that putting a grown woman in the storage cupboard hadn't been part of the plan. *But neither is this.* Standing by the doorway of the girl's bedroom, and watching as Boy B rested a knee on the girl's bed with his tracksuit bottoms down by his ankles, caught Boy A by surprise. The girl was naked from the waist down also, and Boy B covered her mouth with a loose hand. The allure to leave didn't occur until Boy B swooned his manhood down into the young girl's body and made her move rigidly on the bed. She bit his hand, he slapped her face, but he didn't stop. It made him more aggressive and the girl used her own hands to cover her face as Boy B grunted over her.

"Yo, bro. What you doing? We gotta get outta here!" Boy A finally spoke.

Boy B didn't hear him.

Bending over, Boy A didn't want to get too close. It wasn't something he'd seen before, and didn't want the front row ticket. He threw the candle from the carpet at Boy B's back.

"Ahh, what the…?"

"Let's get out of here."

Boy B stared down at the girl and pulled himself out of her lithe body. He slapped her on the face twice and lifted the cover from the floor to put over her. He pulled up his tracksuit bottoms and stood over the bed. The girl moved her body to the side and pulled her legs together.

"Come on..."

Boy B looked around the room to see if there was anything worth stealing. He objected against his thoughts and ran to the door, seeing Boy A watching him nervously. He patted Boy A on the shoulder as he left the room. They had to get their bags and get out of the house now.

2018

Working from home was never going to be easy with Shanice there with him, and when she asked questions he didn't know the answers to. School was a double-edged sword, he gathered, but Michael had no choice *but* to find her somewhere to go if she was unlikely to go back to her mother's anytime soon.

Lewisham Council could provide, and advise him of any school waiting lists. The only schools available weren't the greatest, said the woman on the phone. Her frankness surprised Michael. She mentioned all the online forms he needed to complete to get Shanice transferred to a school of their choice. He tapped into his website and social channels to distract him from the reality of bad parenting 101: getting your child into a rubbish school.

It seemed that Daniel's idea was a good one, and with the front page post on *Dodgy*, Michael owed him massively. His Mindsite and Postya pages were doing well, too, with strong engagement figures, primarily due to the video he recently posted. The comments and views kept flooding in. The video itself wasn't anything special. Recorded and edited on his phone, it was just a 'talking head' piece where he sat in his kitchen and gave a reflective account of why he wanted more sign-ups to his petition, his intent of moving continent and why this was the only solution applicable to black people in the Western world. It worked. The page views on his site were spiking in the right direction and reaching heights he hadn't seen before. With nearly a thousand users per day logging onto his site at some point to learn more about his goal and how to donate to the cause. The money was coming into his Forward Thinking business account at a nice pace, too. He still had a long way to go, but the objective was becoming feasible. He changed his number on the website and Mindsite to another mobile, which he checked approximately four times a day, so he wouldn't be inclined to listen or respond to every message he received.

He hired a freelance accountant to keep an eye of the business's finances to ensure any tax, and liabilities wouldn't sting this new operation. His earnings he made from FirstThing were separate, and he liked it that way, it would allow him to keep some distance between the business capital he was making.

"Er, excuse me, Mr. Featherstone," said the woman from the Council. "It may help if you could come by, bring your daughter and we could discuss the options in full."

Spending time at Lewisham Council wasn't something that he wanted to do, but he had to do the right thing by Shanice. But he had another meeting at FirstThing that he couldn't miss. He looked at his calendar and tried to organise his priorities.

"Hello, Mr. Featherstone. Are you..."

"Yes, yes, I'm here. I don't know when would be the best time to come in to see you."

"Well, you can come by any time during the day, although there's usually a queue. If you'd want to schedule something then you can just say the word."

The woman's voice reminded him of Melanie from *The Stardium*, and how he found it unintentionally erotic. The reporter had followed up on her initial call, probed him with questions around the subject of black experience in the UK, and whether leaving the country to go to a, fundamentally, worse setup in Africa, would be more traumatic than pleasurable. He answered that he'd acknowledge the creature comforts of living in the UK would disappear and the cultural transition wouldn't be easy, but it was a bigger picture he was looking at. It was about *identity*. Raising confident children, who weren't destined to view their skin colour as detrimental to their successes in life. The call lasted around 30 minutes but felt like an hour. *She's good.* But she was a journalist. *Her voice isn't hers.* It was quite off-putting for Michael to think about *The Stardium's* audience while the reporter fielded questions that appeared personal and borderline, insensitive. Working with Subject Publishing and other media owners, he understood the nature of the beast and target audience being everything. Without understanding your audience, he knew he'd have no business plan and his mission to head back home wouldn't exist.

"So, Mr. Featherstone, Thursday at 3pm."

It was the same time as the Balstec video call and knowing that Simon hadn't respond to his email about funding his own project, made it easy for him to say, *Yes, that's fine. I'll be there.*

Sure, the investment Balstec had made with FirstThing was huge and would resonate with a bigger market, but Michael assumed Simon to be smart enough to distinguish between a personal business and a public one, and there was no conflict of interest. And that the personal project may one day outscale the public business of FirstThing.

Her black jumper, blue skirt and black tights had become her go-to outfit of late, and she regretted the decision to wear it as soon as she stepped out of her flat in Hackney that morning. The office banter could be heard from the lift corridor, and Rebecca thought she'd stumbled into the wrong building. She touched her hip and rubbed her skin just above it, and hated herself for doing so. She saw Jason speaking in the far corner to Keeley, a new office junior and fresh out of university. He was flirting, she was sure of it, but couldn't tell if Jason's demeanour meant he'd flirt with anyone as a mechanic to relax them and get them to do what he wanted. He was emotionless at times, and the flirting hid this, and would catch a naive uni grad in the privates if they weren't careful.

She imagined he was probably good in bed, but didn't linger on the thought as he'd sense any opportunity to slide her way and elaborate on the thought without knowing she was even thinking about it. His flirting made him a sexual psychic, using subtle body language to incriminate his victims with huge hands and eyes that never stopped fantasising about his prey.

She walked to her desk, and tried to think about her work. She had a few spreadsheets to run through, to check their numbers equalled to the monthly tally they'd enlisted in the report to send to clients. Michael crept into her mind, and their relationship was nearly over, she knew it. The calls were beyond pathetic and he didn't seem to want her around. She didn't want to be a nuisance, especially with his Africa project taking up so much of his time. Not even her suggestions about it were of any use and would just spark an argument between them. Donations, she said, were great, but why not use the money to invest in something close to home, not far away? That didn't go down well.

What is the Society of Black Politicians, Michael?, she had asked. *And who is Melissa Grant? Why does she want to represent you, and why is she waiting for your petition to reach a significant number before being sent to Downing Street? Is she pretty?*

He hung up on her after that, and it made her furious. She didn't call back. She couldn't. She just wished she hadn't had the abortion now, and wished Michael was more caring about it. He didn't care enough about her. That's it, she thought.

Her phone rang, just as Jason winked in her direction, keen to pop over. She held the phone up to her face, making it obvious she was busy.

"Hey Mum," she said.

"Becky, hello. I don't feel good."

"What do you mean? Where's Marie?" She couldn't bring herself to mention Charlie's name.

"The wedding, it's stressing me out. I mean, I don't think he loves me…"

"What? Mum. Are you okay? Are you home?" Rebecca stood up and headed to the corridor by the lifts. "Where is he?"

"He's left me… ah, I can't take it."

Rebecca stepped back in reaction. "Mum? Mum? Talk to me. What's…"

A tear leaked from Rebecca's face. She heard the dial tone and called Marie. Straight to her sister's voicemail. She tried her other sister, Debbie. No luck.

Whistling in his normal joyous mode, Jason ignored Rebecca's pained expression as he headed toward the lifts. "Everything okay?"

He was surprised, yet thankful when Rebecca gave him a hug and squeezed him tightly without saying a word.

Shanice ate quicker than she spoke and with the evening winding down, Michael knew they couldn't continue on like this. He still hadn't called Annabelle about her daughter's bullying as the situation reverted and was now on his doorstep. He watched Shanice drink her orange cordial and a mild happiness lit up her face. It didn't last long as she clinked with her fingers at her empty glass.

"See what I mean about Mum," said Shanice. "She doesn't care about me."

"What do you mean she doesn't…? Of course, she does."

"No, she doesn't," said Shanice. "She hasn't made any effort to see me, and rarely calls. She thinks it's a holiday but I don't care."

Somewhat evident that Natalie had taken light of the situation, accepting her daughter wasn't in immediate danger, but she did work also, and Michael understood it wasn't so easy to come down and miss work, especially if her daughter was with the father of her child anyhow. The only rationale plausible that could explain Natalie's behaviour.

"We're going to the Council tomorrow, to get this sorted," he said. "You're going back to school."

"Why? I prefer home-schooling."

"This isn't home-schooling."

"But, but, it could be."

Michael recognised the fear of going back to any school would be hard for Shanice, and he had to be sympathetic about it. But he couldn't let her education go to waste also. Her old teachers still sent Michael work for her to complete, but it wasn't the same. She was left to her own devices and that meant she could have been learning nothing at all.

He didn't want to argue with her and breathed a sigh relief as his phone buzzed beside him.

"I'm going to my room," said Shanice.

"Hey Paul, what's up?" said Michael, surprised.

"Sorry, bro. Been meaning to call and explain myself. For the other night."

"Don't worry about it, really."

"I just a bit concerned by it all, Mike."

"What's the issue, dude?"

"You know what the issue is," said Paul, sounding hostile.

"No. I don't. You called me."

"Ah, I don't need this *shit*, you hear me?"

"I'm listening, dude, but you need to calm down a bit."

"I'm calm," said Paul. "Don't tell me to calm down."

"Er, yo..."

"This whole Africa shit, B... I don't need it, now or ever."

Okay. We've finally hit the nail on the head. "If that's what the issue, fine. You don't have to like it. I don't agree with everything you do."

"But I don't drag the mans into it, do I?"

"How am I dragging you into this? You're the one with the attitude about it, bro."

"The media, man," said Paul. "The media is gonna do its research and find out things we don't want them to."

"Come on, man," said Michael. "You've got nothing to worry about. You're as clean as a whistle. Lawrence has done time, but he's a free man now.

There's no demons in the cupboard."

"You don't… ah, fuck this, bro. Thought you were smarter than this. See you soon when this dies down."

"It ain't going nowhere, son… it ain't." But Paul had already hung up. Michael shook his head in disgust.

He heard the HeyBrow app notification and thought Paul was apologising, but saw Finan's name appear on his screen. *Hey, Mike.* Two words at the start of every crime, he thought.

What's good?

Just chilling, she messaged back. She was typing something else. *I'm liking your Mindsite posts. The video was inspirational. Really cool.*

Thank you.

She was typing. *You know, I saw this and think it's amazing.* She forwarded a link. *They say your name, too. I told my sister that I knew you when she sent it to me.*

If he was younger, he would have been blushing. He clicked on the link before replying and saw the headline from a website he hadn't heard of before: 'Is it really time for black people to go back home?' The article started with a Squareview video embedded in it, and a bearded and high-afro'd guy, called Leo McCarthy, a professor from Wolverhampton University, talking to the camera. The man mentioned Michael's name and said how the revolution for change was coming and now was the time more than ever that black people created their own fortunes and existence. Leo even called Michael a prophet and would be the one to lead us to our freedom, just like Jesus.

Michael squirmed. His stomach hadn't fully settled his dinner and wasn't sure if it would digest properly. The responsibility wasn't about one man taking his people to another place, it was about a collective understanding and movement for everyone involved to find their destiny, and ultimately be happy. There was no way he could lead millions of people to Africa as a Pied Piper character. He read the rest of the article and relaxed as he appreciated the balanced tone of voice in it, and explained the possible challenges that Michael had thought about, too.

Thanks for this, Finan. I see I'm famous!

She was a HeyBrow expert and replied in seconds. *You've always been famous to me, Mike.*

He didn't know whether to reply or ignore the message. He decided to go with the 'thumbs up' emoji and didn't look at his phone for the rest of the evening.

Chapter 11

1996

He ran down the stairs, convinced the man was awake and would try to call the police. Boy B didn't wait to discuss it with Boy A. This required immediate action. Boy B ran down the small hallway and into the kitchen, only to notice the man wasn't there. He heard Boy A coming down the stairs, heavy footed. Moving into the living room, Boy B caught the man trying to lean on a door handle. The duct tape was gone from the man's face, and the man balanced upright on the door with the chair still attached to his body. The man looked up and caught eye contact with Boy B like the first time they faced the confrontation. *No time for games*, thought Boy B. He motioned over to the man and punched him repeatedly in the face. The man moaned in pain before toppling over onto the living room floor with the chair vertical and facing the ceiling. The man was still alive, but the boys had to be quick and get out of the house.

Boy A stepped into the room and saw the old man on the floor. He had the bags in his hands, ready to leave.

"What were you doing in there?" asked Boy A.

"In where? Here," said Boy B. "You don't see." He pointed to the man.

"No, in the bedroom…"

Boy B stared at him straight on. "Nothing, man. Don't you worry."

"Is she all right?"

"She'll be fine. Are we going or talking?"

Boy A handed over one of the bags to Boy B.

"Cool," said Boy B. "Was there someone else in there? You were making a lot of noise."

"Yeah, I think the mum."

"The mum. Where is she?" asked Boy B.

"In the cupboard upstairs."

Boy B seemed startled, but nodded with respect. "Okay, my G. G'wan." He looked into the bag. "You ready to bounce?"

Boy A sighed quietly. *Finally.*

2018

They weren't far from The PellyCon, a small theatre house Michael had visited a few times with Madyson and Allen over the years. It'd be a nice place to go to after work and during those times when he needed to take his mind away from business. It also meant he could take Shanice with him, to actually do something together instead of being couped up in the flat all the time.

He took a glance at the road sign opposite him, aware he'd never heard of Idonia Street, or the housing estate that occupied most of the road. A few detached houses along the left side of the road were cornered by a small green and kids' play area. The road itself was seriously in need of some TLC, with potholes, ground contraction and unstable tarmac layering. Indicative of its state, cars were forced to drive slow and with caution, despite any added road bumps.

Not the impression he'd want to give prospective clients, but on a strict budget, it was all he could manage. It didn't make sense if his new office space was lavish, either. That's not what the project was about. And hopefully, people understood that.

"You ready to go and take a look?"

Michael had tagged Lawrence along to assess the IT setup and to also see how his brother was doing. He presumed it meant exchanging money as it often did, but this would be a meaningful catch up, too.

They stood outside a small business unit next to the housing estate with only the door signage providing any inclination of what it was. Michael pressed the door's buzzer and a short overweight man came to open it.

"You're Mr. Featherstone?" he asked.

"Yes, that's me. Us," said Michael. "We're here to see the workspace for our business."

The man refused to open the door fully. "You know the rent is £500 pcm."

Michael smiled. "I think we can manage that."

The man didn't see the funny side. He observed the two tall men in front of him, but couldn't place any concerns against them. As the unit's manager, he'd seen enough people come and go, both long-term and short-term tenants, and knew that they came in all shapes and sizes. He allowed Michael and Lawrence inside the unit's reception area. The pictures that accompanied its website's listing were clearly shot with the best camera possible. Lawrence frowned as the man's guided tour across the four-storey building didn't include the stained carpet, the fingerprints on walls, the loud noise of the other people in cramped booths or at small tables.

"This will be your office," said the man, who still hadn't introduced himself by name, as he opened the door to a side room. It was smaller than the First-Thing office and it had two desks in it. "We are fairly relaxed here. Our prices include absolutely everything. There's no additional rates or service charges or meeting room booking fees. You're good with us… Electricity, heating, cleaner, organic tea and coffee, beer, printing, etc. Everything is covered. The shared kitchen space, toilets, all of it. And the broadband — our core service — is the best fast fibre broadband."

Michael looked at Lawrence to see what he thought, but the body language was unclear.

"Okay, I'll leave you two to think about it, yeah. Go inside, take a seat. I'll be down the hall when you're ready."

They watched the man walk off, whistling away.

"What you think, bro?" asked Michael.

Lawrence shrugged. "It's not heaven on Earth, but it's somewhere. As long as their Wi-Fi and servers are decent and can handle all the site requests you're going to have, then it's good. I know you don't want to spend, but scared money don't…"

"Yeah, I know, but I'm just starting out and I don't want to risk anything at the minute. Bad enough I'm still working at FirstThing, and Bryan's been calling me out."

"What you mean, 'calling you out'?"

"Just that. At meetings, he makes jokes that I'm not fully committed to

Balstec and I'm pushing my own venture more."

"Er, bro. I mean, you're here. You can't keep juggling both worlds. Pretty soon, something's gotta give."

"Thanks, Law. I knew I'd have your support."

Lawrence missed the sarcasm, studying the cable portholes and internet access the room had.

The diverted attention made Michael watch Lawrence for a moment, at the child intrigue he remembered his brother had as they were growing up.

"I'm thinking of resigning."

Lawrence looked in Michael's direction. "For real."

"*Fo real.*"

"Well, if you're ready to do it, then do it, bro. Really, no time like the present."

"Thanks, Law. Means a lot to hear you say that."

"And, I think…" Lawrence was finding the right words. "If you're ready, and I'm ready, then I'm happy to take an advance before I start the work for you…"

It was only a matter of time. Michael knew that much.

Agreeing to the rent and the office space with the short man was the easy part. Deciding what to pay Lawrence was a bit more tricky. As they left the building, the principle of saying yes to Lawrence had been done, but the transfer of money hadn't. As they walked to the car, Michael had to address it.

"Is Shanice okay? I should pop round and see her," said Lawrence.

"Yeah, you should."

"What's up with Natalie, dude? She okay? Mentally?"

"Maybe, I don't know. She hasn't seen Shanice since she run away, and I had this Council appointment about schools the other day, which was pointless."

"Why?" said Lawrence, checking the road as he crossed it.

"They essentially said I should get a tutor for her as the best schools are overcrowded, the fee-paying schools require large deposits and a term's notice in advance, and we're approaching the middle of the school year, which is the worst time to transfer anyway, as we've missed most of the application deadlines."

"Sounds rough."

Michael sighed. "It is what it is. Just gotta find a way. Or she has to go back home."

They reached Michael's car and he opened the door for Lawrence.

"What about you? How are your rugrats? It's been a minute."

Lawrence strapped the seat's belt across his chest. "That's why I need that money, bro. Maxine is stressing me. Says Maxwell is growing, needs trainers. This and that. And then has the nerve to say she's seen Bryce with better clothes than Maxwell, and how Denise is driving a nice car. Joke tings, I swear."

"That's what happens when you get two women pregnant at once, man."

Lawrence resisted getting angry. "I know. I know."

"Other than that, though. You good? I mean, you can help out with my project. I really need you to be focused on this one, Lawrence. No slip-ups."

"We good, bro. Seriously."

As Michael straightened up to start the ignition, his personal phone vibrated in his pocket. More social media notifications, more responses to his posts. He just caught the HeyBrow text from Allen before returning the phone back into his pocket.

You seen this yet?

It was a link to *The Stardium* article by Melanie Watson. He clicked it open and read it for a few moments. With Lawrence beside him, he couldn't read it in full. The mention of his name raised his eyebrows, and Forward Thinking was mentioned, too. Plus the link to goingbackhomesoon.org, and the free publicity. He closed the tab and launched the keyboard to reply back to Allen. However, the following message from Allen came before he could type anything.

Sorry to hear about Rebecca's mum. Heart attack.

"What?!"

Lawrence turned his head from his own phone and looked at Michael. "What's up, Mike?"

"Becky's mum. Had an accident."

Michael didn't elaborate and Lawrence didn't push him on it. He had met Amelia a few times and she seemed like a lovely person, despite her wedding plans. *Why hadn't Rebecca messaged him about it? She'd call when she was ready. Maybe.*

They reached Lawrence's house in Brockley, a house share with two other guys, and said he'd complete the money transfer later that day. Seeing Lawrence grateful made Michael appreciate his brother's struggles in life, and why the road ahead wasn't going to be easy, but didn't have to be hard work at the same time.

Before getting back home to Shanice, he pulled out his business mobile phone and saw two missed calls with one voicemail message. He listened to the message and a smile lifted onto his face as the voice of Melissa Grant echoed onto his ears. She had seen the *The Stardium* article and was asserting the Society of Black Politicians as his advisory board and that he would need them if his petition made it to Parliament. She was keen to ensure that his project "wasn't just the flavour of the month" and with a list of media outlets ready to interview him, starting with BWMTV (Black Women Men Television), he needed to capitalise on his momentum and she would facilitate any untouched areas that his social channels and website couldn't reach. Michael perked up slightly when she mentioned getting Miles Brannigan onboard and how the reputed MP was a SBP member. This would be a great move, as Miles appeared regularly on television representing his Lambeth Labour constituency, and as a frequent soundbyte on London news slots for any preceived injustices for the black community.

What was the gain for SBP by joining him and did they have an agenda of its own, and considering they were working on a voluntary basis, and hadn't discussed any fees, he would use their services for as long as he could.

The other number on his phone he didn't recognise and didn't ponder on it. He had to get home, but Bryan was calling him, on his personal line.

"Hey, Bryan, how it's going?"

"Not good, Michael. Not good."

A thickness of tension surrounded the call, and Bryan only called if he wanted a problem resolved. Quickly.

"Why, what's up?"

"Did you talk to Simon at Balstec about your Africa thing?"

By calling it a 'thing' didn't sway Michael from the subject at hand. Everybody viewed his project differently.

"Yeah, we spoke about it when I went by his house. Why?"

"Well, he says he doesn't want to fully invest the half a million quid, and wants to put some of the money towards your project."

"What?!" Michael couldn't believe it. Simon had read his email and had considered it seriously. *This is major.*

"Yeah, Mike. He wants to reduce the investment by 50% as he's not confident he'll reap the dividends from it as other tech giants are releasing similar products this year."

"What's that got to do with my project?"

"What do you mean? You're the one who put the stupid idea in his head, Mike."

Offended. He held back from saying anything he'd later regret.

"We've accounted for this money to help us reinvest in our business and now I've got to explain to the CEO that it isn't happening and he's going to be pissed. I'm sorry but if Balstec don't complete the paperwork as agreed, we've got a real issue here. Mike, I'm going to have to suspend you until further notice."

"What?! No, you can't do that."

"I can, Mike. I have no choice. Simon seemed genuine about this, and investing our money into your business can't happen, it's beyond a conflict of interest. It's downright theft."

"I'm not stealing anything from FirstThing, Bryan. You know that."

"Yeah, but that's not what it looks like."

"This is crazy. You can't do this, Bryan."

"I need you to rethink your investment with Simon and get him back onto our books with the full amount."

Michael knew the implications of doing such a thing and how his own project could suffer as a result. "I'm not doing that, Bryan."

"You need to do it, Michael, or else. I don't want to suspend you until this is resolved but it's the only justification for such action. We'll need to see any emails you sent and other communication."

"I'm not a criminal, Bryan. This is bullshit. Clients have a change of heart all the time, you know that."

"Not when we're the ones pushing them away. That doesn't make sense, does it?" said Bryan.

"I didn't push anyone away."

"Mike, consider yourself suspended until further notice. I'll be in touch to let you know what the CEO says, but I can't have you working with Balstec in this capacity. You can't be trusted. I'll be in touch."

"Man, fuck…" he held back.

"What was that?"

A silence registered against their ears.

"I'll send you an email soon, but do not come back to the office until I say so."

Michael didn't reply.

"I'm sorry, Mike. Goodbye."

The dial tone lingered in his ear before he moved the phone away. A feeling of stress was mounting but he had to think positive. When one door closes, another one opens. He had to get in touch with Simon and see if what Bryan said was true.

Chapter 12

1996

They took a final glance of the mess they'd caused, but didn't indulge in its outlook. The place ransacked, the furniture overturned, the man still tied up and wriggling uncomfortably on the living room floor. Boy A thought he heard a sound on the landing but ignored it, and tapped Boy B to follow him.

"Let's go," he said.

Boy B looked in their bags to see the value of their robbery, and whether the experience had been worth it. His head felt light, a dizzy spell looming. He waved at Boy A and signalled to head out.

Moving swiftly, Boy A ran into the kitchen, and stood by the shattered door at the back exit. The shards of glass sprinkled on the floor next to his feet. He pulled at the handle and opened the door. He looked back at Boy B, still in the living room.

"There's nothing else..."

Boy B turned, thought he'd heard a noise. *A movement on the landing? Maybe the girl was feeling brave or the mum had regained consciousness?*

The sound of police sirens flooded his mind.

"Come on!" shouted Boy A. "We gotta go!"

It was the reality check he needed. Boy B ran out into the garden, the tidiness a contrast to the cottage they'd just spent a few hours raiding. He pushed Boy A, who was standing by the gate, checking if the car sirens were nearby. Instinctively, Boy B turn around and he thought the dad may have managed to free himself, but he saw a lone figure in the upstairs window. It wasn't the landing floor window, it was the attic window. He tapped Boy A.

"What?!"

"Up there. You see that?"

Boy A twisted his neck to understand what Boy B was referring to. The girl in a white nightie looked like something out of a Japanese horror film, but she was real and she was staring at them. Her eyes remained focused on them both and her expression didn't waver or flinch. A sadness engulfed her. A police car was heading their way.

"Bruv, I'm going. Now..."

Boy A pushed the gate open, clasped onto his bag and didn't look back, unsure if Boy B was behind him or not.

2018

There wouldn't be a sense of repreive happening soon, and Michael needed an avenue to release the stress he was finding unmanageable. *Basketball.* The one place where nobody could interrupt his thoughts, the place where he could be active, competitive and intelligent at the same time. He dribbled the ball down the court and looked for his teammates. Guarded heavily and not faking their decisions, it was too easy for the defenders. *A lack of experience*, as he maintained his dribbling, but was weary of the imaginary shot clock, and that he couldn't keep this up for too long. He put the ball through his legs, changed hands, kept his defender at bay with a loose arm. No help forthcoming. Rotating his move, he spun off the defender's lead foot, watching the opposing player stutter at the change of direction. Once he'd lost his man, he thought twice of pulling up for the jump shot or taking the ball all the way to the basket. His teammates' defenders were observant and moved closer towards him to help out, just enough coverage of their own players to not commit fully to their actions. The ball bounced firmly on the floor, with time running out, Michael decided the best outcome. He dribbled closer to the help defenders, luring them into a false sense of security. Ready to make his move. He paused, lifted his body off the floor and kept his eye on the hoop. A defender jumped up in the air, reacting to the manoeurve, expecting the ability to block the shot to occur. Michael, though, pre-empted the anticipation and dished the ball to his teammate, who was now unmarked, and pushed the ball into the basket via the backboard. He slapped his teammate's hand as they ran down the floor to get back on defense. He caught the opposition bickering among each other as they only had two more opportunities to win, and Michael's team had one. The disagreement meant disharmony and it was a chance to exploit. The other team's point guard forced a pass to its centre from the top of the key, but the big man, two inches taller than Michael, was facing the wrong way and had no idea was what going on, apart from being wide open under the basket. Michael intercepted the pass, saw a teammate running with speed along the sideline. The point guard was still hanging about, trying to steal the ball back, but Michael sensed the player would do this and threw the ball high into the air above everybody. The looping trajectory of the pass was uncertain, until his teammate caught the ball near the hoop and dropped it in the basket. Game over.

"Yes, yes. You African spearchucker!" One of his teammates jeered.

All the players stopped in their tracks and looked over at Michael.

"What you say?!" said Michael, walking towards the white teammate.

The following silence in the hollowed sports hall allowed Michael's words to echo.

"Nothing. You know what it is. It was a great pass, bro." The teammate held out a hand for Michael to slap it, but the gesture was ignored. "What?! Come on, we won."

Yemi hadn't come today, and Michael wondered what his friend would have made of it all. He smiled at his teammate, and the acceptance allowed the volume of the basketball banter to continue at its usual level. Michael sat on the bench, thinking about casual racism and how it could affect anybody's quality of life if they let it be.

The scrimmage now over, and he was thankful. He felt better, as a whole, for going, but the night wouldn't get any smoother. Checked his phone, he saw the missed call and voice message from Madyson. She was in hospital.

Damn, hoping it wasn't serious. Her new West End show had just started. *Bad timing or what.*

Hospitals were depressing on most days, and seeing Madyson in a bed with a tube out of her arm, made the realisation even worse. He checked on Shanice, who was consumed by an Amercian sitcom drama he couldn't remember the name to, but seemed unfazed by his absence from home. The drive to Hammersmith Hospital didn't take too long and he found her in the emergency department. Lying in her gown and appeared knocked out by the blood test she'd taken.

"Hey," he said, grabbing a free chair.

"Hey," said Madyson, turning her head.

"What happened?"

"I've been feeling rough for a while, Mike. That's what I've been meaning to tell you."

"What do you mean? A while. But you've got your show."

Madyson sat up, adjusting her pillow. She looked weak.

"Let me help you," said Michael.

"It's okay, okay. And it's fine, said the production company," she said.

"How?"

"They've got a double for me, who looks like me and knows all my lines."

"A what?"

"A double. It's standard in theatre, Mike."

"Oh, yeah. What's up with you then. Are you going to be here long?"

Madyson glanced at the nearby television set, watching the actors in the adverts, and their drawn-out method techniques. "I've got to tell you something, Mike, and you can't tell anybody else. I was going to tell you the other day, but couldn't find the right time."

"Well, what is it?"

"I'm HIV positive."

"What you say?" he said, removing his attention from the television.

"You heard right. HIV, bro."

Sadness and resent halted his logic, and he couldn't believe she was saying this. *She's beautiful and smart, and isn't silly enough to get it, right?* But he stared at her face, and her eyes not budging, firmly fixed on his.

"No way, Madyson. No way."

"I'm sorry, Mike. It's one of those things. I think I've known for a while, but suddenly I was out of breath onstage, my body was hurting, my trips to the toilet were painful, I had to get checked out. And when they told me, I knew it. I wanted to tell you but I wasn't sure."

He stood up, and saw the other patients on the ward either asleep or in quiet conversations with significant others. Anger arose in him, but he couldn't fight against it. He wanted to punch the television for its horrible depiction of how to wash dishes with a new liquid soap he'd probably never buy.

"Mike, sit down."

"No, no. I can't. This is not happening."

"It's real, Mike. Look at me." He didn't look her way. "I'm going to be fine."

"How did you get it? Do you know?"

"I'll tell you if you sit down."

He thought of Daniel and his crush on Madyson and hoped he hadn't infected her, especially with his jobless existence and domestic crisis. But he resigned to knowing Madyson would have said if those two hooked up. Michael sat on the edge of the bed and inhaled visibly. Still angry, most so at the lack of discimination diseases seemed to have when picking their victims. He restored eye contact, knowing he couldn't do anything at the moment but to listen.

"I've had a rough life, Mike. You know that. Stuff happened before I left to go to America, and stuff happened while I was there. I don't know who gave it to me, and it's hard to pinpoint when I felt like I knew, because I was in denial for a long time. It's not something you tell the world about..."

"Yeah, but Madyson, we talked."

"You're still a guy, Mike. I can't tell you everything."

He shook his head, surrealism taking shape.

"But I gotta say this..." Michael caught a glimpse of the television again. "I have slept with one of the guys..."

Madyson expected the reaction as Michael launched himself from her bed, but his focus was towards the television. He was standing there, nearly blocking her view, and staring at a news clip. He *was* on the screen.

"Is that you?" she asked.

"Oh shit."

They watched as the news reporter described Michael as the leader of a potential black exodus from the UK and what this meant for small to medium businesses in the country. How businesses would suffer in working-class neighbourhoods that had a dispropriate number of ethnic minority residents. They showed his video advert and his advocacy for a petition that pulled the black community from its British roots and led them back to Africa.

"What are they saying, Mike?"

The clip ended with an social media influencer stating how Michael was promoting segregation and wasn't helping the unification of diversity in Britain. *The project is pulling people away.*

"Nothing much."

"Jeez, dude. You're on TV now."

"I'm in a hospital, Mads."

"You know what I mean. This is big. You're gonna have some people calling..."

He didn't want to leave but had to check on Shanice and prayed no reporters were camping outside of his flat. He realised the benefits of being the hot topic, but couldn't let it affect his personal life. He kissed Madyson on the check and hugged her before going back home. The news story had open up some questions about the premise of his project and his calling for people to sign up with him.

FirstThing were soon to pull the plug on his salary and he'd need to use the business's donation to fund his living as well as organising the first wave to Africa. He'd estimated a strong figure but he currently wasn't close, and if he didn't have a job to support him, it was doubtful his project could survive at this rate. He called Simon at Balstec but only got through to his personal assistant, just as she was leaving for the day. She said how Simon was interested in his project and wanted to discuss it with him, and checked his diary for when he had an appropriate time to talk. It was a bit of good news for the day, but *damn, Madyson, what the hell. No bloody way.*

Michael arrived home, partly astounded by the lack of paparazzi hiding in his lift, and by how tidy the place was, even with Shanice living there. It dawned on him that his role as a father had come a little too late. He enjoyed her being there, but his impact in her life wasn't where it needed to be, and she, at least, needed to attend school to deflect the reality of avoiding it and pretending she was better off without it. She had cooked a pasta dish and the smell of it was instant as he walked in. The aroma held strong by its salmon and pesto ingredients, and small additions of basil, thyme and oregano, to soak out the flavour. Michael was impressed.

"Hey, Shanice," he shouted.

"Hey, Dad."

She entered the room in her tracksuit and t-shirt, her posture straight and her head upright. *She's getting older.*

"I've got some bad news. It's Madyson, she's not doing well and I'm not sure if I have a job, too. I've got to take you home, Shanice."

Shanice didn't utter a word, but clearly upset. She turned her body around to walk away.

"Listen. I want you here, but it's not working out. You've got to stay in school and get your education. But you must stand up to the bullies. You can't hide. I'll come to the school, if you need me, but we must face this together. It's too important for you not to go back, Shanice. Do you understand? I'm sure your mum will agree, and I'm sorry, but I'm doing this because I love you. I want you to make something out of your life."

Michael wasn't sure if she'd heard anything he had said, but it was the right decision, he hoped.

They ate the pasta in silence, barely looking at each other. He heard both of his phones vibrating in the kitchen, but ignored them during the dinner. She was angry and probably felt let down, Michael reasoned, but there was no way around it.

The drive to Milton Keynes quiet, painful as the radio presenters and CD music widen the generation gap between them even further, but the drive was quicker than expected. Heading into Bletchley, the scene didn't resemble Deptford one bit, the terrace houses bigger and probably cheaper. A glance at his phone, and he didn't read Melissa from SBP's text message as it was long, detailed and couldn't be digested at that moment, and he swiped away Tyler's, his accountant, email, too.

As they waited for Natalie to answer the door, Michael built up first impressions and how he could react to them. He didn't want to be judgmental or pick a fight with Natalie. He just wanted to explain that Shanice was the priority here, and if she stuck with the school the consistency would be better for her than waiting for something to happen at his flat in London. It was about her, not about them as parents.

He seemed to forget this, however, as Natalie emerged at the door, radiating a glow he hadn't seen before. She wore a floral casual v-neckline blouse, with tightly-fitted blue jeans that hinted at her body shape, and a confidence he hadn't predicted. Gladiator sandals on, her feet well-pedicured. Her make-up flawless, also. Her eyebrows natural. Hair neatly done. Skin care, too, impressive. She looked good. Happy. He smiled.

"Oh, hi. Natalie."

"Michael." Her attention turned to her sullen daughter. "Shanice. Get inside, please. We'll talk in a minute."

Michael sensed he'd have to continue to talk with Natalie on the doorstep for some reason. As Shanice bowed her head further, she glanced at her father. He took the initiative.

"Hey, I love you. Know that. And I'll be back really soon. I'm going to see what the school situation is like, and get you back once I get a place. But you need to stick it out here for a bit, okay."

Shanice nodded, a loose tear rolling across her face.

"Keep talking to me, so I know what's going on. We'll sort out the bully, okay. No need to worry about that. You're smart and beautiful and it's what's inside that counts. I'm here for you, always."

He reached over and hugged her, not seeing Natalie turn back into the house as he did so. Shanice pulled away, wiping her face and avoiding eye contact with him as she entered her home. Michael watched her fondly, but the feeling was interrupted.

"Oh, er, hi." A male voice coming from behind Natalie. She turned and held his hand.

"Sorry, babes. But I gots to go. The boiler guy's at my house."

Michael took a step back, aware he wasn't invited to this party. He wanted to be cool about it as Natalie was a grown woman, and having a man at her house shouldn't have surprised him, but it did. The man looked at him: as if trying to see if there was any mirror reflection. The same skin tone, not too much difference in height, the snazzy dress code, and the quiet sense of confidence. It was a flawed generisation but both men appreciated that Natalie had a type.

"Oh yes, of course, Reggie."

Michael knew then that the guy was a sports player (or former) and wasn't British. The accent had a Brit twang to it, but he didn't know any English-born people called Reggie, or Reginald. *Such an American name.*

Natalie leaned forward to give Reggie a kiss and was rewarded with an embrace so strong that Michael turned towards the gate and pretended not to notice. He heard Natalie giggle, a mixture of surprise and enjoyment.

"See you later, big boy."

Wow. He is still standing there.

Reggie moved from Natalie and walked onto the small garden path near where Michael was standing by the gate. "Hey, man. I'm Reggie." Michael faced him.

"Michael."

"Sorry, I've got to run, but nice to meet you."

"Likewise."

Reggie held out his hand and Michael took it. It was a firm grip. Somebody who caught some kind of balls for a living. Reggie clasped tight and nodded. Natalie waited patiently.

“Bye, mate.” Reggie finally let go of Michael’s hand and made his way through the gate and into his nearby car.

Mate, thought Michael. *I’m not your mate. You’re not even from here.*

Knowing it was all clear, Michael approached Natalie and wanted to lambast her about making time to have a fella at her house, but not enough time to even come down and see how her daughter was doing. It just defeated the purpose of him bringing Shanice back home. Shouting at her would do no good, either. Even being jealous of her happiness would do him no good. Shanice’s education was the priority here.

“Thanks for bringing her home, Mike.”

“No worries. She didn’t want to come back, you know that?”

“I know, but she’s lived here most of her life, so she’ll get back into it. I’ll talk to the school to keep a close eye on her and let you know what they say.”

“Appreciate it.”

“And… me and Reggie. It’s not serious, but I like him.”

Michael held his opinion. “I’m not one to judge. Just let Shanice get back to normal, please.”

“What does that mean?” said Natalie.

“Nothing,” said Michael, realising the wrong tone was used. “Shanice is quite fragile. Seen a lot, so just that. Mentally she needs support.”

Natalie folded her arms, and her stance uncompromising. “Well, thank you, part-time Daddy.”

"Come on, I didn't mean it like..."

"Whatever, Mike. You do your thing, and I'll look after our daughter. Thanks for bringing her back. I'll speak to you soon." She turned away from the door and closed it.

Michael stood still, half-expecting a smile or even a goodbye. He looked to the closest window, not spotting Shanice watching him from the window above. 15 seconds passed and Michael headed to the gate and walked to his car. He hoped he was doing the right thing and not sending Shanice back to the lions. He thought back to Madyson and worried about her health, even though she'd recently seemed fine at Yemi's party.

The long text message from Melissa from the Society of Black Politicians reaffirmed their alignment in representing his cause, and that his petition target needed to reach 100,000 signatures before they took it to Parliament. It was currently on 25,000. She had wondered if he saw the news report about his video, and if he checked the video views on his phone. He'd had to turn off his social media notifications to eliminate the distraction. But as he checked in on his video, it'd had risen to 150k views. But he couldn't celebrate.

Crap, Madyson...

Reaching home to an empty flat felt unusual, the lack of voices made him feel lonely. He'd fill the air with television noise and grabbed at the remote control, tapping the guide button to see what was coming on. He stopped at a news channel. The lone black voice from the panel on the show, *An-*

swer Time, and it was from Miles Brannigan from the SBP. Michael had missed most the debate but kept watching. The audience and panel were discussing the implications of a minority exodus in the UK. He wondered if his video had been the catalyst of the debate. The show's producers hadn't called, on either of his phones. He had to keep his ego in check. Miles was speaking about how immigrants in England had helped the economy, not lessened it in any way, and the truth, as he saw it, was generations of white working-class people, who couldn't break their class cycle were angry with its chosen government, and found it easy to vent at foreigners, whose differences were a distraction for the natives, and were too absent-minded to stick with their original agenda and make the government work for its money. And, Miles continued, if there was an exodus of minorities, how would this country survive, and could it really do the essential work as necessary when all the mining work and textile factories were being shut down due to an overreliance on education, and the oversaturated information age. The exodus would return to Britain its own sense of identity with jobs and poverty the only real issue for those who decided to leave England. The audience paused, before it clapped for Miles. *Did they really understand what he was talking about?*

One person who didn't understand, thought Michael, partly impressed with Miles, was the unexpected surprise guest, who was in his office in Downing Street. *At this time?*

"Well, err, this is completely fantastical, isn't it?" It was the prime minister, Gerald James, talking. "This is something that's never going to happen, so what's the point in discussing it?"

Michael saw Miles keen to interrupt and to say something, but the programme's host, Beverly Parsons, got there first.

"The reason we're talking about it, Prime Minister, is that racism and racist crimes towards minorities are at a high," said Beverly, "and it's a valid discussion point for Britain's future, especially when skills shortage is so prevalent, meaning the country will need to spend more money to keep people in education and training."

"Well, really," said Gerald. "I think we're in a pretty good place. And anybody who doesn't like England, should leave. Now."

Miles saw his cue. "Well, we are, Mr. Prime Minister. My organisation, Society of Black Politicians and another organiser, Michael Featherstone, are declaring that black people leave the United Kingdom as soon as possible."

"What?" It was another panelist. But Michael didn't recognise the name.

"Excuse me," said the prime minister.

Miles tried to talk, but he couldn't be heard. The clip microphone on his shirt top button had been switched off. There was an uncomfortable hushing around the studio as Beverly jumped in, and changed the subject with the next discussion point.

Michael leaned back into his couch. *Oh, shit.* The Prime Minister knew his name. He picked up his phone and found Melissa Grant's number. He threw it back on his sofa once the busy tone surrounded his ear. Frustrated, he wondered what Miles was thinking by calling him out, and whether Melissa had set Miles up to do as such.

Reaching back, Michael stretched at his phone, angered by his dependence on it and why he couldn't leave it alone. He called a familiar number and hoped it'd would allow him to reorder his thoughts, and if he was doing the right thing: with everything in his life. But the line just kept ringing and Michael assumed the person was ignoring his call. He stopped the call, deciding to send a text message instead to show he wasn't a completely discompassionate person. Texting Rebecca seemed weird to Michael as she wasn't his girlfriend anymore, whether he'd told her or not. Missing her a bit, or just missing having somebody there to talk to. He wrote how he was sorry to hear about her mother and hoped they could stay friends despite recent events. She didn't respond back and he wasn't surprised.

The quest to go to Africa was real, and was it the reason why he didn't want her as a girlfriend anymore? Admitting it was painful, but her white skin didn't fit the bill with what Africa represented in everyone's mind. The reality of image, the results and comments from his video, proved that the perspective of what Africa was and is, limited in the mind of many and he couldn't convert that view with just video, or even a return home project. He *needed* people. He couldn't afford to alienate them.

Noting the time and his body required a shower, he was in the process of switching off the phone for the night, but remembered that Tyler, his freelance accountant, had emailed him.

"What? No way!" he said aloud. He flopped on his couch, feeling a new level of stress.

We're being audited, Michael. I got a call from HM Revenue & Customs, and they want to know what's going on. We should be fine, but thought you should know.

Being a professional basketball player and self-employed, Michael had briefly dealt with paying annual taxes and how he had to register his income on a regular basis, but as a limited company by guarantee, he knew it'd be different and hoped Tyler could work it out for them. The auditors were a direct affiliation of the government and any wrongdoings meant his project to start something amazing would be doomed before it even began. And for whatever the reason, it just didn't make sense why he was being audited so soon. *Who the hell set this up?*

Chapter 13

1996

It was as if a KRS-One song was playing throughout his mind.

Woop-woop! That's the sound of da police! Woop-woop! That's the sound of the beast!

Panting, sweating, running, bags jingling beside them, Boy A could hear the footsteps from Boy B, the heavy stampede of a long night's activity trawling every step that was taken. Boy A couldn't believe they were finally out of the house. He reflected, and pondered on if the woman had been found, or still in the hallway storage space. And the girl at the window: *Who was that? Would she tell all to the feds?*

The sound of the police dimmed for a moment as the darkness and soft stench of the alleyway enthralled their sensibilities, removing them from their thoughts. Smack in the middle of the alleyway, unable to see the exit or entrance. Boy B pressed closer to Boy A, denying proximity between them.

"You good, bro?" Boy B puffed.

Boy A nodded.

"You think we're clear?" asked Boy A.

Boy B kept silent. His eyes not aligning with the odd rhythm of his body. His attention span akin to the quietness surrounding them.

Boy A held a bag up to his waist, signalling victory. "We did it."

Boy B returned, "Yeah, we did, soldier."

Whether a compliment or not, Boy A couldn't wait for an affirmation. They needed to work out the next step, and figure out where to go and what to do with the items they'd stolen.

The dim light etching through the narrow gap of the alleyway meant they were hidden from the main street. It was gloomy and unpleasant, but the perfect place to catch their breaths. The old stone bricks and smell began to take form in Boy A's senses, looking at the surrounding of disgust and area of misuse. The dirt and piss-infused slabs of concrete made the experience less enjoyable, but he accepted why they were there, why they needed this dark, arched and gothic walk-through.

"You wanna do this now?" Boy A said.

"Nah, nah. Let's find a better place," said Boy B. "I know a better place where we can."

"You sure?"

Another police siren hindered their movements. The sound soon faded again, and their chance to escape had been revived.

"Let's do this, bro. Gotta keep moving."

Boy B ran to the opposite end of the alleyway to which they'd come from, and seemed to keep running. Boy A huffed, before following absentmindely. Boy B crossed a road once leaving the alleyway and didn't look back. The assumption that Boy A was behind him was enough. A block of flats was now his target and he pulled out keys from his pocket. He used a fob key to pull open the door to the flats, and turned his head as he saw Boy A catching him up.

"You good?"

Boy A nodded.

"Let's sort out the stuff here, nobody will come by for a while. Sit by the stairs."

Unsure if it was a suggestion or instruction, Boy A was too out of breath to argue. The stairs were cleaner than the alleyway and he hoped nobody saw them there. He had some confidence in the tower blocks as he lived in a similar block not too far away.

"Cool."

2018

On the video call with Tyler, it would appear that Michael had nothing legally to worry about. For a business that had only just begun its operation, his taxes were small and the audit required very minimal effort to ensure they could continue as planned. Tyler expressed their shared fears, asking if Michael if he had any knowledge of why this was happening so soon, but a blank expression summed up the whole story.

"All companies in the UK are legally obliged to send copies of their statutory accounts to their shareholders, anyone who can go to their annual general meeting, HMRC and Companies House," said Tyler, unsure of Michael's knowledge of accounting and if Michael's quietness lent an affirmative on the subject. "The statutory accounts must include a balance sheet, showing the value of everything the company owns, what it owes and how much it is owed."

"This is boring, Tyler. Are we in the clear or not?"

"Yes, but..."

"But what..."

"If you don't send over a profit and loss report that shows the company's sales, costs and the profits or losses it has made over the financial year, then we could be in trouble."

"But we just started."

"Yes, I know and that's our argument. And as a small company, you only need to show your abbreviated accounts as you're a micro-entity with less than 10 employees and less than £300k on the balance sheet. I'll go back and confirm this so it applies for the following quarter or next financial year."

"Please. Thanks, Tyler. Let me know."

"One question: do you have a director's report?"

"You know I don't."

"Okay, no worries. But one thing. Is everything alright?"

Michael knew what he meant. *Was his business idea strong enough? Was it right? Could he afford to have a freelance accountant?* The request of an audit, in his mind, was unnecessary and thanks to the SBP boosting his profile, the reasoning behind it could have been triggered by anybody.

Sure, Michael thought of Paul, Rebecca and maybe the government as the conspirators of such an act, and would aim to shut him down and deflate his dream. Paul hadn't been much of a friend since the outburst in the pub; Rebecca could have been bitter due to their relationship crumbling and her ill mother; and well, the prime minister now knew his name and indeed anything was possible.

Michael stood in his small office suite, noting its difference with FirstThing.com and tried to explain the difference in his thoughts. It was a stepping stone. Nothing came overnight. But if somebody could simply call the government and have his company think about closing with just a call, it meant he needed to get his idea protected and get some liability insurance in place.

A familiar vibration in his pocket meant it was his phone. He smiled at seeing the name on the screen.

"Hey Mike, how are you doing?" It was Franklin, Michael's father.

"Hey, Pops. What's up? Haven't spoken to you in a few days. Everything okay?"

"Yeah, me and your mum are well. Just wondering about your business and Africa ting."

"Well, you wouldn't believe it if I told you but somebody or something is trying to take us down before we start."

"What you mean?"

Michael didn't hesitate, but knew his thoughts weren't cohesive. "I don't know, really, Pops, but the government been sending us letters about tax collection and putting pressures on our finances."

"You gotta get that money right, son. You know, public money is government money."

"What does that mean?"

"I mean, you can't just take people's money and not do nothing with it, you see. The government always want 50 percent of everything. It's modern-day…"

"Don't say it, Pops. Just don't."

Franklin paused and held his tongue.

"Well, I tink you should just do what they say and pay the man."

"But there's no case. I've got to make money for them to be able to tax it. We're not a conglomerate just yet, Pops. I don't know…"

"Just be careful, son. A lot of fraudsters out there…"

"Don't remind me."

"We catch up soon, yeah."

"Yeah."

The dead tone lingered as he decided to text Miles as Melissa said he should, and seeing Miles jump on the text thread and replying quickly was great for him. Miles asked him about the television appearance and whether he'd seen it. The ramifications of "celebrity life" and being recognised was the top of their agenda, and Miles warned Michael to continue with his business, but to be cautious at every given step. People by nature were keen to see him fail. Michael sensed this was beginning to come true. He asked Miles if he really needed to mention him on TV, but Miles said, "No publicity was bad publicity, and the SBP were there to ensure Going Back Home would get the opportunity it deserved."

Michael huffed. He could hear other people outside his office room by the outside printer and knew this shared occupancy in the business unit wasn't ideal. He'd need to buy a printer for himself. Any documents could be seen, and this wasn't something he had the time to get into it. He remembered Allen said he was thinking of selling his, and it meant getting it for cheaper than the standard price for one.

He called Allen but there was a busy tone. He began typing a message so he didn't forget to ask his friend, but was interrupted upon his phone ringing.

"Hey Allen. I was just sending you a HeyBrow text."

"Yeah, what it say?"

"I haven't sent it, but was going to ask about your… "

"My love life. Bro, you don't want to know."

"No, no," said Michael.

Allen wasn't listening. "Mate, the wedding's still off. Michelle still thinks I'm seeing that girl from work. I wasn't even to begin with."

Michael pictured Allen with his head in his hands and Allen feeling sorry and sickly.

"The kids okay?"

Allen didn't hear him.

"I can't do this. I need to get married. I want to get married. Maybe Maya will marry me. I don't know. Bro, are you there?"

"Yeah," said Michael, helpless. "I've been here all the time."

"What should I do? I mean, Michelle's not answering any calls and I've got the children with me."

"Huh? Where's Michelle?"

"I don't know, Mike. Her mum says she's fine, but she's not taking my calls."

"Are you at work?"

"No! Aren't you listening?!"

"What?!"

"Michelle is gone. Left me with Markie and Jeanette. I don't even want them to go to school in case she picks them up early and runs off."

"Ah, man, dude. Sorry… you okay?"

Allen breathed hard into the receiver and Michael pulled the phone away from his ear. The answer came without a sound and he knew it was a tough situation for Allen.

"Errm, you seen Madyson?"

The thought of Madyson may distract Allen for a moment.

"No, how is she?"

"Getting worse, I think. It's not good…"

Allen didn't reply. He was talking to his children and leaning away from the phone. Michael could barely hear his voice.

"Sorry, Mike. I gotta go," said Allen. "They need some parental guidance."

"Sure. No worries. Oh," said Michael. "Yeah, I meant to say. Do you still have that printer on offer? I need a printer…"

"Okay, you need to come by and get it. Anytime. Yeah? I gotta go."

And with that, another dead tone ran by his ear. Michael wasn't sure if going to see Allen was a good idea or if he should buy a printer himself. Too many things going on. He had to check on Shanice, Madyson,

Lawrence and of course, the new business. He almost had forgotten about Daniel and his job situation. And his mum, Glenda, had reminded him about the 91st birthday party for his grandmother coming soon, and family members wanted to see him and support him. *Too many things...*

Scrolling through his Mindsite feed, Michael thought back to what Miles had said about publicity and how crucial it was for his small organisation to survive and create a buzz, and without marketing, there was no organisation, no money and no chance to go back to Africa. Miles said how the SBP could advise Michael to think about running for London mayor to boost the petition and awareness of his campaign.

"This will help raise money for everything," Miles had said.

"Won't it be a conflict of interest?" Michael asked.

He could feel Miles shaking his head via the text message. "No, because you're London-centric, AND you're also doing the best for the city by creating a channel of communication between Africa and London. By the time the results of nominations are announced, you'll have enough support and backing to make your Africa campaign really have some fruition and legs to make it work..."

It was a great idea, but too political, maybe? Michael needed to make more noise first before running into the mayoral race, but he'd keep that lane open.

He tapped at his phone and opened a digital radio app to listen to his favourite radio station. To shut down some of the outside sounds of the other small businesses, he grabbed his earphones and placed them into his ears.

Some music and commentary would relax him, allow him to think and fully concentrate on expanding the ways to create interest in the company. The social media posts and media coverage were doing well, but there were too many spikes and dips in the website's visitors and their subsequent signage or donations. Regardless of the number of sign-ups, Michael had to elaborate on his business plan and the execution of how a wave of immigrants would suddenly disrupt the local economies they landed on, and how he needed to stagger such an approach to making it work.

The music of Beyoncé wasn't really to his liking, but her songs were so familiar it meant not paying too much attention to them. He thought of Yemi, and the understanding of African culture was closer to his friend than his own knowledge. The problem of living in Europe or a non-African country meant an isolation away from the everyday traditions, languages and overall behaviour that would be necessary for Westerners like himself coming over to Africa without being too reliant on their old Diasporic practices.

Pulling up his keypad on his phone screen, he typed in Yemi's number and waited to see if the ringing would eventually go to voicemail. The music from the digital radio app stopped.

"My man, Michael," Yemi's accent pulsating against the phone.

"Hey, Yemi. You good?"

"Of course, man. What can I assist you with? You coming ball?"

"Ah, not today. You going?"

"Haha. Not me either."

"Um."

"You okay, bro?" said Yemi. "What you doing? You wanted to give me

Madyson Peck's number? I *didn't* know you knew her..."

"Yeah, we've been friends for a while."

"Really?"

"She's fine, dude. Really hot."

"Well, um..." Michael knew he couldn't go into detail about Madyson's condition as it'd spark too many questions around his relationship with her, and also her privacy as well. "I called to see if you could enlighten me about Nigeria. I just need some information about housing, government, social-economics, etc."

"What you need to know?"

"Everything. I can't do this project without the knowledge, bro."

The next hour was an education in Nigeria economics and the reality of what was lying ahead for any plans Michael made. Would he just focus on the richer countries of Africa as places to immigrate to?

Based on housing figures, Lagos was the most expensive city in Africa, and the average price of three-bed homes were approximately NG 140m. Abuja, the capital city of Nigeria, had been experiencing interest increases from both local and foreign investors, which caused the prices of housing to rise and build better chances of return on investment for those investors.

The Nigerian economy had expanded by 1.9 percent in the past year, and this was an improvement from the minuscule growth of 0.8 percent just a year earlier. The increase helped by improvements in manufacturing and services, supported by the continued recovery in the oil sector. Check with the International Monetary Fund (IMF), said Yemi, who admitted to getting his information mainly from *Routers* and its African correspondents. *The economy in Nigeria is projected to improve further, based on IMF estimates, and the Central Bank of Nigeria has been more optimistic, projecting a 3 percent in the coming year.*

Michael kept taking notes, realising his call to Yemi was great research and it was just what his visitors wanted to know, and he'd plan a trip to Nigeria in the near future to establish a network of contacts to able his facilitation of the big move.

Yemi added how the real estate sector in Nigeria struggled for decades and wasn't sure if it really contributed any more than 10 percent to Nigeria's GDP. The sector had been in decline for the better part of the last five years, and even with the National Housing Fund the struggle had continued.

Michael asked Yemi about the migration status of Nigeria and its neighbouring countries, and whether it was in a manageable state. According to the Government of Nigeria, said Yemi, it had given more attention to migration management as rumours about border control had been horrendous for years. Even with additional responsibilities to the National Commission for Refugees, ongoing dialogue with the European Union, the planned projects with the National European Union Development Fund (EDF) and the President on Diaspora Affairs on the case, high internal and external migration was still high mainly due to the size of its population, economic climate, as well as its porous borders.

"And how's the employment rate? Good, or could it use more labour?"

"I don't know everything, bro."

Michael grinned. Of course, Yemi didn't. He was just a gateway to further information he would need. Michael typed up 'employment rate in Nigeria' on Huddle from his laptop and saw there was a good, high employment rate average of 85 percent over the past five years with its peak almost doing over 90 percent.

"Says here employment is good."

Yemi hesitated. "Statistics aren't everything, my friend. But it depends what reinforcement you seek."

"What you mean, Yemi?"

"Not everyone will find work when they come here, and if your plan relies on it, then you're doomed to fail."

"To be honest, it's about creating an infrastructure where new jobs will emerge because of the skills that people will bring with them."

"And money? This doesn't come out of thin air."

"As long as the immigrants are benefiting the country or wherever, and bringing money in, then what's the problem?"

"Hmmm," mumbled Yemi.

"If there's no jobs, money and we're taking away from the economy, then it's a problem. That'll be the challenge, and the idea is to only have people who are ready to contribute to the country, not take from it."

"Okay, I see," said Yemi. "When is this all happening?"

Michael tsshed. "You mean you haven't been on the website, or signed up for the petition?"

"Of course, I… haven't. Sorry, brother."

"No worries. I understand, but first wave of people will be in 2025, when we'll have 80,000 people a month shipping to Africa."

"80,000!"

It was a massive number and made his feat feel impossible, but it was an estimate, Michael knew, and a top-end of the number with the likelihood becoming much lower.

"Yep, we'll achieve it, don't you worry," Michael said with confidence.

"I'm sure you will."

Michael heard the doubt in his friend's voice, and it was something he'd become accustomed to recently. He put down the phone after saying his byes, and tapped at the radio app again to get his mind relaxed and to downsize the enomority of his task.

The sounds from outside his office had died down due to the time of day, so Michael decided to play the radio app without any earphones.

Unfortunately the music hour he'd hoped for had gone, and there was a panel discussion going on. The subject for the discussion was his idea, where they were questioning if black people moving to Africa was a good thing or not. He didn't catch their names or why they were talking about it, but clearly the word was getting around.

"It's like, slavery reversed," somebody said, and it made Michael grimace. *They don't get it.*

He listened for another five minutes before switching the app off. The media would either help or hinder my goal, he thought, but people logged into media to hear those opinions and would base their own feelings off the back of their chosen media source.

He put down his laptop and moved his phone away from his reach. It'd been a busy day, but he was going to be much busier down the line. He wanted to check on Shanice, but didn't want to talk to Natalie, who could provide him with more detail than Shanice probably would. Was Shanice enjoying school again? He'd send a text message later, he decided.

A knock at his door.

"Hello."

Lawrence opened the door and poked his head through. "You okay, bro?"

"Yeah, where you been? Thought you were coming by today to run through things."

Lawrence entered the room with his rucksack on and kept his head down. "Sorry, yeah. That was the plan, but got caught up."

"With what…?"

Lawrence didn't answer and sat in a free nearby seat. He remained quiet and didn't look at Michael. He sensed there would be more words but was surprised when Michael didn't continue. He had a headache and shouldn't have turned up unannounced.

"I need to go to the toilet," said Lawrence, standing up and heading out of the room.

It was a risky move with Lawrence, he knew and watched as Lawrence left the room nearly as swiftly as his brother had just entered it. He leaned over his small desk, and saw Lawrence's rucksack on the floor and it was partially unzipped. He wanted to trust his brother but nothing lately had helped build that trust. He moved over to the rucksack and opened it to see cannabis and cocaine baggies inside it. He sighed. Michael returned back to his chair by his desk.

Lawrence finally came back into the room, and appeared to have splashed water over his face.

"I had a thought, bro."

"What?" Michael said, disappointed by the discovery of drugs.

"There's a company that does media monitoring and I thought it could be of benefit to you so you know what people are writing and saying about this business."

"Yeah?"

"Yeah, BSN. They compile reports for a monthly fee and have editors to upload stuff in real-time, too."

It was actually a good idea, but he had other things to address.

"Lawrence, you doing drugs again?"

Lawrence irked his body uncomfortably. "What?"

"I saw the drugs in your bag."

"Why you going down my bag?"

"Why *do you* have drugs in your bag?"

"Man, fuck you, bro. I don't need to tell you anything."

"You working with me, man. I can't have no addict on my team, you know that!"

"I'm not an addict…" Lawrence bit his tongue, careful of getting his words right.

"So, what, you supplying now?"

"Maybe…"

Michael threw his hands in the air. "Ahhh. No way. I can't have this…"

Lawrence admitted defeat in his stance. "I'm sorry, bro. I need the money. I got these kids to pay for, you know. I got rent to take care of. Shit is tough…"

"But you can't do this here, Law. We gotta keep this business clean as candy. The media will start sniffing around soon and you can't bring this shit here, bro. Seriously..."

Lawrence was quiet and put his head down. It was something he needed to think about and whether he really believed in his brother's business or not. *I need to sell this shit, quick.*

Chapter 14

1996

They looked inside the bags, and believed that they had struck gold, winning the lottery. Still brimming with the VCR player, diamond necklace, marble ashtray, glasses, the ring, blender and other things from the house, they marvelled at the task that was finally coming to an end. Boy B was taking control and adjusting the stolen goods between each bags.

"What you doing?" said Boy A.

"What does it look like?"

That's why I asked, duh.

Boy A didn't reply. Boy B didn't elaborate. They sat next to each other on the first step, heard a shuffling noise above them. The sound translated into footsteps and were moving into their direction.

Boy B remained calm and continued to place the goods into the respective bags of prominence and difference. Boy A looked up. All of their hard work would be discovered, and they'd be reported to the police.

The owner of the footsteps came closer, Boy B raised his head up and laughed. He recognised the steps pattern and was confirmed correctly when he saw their face.

"What's good, Bill? You up early?"

Billy Marshall worked on a construction site and had to report in at 6am every morning.

"New job, innit. Can't do what you mans is doing, or I'm back in the clink."

"We ain't doing nothing but having a chat," said Boy B, looking over at Boy A. "Ain't that right?"

Boy A moved his head in unison, watching Billy, checking them out and studying the bags in front of them.

Billy squeezed between them and headed towards the door. "Haha. Yes, indeed. Looks like you're having a chat, all right. Be safe, guys. I gotta go."

The door slammed and Boy A felt his pulse slowing down.

"Yo, I betta make it home. Sounds quiet out there," said Boy A.

Boy B stared at Boy A, and then above him at the empty and dusty staircase. "Hmmph."

"What?"

"Nothing, bro. You good. Take your bags and we link up another time, yeah. To talk and ting. I know mans who can give us good Ps for this stuff."

Finally. A plan.

He assumed Boy B lived in this block, from the fob key, but it could have been anybody's. His own block was about five minutes away, and he would pray that his mother hadn't checked his room that night, or she'd be asking all sorts of questions. He raised his hand to give Boy B his fist of respect, but Boy B didn't accept it. After everything. Sure, it didn't matter, but it'd be a night to remember, at least. He didn't check his bag and just wanted to leave as soon as. Boy A stood up and mumbled before walking towards the door.

"Remember, bro," said Boy B, keeping his head down. "No words, yeah."

"Yeah."

Boy A pushed the handle down and the door opened. Boy B moved up a staircase, cautious of being seen by a passing stranger. The sunlight appeared stronger than before, and there were more cars appearing on the road. Boy A entered the street, and hearing the door shut behind him. Time to get home. His bearings took a minute, and when he reached the corner by a closed pub, he remembered where he was, and how he'd get home. The bags were noticeable but there was nothing he could do about it. It was something that they'd badly planned.

A sound, a voice, maybe. In his path, or direction. The echo trembled against the bridge he walked under, and it bounced back into his path. He wanted to turn around, but he had to keep walking. It could have been anybody and anyone, and to get involved would not be a good idea.

"Hey, mate."

Shit. Clearly not a man from the manor. Clearly not one of his elderly white neighbours too poor to move from the ends. And it was the sound of somebody in their 30s or 40s, trying to be cool. He increased his walking speed, not too obvious as so to attract further attention.

"Yo, mate."

The voice getting closer, and accompanied by a vehicle.

Boy A ran. There was no point in looking back. He was near his gates and he could make it. The bags bounced against his legs and he scarpered. Cutting through the housing estate before him helped as the voice disappeared, and he hid by a kids' playground, behind an old car, breathing heavily. He had no idea of where he was as he never hung out around this part of the estate, having outgrown certain parts of the district he called home.

The thought to wait until the voice was long gone was top of his mind. Boy A wondered if they'd seen him leave Boy B's tower block and had followed him all this way. Had they taken pictures? Recorded his clothing and every step? *Fuck. Man.*

A heavy hand grabbed his shoulder and it was firm. He looked down at the ground via the car's reflection and knew it wasn't good. He would have to give up the goods, his night over. He couldn't fight his way out of this situation.

"Mate, why would you run unless you've got something to hide? Me and my colleagues just wanted a word. But it seems you can actually help us out with our investigation. Lovely."

The sounds of handcuffs throttled Boy A's ears and the reality of the end game was emerging over his thoughts.

2018

It occurred to Michael that doing the right thing didn't bring him immediate gratification or a sense of happiness as he thought he would. He stood alone in his flat and watched the material possessions he owned failing to respond to his melancholic mood. Their one-dimensional purpose and lack of interactive qualities meant zero resemblance to human emotion or feelings, a painful quietness filling his home. Of course, he knew the media he'd switch on every day could defer his loneliness for a while, and yes, his mobile phones appeared to contain the capability to create a real-life android, but it wasn't the same. Shanice, for all her youthful sins, was gone. Rebecca, too, gone. Madyson, although she never stayed over, going, slowly. Friends? They were disappearing as well, weren't they? Something about Shanice's antagonistic body language towards anything reminded him of when he wanted to get through that awkward period, and just become an adult already. Money and freedom to do whatever he wanted. The mental burden of growing up to rely on others to do what you needed to achieve, and to accept their failings, too, along the way was probably how she felt. He had let her down, but it wasn't because he hadn't made it up to her for being an absent father. It was his blurred intentions with Natalie, and his failure to understand her beauty wasn't singular, but it came with a personality and an understanding that making love to her would equate a memory for the rest of his life he'd never forget. That was Shanice, and that was his ignorance.

He circled his body, unable to decide where to sit and to whether he'd jump on a device or turn on a medium of some sort. His attention was taken away by the shuffling of feet outside his front door and then the rattling of his letterbox. The time of the day didn't explain why the postwoman was not on her appropriate shift time, and the unusual-looking nature of the letter that faced his hallway floor. The possibility of another tax audit or company registration letter ran across Michael's mind, and he walked away from it, knowing he'd address the situation later. He reached at his TV screen and switched it on. He picked up the phone from his couch and noticed a voicemail waiting to be listened to.

It was from Bryan. Said he wanted some help with Balstec as Simon wasn't playing ball. Not surprising, thought Michael. *I'll call back tomorrow.*

He wanted to try Madyson and see how she was doing, but she'd told him he didn't need to check on her every five minutes. She'd been in touch with other family relatives and some old girlfriends, so she'd be okay. She wasn't on a life-support machine, she just had a terminal illness. She would return to work and be able to do normal things until her symptoms became too much.

Michael shook his head, unable to understand the timing of it all. *Why now? Had she hidden it? Why didn't she say something before?* There were too many questions he wanted to ask her and for some reason knew he couldn't ask her now for being labelled insensitive. He tried to switch off and make space in his mind, and channel surfed until he came across a dating show he'd found himself liking for no apparent reason.

He woke up three hours in the same position, although his head tilted back on his couch. The dating show had turned into a casino gambling show with a strange fluorescent backdrop and a well-dressed host. He had no idea what had happened until pain in the neck from sleeping while sitting erupted. More phone notifications from his regular apps, but sleep was required and he switched off the sound from his devices. As he walked to the bedroom, the sense of something he needed to do arose, but then escaped him. He fell onto his bed, not brushing his teeth or showering and quickly undressed, lying down in his t-shirt and briefs. The light was on and it disallowed sleep from overwhelming him as he closed his eyes, and a brightness flickered. He rolled over, knowing he had to get up again to switch off the light if he was going to have a decent sleep. His body cradled like a baby and the remembrance of how he used to suck his thumb as a child entered his mind. Reaching for the cover, his body temperature dropped and even as the duvet warmed his body, he was uncomfortable. His thoughts dominating his ability to relax so he sat up. *The letter. Go get it*, he told himself. He rose from the bed, and stood next to the light switch, deliberating for a second. He clicked the switch and the room fell into darkness. He returned back to the bed and allowed his eyes to close to aid the start of his sleep.

The morning crept up before his dream had ended. The image of little men running across an athletic track with no batons and no visible crowd made no sense. He swung his legs over the bed, willing himself to be active and to make the most of the day. He couldn't find his phone but didn't worry too much about it. His other phone was on the dining table. Michael ignored the fact his teeth needed brushing and walked into the lounge. He stared at his front door before heading back to his bedroom.

He had to make a call.

"Hey Mike. How you doing?"

"Hey, Allen, you free? Let's meet up in Rosie's for a coffee."

"Now. It's barely 8am."

"I know but I got this letter and I need to talk to somebody about it," said Michael.

Michael spotted Allen as he walked towards him in the coffee shop. Packed and busy. Michael wondered if he was in the right business. People's drinking habits definitely had caught up with them and the price to pay was isolation and a hot cuppa at the same time. Making a mint, for sure.

"Hey Mike," said Allen as he sat down. "You look like crap, dude."

That's funny, I was just thinking that about you, Allen.

"Seriously," said Michael.

Allen wrinkled his face to indicate a response, and Michael tried to acknowledge whether there was any truth in the statement, and to whether he'd had a good night's sleep or not.

"Anyway, you ordered?"

"I don't want anything."

"You sure? I think you'll need it in a bit," said Michael.

"No, no. I'm good. Really. Had a chance to drink and eat a bit this morning."

"Okay."

Michael hesitated with the next move, indecision upholding his thoughts and execution of his delivery. He was the organiser, and had to conduct himself appropriately. Sliding his hand into his pocket, he pulled out a letter and handed into Allen.

Bemusement covered Allen's face. "Okay. What's this?"

"Read it."

The second guessing that morning as to whether to meet Michael at all came back to Allen's mind. He studied the envelope and noticed its officiality. It wasn't as a regular letter.

"Oh, man," he said, as he pulled the letter out of the envelope. It was from the prime minister. "Gerald James."

The volume of Allen's voice led a woman sitting nearby to look over at the both of them.

"What is this, bro?" Allen said.

"I'm not sure if it's a good or bad thing."

“From the prime minister! Are you kidding me?”

A staff worker from the coffee shop approached the table.

“Coffee. Latte. Allen.”

“Thanks,” said Allen, looking up at the woman serving him.

Even as she walked away, Allen stared at her. Michael understood why Allen was having problems at home.

“Yo, the letter.”

“Err, yeah. Let me have a read.”

The expression on his friend’s face. It was clear Allen was confused by it all, and why this letter had been sent to Michael at all.

“He wants to arrange a meeting with you! *Michael Featherstone!*”

Michael could hear Allen’s voice raising and saw people peaking over in their direction.

“What the bumba, bredrin?! This is bigtime.”

“Yeah,” sighed Michael. “But you’ve read it all?”

“Err, okay. So while it’s totally commendable that your activity is raising awareness for ethnic minorities in the UK…” Allen stopped. “He didn’t write this, did he?”

“Probably not.”

“...we would like to discuss further the policies of your petition and website to where the government could support your plans, and establish a suitable criteria to follow and uphold. This is a protocol measure we take with every new political activity and something we believe you could reap the benefits from as it would allow an invested interest from the right people. Whoa.”

“Yes. Whoa.”

"What the fuck does that mean?"

"I have no idea, but the Society of Black Politicians warned me this could happen," said Michael.

"You gonna meet him?"

"Got no choice, right?"

Allen dropped his head and drank some of his coffee. "All got choices, man."

"Sorry, Allen. I didn't mean it like that." He extended his hand and tapped his friend's elbow. "How's it all going at home? Michelle?"

Allen raised his head. "Still mad. No wedding. Knows I'm not there emotionally."

"Does she know about the girl?"

"Not directly."

"So, you're good, right?"

"Well, I kinda made a pass to the girl, didn't I?"

A pause, a quietness swarming them both, as if the whole shop was listening.

"... And she rejected me. Said she'll tell Michelle if..."

"What?" Michael couldn't believe his ears. "No way."

"... I didn't leave her alone."

"But that's good, bro..."

"I'm not sure if it is," shrugged Allen. "I'm not sure about it."

Stumped. Something wrong was happening with Allen and there was no rationale as to the real problem.

"I think I love her."

"So, tell her: it's what Michelle wants to hear."

"Not Michelle, bro…"

"Oh…"

The rest of the morning allowed an air of discomfort to surround their respective issues. They drank their coffees silently, not wishing to disturb the other person. They allowed minimum eye contact and raising of eyebrows. *Gerald James is up to something*, thought Michael. *My work crush is going to do something*, thought Allen. They didn't say a word to each other for the next five minutes as silence took ahold of the shop but the volume of everybody else around them picked up and distorted their understanding of where they were, and why a cloud of anxiety seemed to simultaneously sit above them.

"What's up with Lawrence?" asked Allen, breaking the silence. "Heard he was returning to his old ways."

News travels fast. "Yeah, he's been dealing again. And I got a message last night saying he's not sure when he's going to come back to Going Back Home."

Allen wasn't too surprised. "You think it's serious?"

"You never know with that guy. Never know. Just hope he hasn't met the wrong person. His kids need him. He doesn't realise that."

"Yeah," said Allen. "Kids need their fathers."

Shanice entered Michael's mind, and he thought why his dad never told him how hard fatherhood actually was. "They sure do, bro."

His contemplation broke as a vibration from his phone, a text message via HeyBrow.

"You okay?" asked Allen, spotting concern on Michael's face.

He wanted to say something negative and really digusting but knowing that Daniel had had his world turned upside down, primarily due to his African project, it was wise to remain neutral in his reasoning until he had other evidence to behave less than so.

"It's from Daniel. He's spitting a gut at me."

"What you mean?"

"Vex. Says he's officially been fired and blames me for it."

"But he *did* the posting…"

"I know, but if I hadn't come up with my petition, regardless of whether he covered up his identity on his company's CMS or not, he says this ludicrous game I'm playing has cost him a lot, and maybe his family and home."

"Jeez."

"I didn't ask him to do it, Allen. The guy, well, you know, Daniel…"

"Yeah, I know him. He's just letting off steam. He'll come around, you'll see."

"He did get my site some good traffic as well…"

"Yo, that's not the point, man."

"I know, but truth is truth…."

"Drink up. I told Michelle I wouldn't be too long. Gotta build up those trust walls again."

After saying goodbye to Allen, Michael knew he needed some light relief. So much thought to his business, the prime minster's letter, organising the scale of this ambition dream, not to mention Madyson, Daniel and Paul. He just needed to zone out for a bit. Rebecca would have been the perfect counter punch to lighten this mood, but that wasn't happening. The last time they spoke, she rambled on about her friend, Michaela, acting weirdly when they went out, especially around black guys. Then she said her mum and Charlie were still getting married, although it was postponed due to her mum's health. And she missed him, a bit, but not enough to get back together again. He respected her honesty, even if it wasn't what he wanted to hear.

He ended up at his local street market in Deptford, where over 300 stalls served tons of customers each weekend. The great diversity of people and products for sale, and being outdoors, meant it was a good place to take a walk and distract the mind. Inhaling the air, thick and smokey, he was glad the market had finally reopened after a small closure of a couple of weeks due to a bomb threat. He had missed it. Everyone respecting each others space within the crowded environment, forming a sensible one-way system. In fact, thought Michael, it was much more pleasant and easy that way. Space was given its freedom. Much more airy. A pleasure to walk and quietly analyse the area. He bought a cheap phone charger and fake iPhone earphones. A very well-run market, and had a great ribs stall, too, but it was still a market, and Michael knew what his conscious bias about them meant.

Leaving the market, he had to get back to his reality. He was going to become famous, and was going to be a platform to take him to where his ambition wanted to go, and it wasn't about the money. Getting distracted again, his phone rang.

"Hey, Mum."

"Mikey, boy. What you doing? Still causing trouble?"

He was a little taken aback. She wasn't talking to Lawrence.

"No, Mum."

"We having a surprise party for Mummy. You haffi be there, right?"

Mummy was Michael's mum's mother.

Family functions weren't his idea of having a good time but he hadn't made an effort in a while, and his Africa project was something to talk about with people who would speak with him honestly and frankly.

"I'll be there."

"You better."

"I'll be there."

He could hear her saying something else but her voice was interrupted by a distracting beep. Another call. Michael held the phone at a distance and saw Rebecca's number ringing.

"Mum, I love you, but someone's calling me. Speak to you later."

"Son…."

"Hello."

The wait for her response took forever.

"Mike."

"Hey."

Something about talking with Rebecca made Michael feel good and bad in the same breath.

"Mike."

"You okay? Where are you?"

"I'm at home."

He didn't answer, knowing the delay in her voice meant a slow continuation.

"Mike, sorry, I don't mean to call, but you're the only person I thought would understand."

"What do you mean? Is it your mum?"

"No, it's not. It's just life, you know. Everything feels like it's coming down, slowly. I can't pinpoint it yet, but I can feel it."

Michael paused, then spoke. "I know what you're saying. It's like a lack of controlling things…"

Her voice perked up. "That's it. Exactly. I mean, Mum. Michaela. Work. You."

"Me?"

"Yes, you, Mike. Things have changed, but I still feel the same. And everyone else around me is doing something, but it doesn't work with how I'm feeling."

"I'm sorry, Becky, but things are crazy. I can't control it either, but I'm trying to make a breakthrough with my African project."

"And you couldn't include me…?"

Michael knew he had been in this conversation with her before, but he couldn't remember when. There was a reason why they weren't together, and why he couldn't see her understanding his need for moving on. He decided to change the subject.

"You said Michaela? What's up with her?"

Rebecca noted the switch of subject. "This isn't… ergh, anyway. She's going through it — and doesn't say exactly what it is. Something that happened when she was younger — and she's not getting help about it."

"When she was younger?"

"She was burgled and was in the house when it happened, and is still scarred by it. Got severe trust issues."

"I can imagine."

"But she can't keep talking about it — and not doing anything about it. We've all got our issues…"

"Yes, we have. And Becky, thanks for the call. I know it's not easy, all this stuff."

They continued talking for another three minutes before the awkward silence intervened and dismissed any reunion chat that Rebecca quietly wanted. Michael put the phone down and sensed this, but the time wasn't right — and he didn't have time to deal with her issues, let alone his.

He saw an email pop up on his phone and quickly studied it. It was from SBP's Miles but it was a personal email address. He studied it with intent and wondered if it was still about the mayoral plan they had mentioned, and how he should expand his campaign's goals. They had already informed Michael that the mayor would be elected by the supplementary vote method for a fixed term of four years, with elections taking place in the May of its relevant year. He half knew this, but he'd need to give a deposit of £10,000, which was returnable on the candidate's winning at least 5 percent of the first-choice votes cast. An investment, but a non-guaranteed one.

Each candidate required 66 signatures of people on the electoral register in London supporting the nomination, two from each of the 32 London boroughs and two from the City of London. The campaign for mayor would involve uprooting the current mayor, Ronnie Khatoon, who seemed to have a stranglehold on the position.

"London gave me the opportunities to go from the council estate where I grew up to being Mayor of the greatest city on earth. I still wake up every morning passionate about delivering my promise to Londoners: to make London a fairer city where all Londoners get the opportunities that our city gave to me and my family."

This was the quote of Khatoon — and it was one that resonated with his voters and those who ever vowed they could knock him off his mantle.

Miles's email was strangely wrritten. It wasn't clear to Michael. But maybe Miles was trying to present a coded message. But it soon became apparent. Miles had been removed from the Society of Black Politicians. And Miles thought it was down to the prime minister, who had been in touch with SBP. Michael was unsure what the removal meant or why it took place, but it was clear that it was probably no coincidence that he'd received that letter from the prime minster shortly before Miles was dropped from SBP. *No way.*

Chapter 15

1996

Looking back, Boy B knew he couldn't worry about Boy A. He had to take care of himself first and foremost. Getting their stolen goods home was his best chance to make money, and to help get the things he needed to better his life. He'd sat at the college lectures and read how studies by bored professors showed the impacts on physical health that people in poorer communities lived with. Poor conditions from overcrowding, damp, indoor pollutants and cold environment were all associated with physical illnesses, including eczema, hypothermia and heart disease, even though he hadn't experienced any of those yet. He was young and healthy, and just needed some cash to live better while he figured a way out of the area he lived.

"A-yo, bredda."

Boy B glanced around, surprised at being addressed at such early hours from the same block he lived in. A tall and skinny individual, maybe a few years older, approached him.

Boy C raised his fist and indicated a form of respect so to appear in affinity with Boy B.

"Yes, yes, my fam," said Boy B, upon recognition.

Boy C eyed the bags in his hand. "What you doing, bro?"

Boy B followed the gaze. "Just a bit of business, that's all."

"Yeah."

"Yeah."

Boy B quickly told Boy C about how he came to have the bags of product in his hands, and how Boy A was a nightmare and the worst wingman any crook could ask for. Boy C laughed but held most of it in, scanning the bags and wondered if there was something to be taken. Boy B said it was mainly small items, and Boy C resisted the temptation to beat up Boy B and take the bags anyway. Heading off to work with a possible black eye from Boy B would mean instant suspension, and holding down stolen goods, meant the crime doubled in trouble and a knock on the door from the old bill. Trying to leave the illegal life behind proved mentally taxing for Boy C.

"You guys are crazy. Be careful. You know what the feds are like round here, brotha."

"Yes, that why I'm stashing this stuff now, ya get me."

"I hear that," said Boy C. "I gotta run, got things to do but catch up later when the heat's died down, yeah."

"Cool," said Boy B. He raised his fist at Boy C and waited as Boy C's fists connected with his. He knew Boy C from many years from local football games to house parties they attended, and Boy C had only recently moved into the block, so they barely ever spoke to each other. He analysed Boy C's dress sense, and understood the system was now Boy C's provider. They headed off in different directions, and it meant Boy B would probably never see Boy C for another few months, at least, and then the drama from the burglary would have disappeared.

The front door of Boy B opened. He did it quietly, conscious of not waking his mother and younger brother. He could hear the dripping, the faint sound of emptiness accommodating the sound. It had been like this for months. There was a tortuous, continuous drip of dirty water into buckets his mother had put down. The neighbours above claimed it wasn't their doing and the local council kept saying there were more urgent cases. It made Boy B embarassed to live there, and he could never bring a girl home. His mum worked and what for, he wondered. Just to sit there as the drip interrupted their daily sitdown at the dinner table, so they were forced to eat in their bedrooms, alone. Closing the door, he held the bags with care and headed to his room and hid them in his wardrobe. He rolled over a couple of tracksuits to disguise the presence of the bags, knowing he had to sell the items as quickly as he had obtained them. The floor outside of his room creaked and Boy B wasn't sure if it was the dripping or if it was his mum.

His 11-year-old brother was staring at him.

"What you doing?" he asked.

"I couldn't sleep. I was going to get a drink," said his brother.

Boy B kissed his teeth, and sensed this wasn't the truth, and he closed his door before falling onto his bed. He had no idea of what to do next, but sleep overcame his consciousness, and a dream of selling the goods at a local market came to him.

2018

Not working at FirstThing.com ultimately meant Michael had plenty of downtime, but being at home to concentrate on his African mission seemed to be counterproductive. He hadn't been to his Idonia Street office in a couple of days and wondered if it served to benefit or hinder his business progression. Part of him wanted to quit this path he'd set out for himself, believing the journey was too massive to ascertain. He questioned whether he was really the man to lead a revolution from a system that had been established for hundreds and thousands of years. *But, if I don't do it, who will?*

The logistics needed to be thorough and he wasn't just building a small block of flats. The lifestyles, the food, the travel, the accommodation, the third parties and sponsors and most of all, the people, who would commit their lives towards the unknown; these were the things that he needed to have ownership over, or else the entire movement would be a flop — and only he would be responsible for it.

He grabbed a yellow notepad from his desk. He drew a familiar spider web graph with himself this time in the middle. The web started with him and then linked out to the requirements he needed to get into place. Who to be contacted, and who would require paying for their services. The web grew bigger than the space available on the notepad and he drifted into a second sheet from the pad, aware it was pertinent to quickly include everything he saw as necessary. Of course, he'd done this previously — but writing it again brought home the reality and the scale of the movement. And whether he had the nerve to really pull it off.

The vibration of his phone broke his thoughts and he threw the notepad down onto his couch.

"Hello," he said, answering quickly.

"Hello. Is that Michael Featherstone?" The voice wasn't recognisable, and had a hoarse edge to it.

"Yes, it is. Who's this?"

"Mr. Featherstone. You don't me, but I know you. I've been watching you."

Michael sat up further in his seat. "What?!"

"Don't be alarmed. I just want you to know there are people out there who are watching your project to Africa closely."

"What do you mean? And who are you?"

"My name and occupation isn't of importance to you, Mr. Featherstone. Just know your business idea is under surveillance, and we've done our research on you."

"Research?! Surveillance?! What are you talking about?"

"Mr. Featherstone. I'm talking about *stopping your project.* It needs *to stop.* It won't help anybody if you decide to go ahead with it. Is that clear?"

"I don't know who you think you are, but I'm going to hang up," said Michael. "I don't do prank calls."

"We know you, Mr. Featherstone. We've sent a letter to your office with a reminder of your past. The time you were in the police line-up as a teenager."

A quietness.

"Yes, we know about that. We know about how you cheated on your pregnant girlfriend and how you falsely claimed insurance on your mother's car.

We know that."

Michael looked around his room and wondered if there were hidden cameras planted. "Okay. So, you know that stuff. What do you want?"

"Stop this Africa project. Shut down the website. Stop your mayoral campaign. Stop it all. Or else, we'll go public with what we know."

"You're chatting faff, bro," said Michael. "You have nothing to gain by going public. Like I said, I don't do prank calls."

"This isn't a prank. Your life will be exposed…"

The anger rose within Michael. "Man, shut up!"

As if ignoring him, the voice said: "The letter says, We Know. And it has pictures... Then see if it's a prank…"

The phone died, the call ended. Michael held up the phone to check if there was a problem with his device. He realised it was intentional. *Who is this guy?*

There was only one way to find out. Lawrence. Finally getting through to his brother, he escaped the usual pleasantries and persuaded Lawrence to visit the office to see if there was a letter.

"Hey, bro. You want me to open it?" Lawrence asked.

"Yes, please."

"Okay."

The rustling of an envelope and the crinkling of bended paper meant Lawrence struggled to open the letter in his hands. Michael knew patience was a virtue and didn't ask Lawrence to hurry up, although the tension of the letter's identity was biding and painful.

"It's just some pictures, Mike."

"What of?"

"Err, a younger you…"

A vision of a more reckless version of himself filled his mind. Michael knew the caller had been telling the truth, but why they had gone to this extreme to shut him down, made no sense to him whatsoever. Of course, it was business. But he was ultimately doing a good thing — and it shouldn't affect anybody, only those people who were interested.

Lawrence was talking: "You want me to do something with it?"

"No, no," said Michael. "Thank you. Just keep it on a table so I can see it when I come in."

"Everything all right?"

Michael wanted to tell the truth but he couldn't. "Yeah, everything is all good, bro."

Hanging up to Lawrence, he sat still for a short period of time, knowing calls like this were soon to follow any political campaign, *but why should I change my number?* It was a firm rationale he held onto from the start — the attention would change him. Sure, he'd had a couple of sales or prank calls but not one so threatening and one that had gone to such lengths to put the fighteners on him. He huffed, and he knew until he saw the pictures that he would then make a better decision. Plus, he had come too far to change his number based off a call where he didn't know the caller's identity.

"Ahh," he moaned. Walking around his flat, trying to dismiss any reasoning to deal with his work problems and unidentified callers, he kept coming back to them. They were consuming his mind, and he didn't like it. It was then he remembered Madyson, and how she had been released from hospital and he had to check up on her. Grabbing his jacket and car keys, it was the perfect distraction. She said she was staying with her cousin in east London.

As he drove through, he saw it was the modern East End, with one of the highest ethnic minority populations in London and the most prominent and established British Bangladeshis business and residential communities within the UK. Literally, just driving through it, he could tell the large number of Bangladeshi expatriates, including a significant number of foreigners of Indian origin, dominated its landscape. Michael didn't know the borough had a population of nearly two million people, and as he drove down Whitechapel, and into Shadwell, it became apparent to him, these were the people who probably had similar cause to deliver their own plights back to their own native homes. Or, the bigger question was: was east London the new Asian and ethnic minority home — and could they really survive long term like this? The rundown buildings, next to the reupdated hospitals and food chain shops, indicated otherwise, but Michael had to think selfishly and maintain his own struggle right now than to consider others.

"Damn, this is it." Michael had parked and stood on the pavement, facing a 26-storey high-rise building, looking like it was reaching the clouds and touching the planes as they flew past.

Parts of the block were boarded up and abandoned, and he noted that city workers looking for cheap accommodation were still settling here, before moving on once they were promoted or were thinking of starting a family. Part of the area nearby reminded Michael of his youth when he'd hang around the older guys and tried to be cooler than he was — and didn't like to listen to the wise words of his parents. It was then he realised that he had been here before: many years ago. It wasn't her cousin's flat, it was the one Madyson lived in before she moved to America. *Maybe she was subletting it to her cousin.*

He walked closely to the block and pressed the buzzer to her flat. There was no answer, but he calmly entered the building as somebody was coming out and held it open for him.

"Thanks." The person barely acknowledged him.

Following the signs to her floor, he waited as the dirty lift went too slowly to reach there. He escaped the urine smell and tapped at her door. He checked his phone and called her number. No response. He hadn't spoken with her in a few days but knew she wasn't working as her show producer had told her to take time off.

He peered through her letterbox. "Hey, Madyson."

Part of him said to give up and go home. Maybe the cousin wasn't there, either. It wasn't worth the effort, but he owed it to her to keep trying. Her phone still wasn't responding.

"Mady…son." He stopped, briefly. Holding the letterbox ajar, something out of the corner of the room. She's there. Arm hanging off her bed. Pills near her fingertips. *Crap.*

"Madyson!!!"

He sat on the floor and cried by her doorstep while the police and paramedics broke her door down and whizzed through to try to resuscitate her. They took her to the hospital, but little could be done as she was pronounced dead on arrival. Turned out she didn't have a cousin in the flat, too. Michael broke down in tears, aware he had to call someone from her little-known family. The doctor said it was a brain haemorrhage, but Michael wondered if the HIV had been a contributor as well, not just the overdose on pills. *What had happened to her?* He had let her down. They were meant to be friends, to be partners for life, but life had not chosen it for them. And now…

"Hey, hey, Mike," Paul was staring at him. The hospital hallway strangely busy and Michael engulfed in a world that wasn't his own. He turned to see Paul. *Why?*

"Mike, brother. You okay? I came as soon as I heard the news."

"Yeah, thanks. But she's gone, dude."

Paul covered his mouth realising one of the team had been taken away. He truly liked Madyson and wished they had been closer. "What was it?"

Michael spoke softly: "Her brain. She had… HIV, man — and she popped these pills. I don't know…" The tears from his face fell onto his hands.

Paul didn't know. She had HIV. *Whoa, what did that mean?* Pills, too. It was worse than he had expected. A drink-driving incident, maybe. A falling over in a club, maybe. *No. This.*

"Mike, HIV? What the fu?"

"Long story, mate," said Michael. "She'd been carrying it for years. I didn't know…"

"Is that the reason?"

"I don't know and I don't care, man. She's gone…"

"She's…"

Paul couldn't bring himself to interrogate Michael any further. It was the worse of any bad situation they would face regarding Madyson. Her life was over. Nothing could bring her back.

"Hey mate," Paul said.

"Yeah."

"Maybe it's time to shut down the Africa business and the mayor stuff. This is too much for you."

There was an air of sympathy in Paul's voice, which made Michael consider the words for a short spell. *Could Paul be right?*

Thinking of Maydson and the discussions he'd with her, meant Michael had to keep going. It wouldn't make sense to simply stop the project despite all the work he'd been through to get it this far, and to know Madyson would still be dead, regardless of its outcome.

"Nah, bro. Africa is still the plan. Just need a couple of minutes on this." Michael's phone flashed a notification and saw his mother asking him a question. He had to attend the family party tomorrow. The timing impeccable, he thought.

"Come on, Mike. This is all madness. We don't need any more drama…"

"What are you talking about, Paul. Madyson has just died… We need to do this for her. But I wouldn't expect you to understand." Michael stood up and walked down the corridor. A doctor stopped him as Paul watched them both, discussing Madyson's situation. It was clear she was not coming back. Ever.

The pub seemed smaller than it was. Busier, maybe. But something made it more intimate than it really was. She stood empty-handed, alone, and then realised why the environment clouded her vision. He approached her, gave her a drink and kissed her cheek. Rebecca liked it. It'd been a while since she'd felt wanted. The drink disappeared from her hand, and was placed on the nearby table, her body whisked away into a solace of emotion she wanted to remain in forever.

"Oh, Jason," she playfully jeered as he pulled her close to him.

They kissed, heavily, unaware and uncaring of the eyes following them in the small pub. It was the best feeling she'd had for weeks and she would enjoy it for everything it was worth.

They parted lips, and stared at each other. Rebecca blinked her eyes, unsure why Jason now looked like Michael and Charlie. She continued to blink, but yet, nothing. Slowly…

"Hey, Becca," it was Jason, finally. "You good?"

"Yes, thank you."

Jason leaned over to kiss her again, and she obliged, though knowing the pleasure was fading. She needed to go back. To revisit what she wanted. Her friend Michaela was still acting unusual around her and didn't disguise the feeling when they were out together.

A few moments later, Rebecca typed a one-handed message on her phone, out of sight from Jason: "Mike, I must see you…"

Chapter 16

1996

Police station, London, 6am. The sound of hard-soled shoes on the floor, quick and urgent. A corridor, dimly lit. The sound of a phone ringing. The call is from somebody he knows, asking for his whereabouts and if he's okay, but they don't get through.

Boy A was being questioned by police officers about his suspicious behaviour, in a chair, in an interrogation room. The conversation disappeared as nothing came from it and soon he was alone.

"Get in that cell, nigger."

The cell cold, freezing, no raditator in sight. Thank god for his hoodie. He wrapped his arms underneath. He remembered, the cops talking about a robbery — another robbery, and he was telling the truth-ish. But they didn't believe him. He closed his eyes and thought of Boy B, getting away and having the goods they stole. *Should he snitch? Should he talk about the dad and family they'd scared during their burglary?*

They would question him further in the morning — and see if he wanted to confess. But it was the wrong crime they were trying to pin on him — and they had zero evidence. Zero. He had to remember that.

2018

He thought back to the call and the 'We Know' letter. Michael had picked it up while at the office, and flicked through the photos. Somehow, the caller was right —and had images of a younger Michael and how he was engaged in furtive activities back then. But it wasn't enough. It wasn't concrete evidence. Just photos — and they all needed the backstory to justify what the pictures actually contained, and represented. Michael decided not to act upon the caller's request — believing it would just go away.

Since the death of Madyson, there had been an indirect slew of interest from his friends around his project and whether it would continue. He was struggling to maintain his emotions about her death, but found a release from it with his Africa plight. It gave him more focus, a bit more drive, something he had to do in her honour.

Sitting at his office desk, the text from Rebecca was unexpected but he chose to ignore it. It would slow down his goal. He sensed it wasn't a booty call, but a distraction nonetheless. And thinking of Paul at the hospital meant some of his friends weren't as focused on the goal as he was, but losing Madyson hurt like hell. And it made no sense.

The landline phone rang. It was as if an earthquake happened and his whole office shook. The landline never rang.

"Hello."

"Yo, what's up, what's up? Is that Michael Featherstone? The man going *Back To Africa?*"

"Err, yeah," said Michael, cautious yet suspicious, too.

"It's B Didzy here, *baby*. BABY!"

Oh, another prank call. He looked around his small office, thought if the rent costs were really worth it, and if he had the capacity to fulfil the intentions of a worldwide migration. The website had enough subscribers to start a meaningful trip to Africa, but an exodus was far from reach.

"B Didzy?! You sure?" The outlandish New York accent must have been fake.

"Yo, man. I know you're thinking, Why is B Didzy phoning me? But I seen your posts, man. I seen your vision. Your revolutionary plan, man. You are *the one!*"

Complimented or being mocked? "Err, go on."

"Yo, my man, Hype, tracked down this number for me, man. I see you got people ready for this. This is what I've been looking for my whole life."

"Eerr, thanks."

"Er, listen, man." Silence dominated the call. "Listen."

"I can't hear anything…"

"That, man. Is what is going to happen when I send out a post about this later today, man. The world is going to stand up to us. Take the black man serious. You understand me."

Michael moved uncomfortably in his seat. "Look, I don't know who you are, but if you're really who you say you're are, I appreciate it. I really do."

"Go to any video online and compare our voices. It's me, man. But 6pm GMT, I'm gonna do this alright. Please be ready. Get your IT ready. Get your assistants ready. Get your PR team ready. *We're going to blow this up.* And

I'mma call you back and do a video call with you to tell you again: *I don't play.* This is too important, man. Our people need this. I'm all in, bro. You just gotta take us there!"

The phone line went dead.

Michael spung around in his chair. *What?! Was it real? Am I ready? Really ready? Bro. Bro.*

He quickly called and told Lawrence to monitor the site and social media — and prepare for an avalanche of calls and internet traffic. He had to up the TBs of the server so the site didn't crash. Lawrence was ready. Working remotely, he said he could manage it. Michael had no choice but to go with it.

6.15pm GMT and nothing. Not a peep.

6.16pm GMT.

Oh shit.

It was as if simultaneously the globe had gone crazy. Everyone had been bitten by a similar bug. Everyone was online at the same time, or were either communicating with each other in a strange but normal way. Everyone was connected.

Michael listened on a call to Lawrence when his brother told him to check the site's dashboard. The unique visitors graph was rapidly increasing by the second. He had previously viewed it when it was in the hundreds, but it was pushing to the mid-thousand thousands easily. The sign-ups were also growing. People declaring their interests. Wanting to join Michael back to the motherland. *Back home.* It was beautiful and he couldn't think straight.

What if he got a million people to sign up for it? Would they all really come? Would the logistics be logical for everyone? Was Africa ready for such a move? But *Wow*. It really was B Didzy.

That's all Michael could think about it. B Didzy, the guy who had American popular culture on lock and had the media eating out of his hands whenever he chose. A producer, an artist, an entrepreneur, who had made millions from the entertainment business. Michael did a quick social media search on Didzy, and the man had done as he declared he would. Didzy had posted about the site, added a link and even mentioned Michael's name. It was only a matter of seconds before…

… The landline rang again. It was *The Stardium*, asking for a quote: "What did think of the post?" Then the BCB: "What did you think of the post? Your thoughts." Then the reporter from *The Choice* was back in touch: "What did you think of the post? Your thoughts. And you're going to be front page next week."

He had to give it to B Didzy. Funny how one post could generate so much noise. But he realised it was the content of the post that caused the spike. His vision, and just supported by B Didzy. It was all him: the website, Lawrence, Madyson, the possibility of creating an influx of confused airport staff with the volume of black people leaving their unnative countries.

A text message appeared on his mobile. *We Know* was the message. *It's time to stop it. Or else.* Michael couldn't sit there and do nothing, and decided to call Daniel to vent out his thoughts.

The car moved slowly at the car drive through.

"Can I take your order, please?"

"Umm," he looked at Daniel. "Two strawberry milkshakes, please."

"Anything else?"

"No, thanks."

"Drive through to the next window, please."

Nothing like recountering your youth with another friend and talking over some milkshakes. Something nostalgic and childish all at once. Michael sipped slowly, whilst Daniel seemed to finish the shake as soon as he started it. They were in a virtually empty car park.

"Yooo, these are good."

"Hey, man, I need to talk to you."

"What's up, Mike. Don't worry about it. I'm freelance now. That other stuff wasn't too smart of me. I tried to help your thing but I did it wrongly. You know. Next time, I'll think it through a bit."

"I appreciate that, Dan. I do, but did you hear about the B Didzy post?"

"B Didzy? No. He talking about your mayoral run?"

"No, man. He's gon and told the world that all black people need to sign up to my site so they can be a part of the Going Back Home movement. Dude, it's major!"

"Mike, it's been major for a minute. You just gotta bring it home."

"No, Dan. Listen. Yeah, it's been going okay, but you gotta understand. B Didzy has, like, 60 million followers, and the site has thousands of sign-ups in a matter of hours. I can't fail people, man. We really gotta do this."

"60 mil. Shit. Err, yeah. You gotta do something. Or you'll be a fried fish for the rest of your life."

"Fried fish?"

"Or something… Your rep is on the line, big time."

"But what if it doesn't work out? What if…"

At that moment, a car pulled up next to them. Michael looked at Daniel in bemusement. *Why? It's an empty car park.* The car dropped its driver-side window.

"Hey, Mike."

Michael lowered his window.

"Hello… err, yo! What's up, man?" He recognised him. It was the other black guy from FirstThing.com. "What you doing here?"

"I live around the corner and came by to get…" he looked at the drink Michael was holding. "...an evening milkshake."

Michael smiled. "Okay. I hear you. What you really doing?"

"I'm not following you or anything, bro, but I saw your car and came by to say hi. We miss you over at FirstThing. You need to stop by."

"Yeah, I've been meaning to, but busy times."

"So, I see… you know, Balstec pulled out of their deal since you left?"

Yes, he had heard.

"Bryan is thinking of leaving, too."

Yes, he had heard.

"And Finan keeps asking about you."

He hadn't heard that one.

"Listen," said the man. "I know you're really busy but if you could pass by and do a short presentation on how to blow up a campaign, especially with stars like B Didzy, then we'd be forever grateful. Really."

"No worries, man. I'll speak to Bryan to see what's going on."

"Appreciate it. Let me get my milkshake. You guys have a good evening."

"We will. Thanks."

Michael looked back at Daniel, knowing that was one of the strangest encounter they've been involved in. He checked his watch.

"Crikes. I've got a party to go to."

The room stopped when he walked into it with Daniel. Faces swooped to him, absorbing his style, texture, grace, nodding as he strolled past them.

"Hey, hey." "Good job." "You getting that money?" "Good to see you doing it." "Keep going, youngblood."

Ultimately positive vibes, but the attention overbearing. Michael hunted for his mum, who was stirring a massive pot in the kitchen. His dad bopped soulfully down the stairs as R&B music played from the corner speakers.

"Mum!"

Glenda turned around to face her son. "You made it, baby. Thank you."

He gave her an awkward hug and tried to explain how everyone was talking about him, but she didn't think it was true.

"They just haven't seen you in a long time, that's all."

It was more than that, but with family, it was often hard to tell. They were there to celebrate the birthday of his grandmother after all, and was sure half of them didn't read the papers or sites that he read. But you never know.

"Is that brother of yours coming?" Franklin asked.

"He's busy, Dad. Got to take care of his family."

"What about this family?"

"He's just busy…"

"I see you brought Daniel with you. Where's Allen? You know his dad's in there somewhere. How about the pretty girl?"

"Rebecca."

"Who? Maddy, the actress."

It dawned on him that he hadn't told his parents about her death and wasn't sure if now was a good time. Maybe, it was.

"She died the other day, Pops."

"She what? What about her body?"

"Her family want to cremate her. I can't get involved. It's their wish."

"You all right, son? Sounds like a lot going on with you."

"Yeah. Just a bit."

"How's my granddaughter, Shanice? I called last week, but she didn't return my call."

"Same as before, Dad. She'll come round when she's ready. It's just situations and things. But she's doing all right. Back at school."

"Listen, Michael. You can't be doing this Africa thing with so much of your life in the balance. Family is saying that pop stars are getting involved. Saying you trying to be mayor. What is it, boy?"

"Dad, you said I could do it, didn't you? But things are fitting in the right places and I just gotta keep on going, that's all. That's it."

Michael saw Daniel sitting alone in the corner and decided to approach him, but was stopped by one of his cousins, Oscar.

"Hey, man. I know you famous and all, but you come to my kids' school and give them a talk or something?"

"Hey, Oscar, that sounds cool."

"Yes, great. Perfect. That means little junior will get free school lunches for the rest of the year!"

Michael looked at Daniel and shook his head.

Chapter 17

1996

Boy B had crept into his bedroom, anxious about what his mum would say when she saw the stolen goods, and fallen asleep. However, when she saw the stolen items, her demeanour changed dramatically. She seemed to be excited about what he had managed to get for them. He was surprised to find her sitting on the edge of his bed, but her expression was soft and non-critical. Boy B thought he was in so much trouble — he'd been caught stealing again. But finally mustered the courage to face her, he found her looking at him with curiosity. Calm, she asked him to tell her what happened. Boy B explained that he had found the goods in the house of "a friend". Instead of contemplating punishment for Boy B, his mother praised him for his honesty. Then quietly left the room.

Shocked, but he wasn't. The fact his mother was in his room meant that she was looking for something. So he had *actually* caught her. With bags full of stolen goods in his wardrobe, it was hard to accuse her of anything.

Those lost weekends with his mother, and with his brother in tow, developed a sibling relationship instead of a mother/son one. Her role was confusing, unsteady and a mixture of pain and anguish. He found it hard to figure out. Boy B remained on his bed, and thought to Boy A. *Why had their friends encouraged them to do the burglary together? Would this night for-*

ever keep them joined at the hip? He sincerely hoped not.

2018

 Hey, Mike.”

“Lawrence, thanks for the other day. And going to the office and that. But where you been?”

“What you mean, bro?”

Michael glared at his cereal bowl, half-empty and something he should have grown out of by now. “The party. You weren’t at Gran’s party. Mum was mad at me for you not showing up!”

“Oh.” Pause. “Sorry.”

“You see the traffic lately?”

“Huh?”

“The website. B Didzy gave us the shout-out and it’s going bananas. We got momentum on this now.”

Michael didn’t know exactly where Lawrence was — and wanted to ask but he was used to being confused by his own brother’s life. He tried to focus on the positive things they shared or had in common.

“Sorry, Mike.”

The tone of voice and hesitancy threw him off. “You ain’t seen it. You’re supposed to be on these servers night and day, ensuring the site doesn’t crash and any payment we can handle.”

“Yo, easy on the vocals, bruv.”

"Easy on the…? Nah, what?!"

"I'm here at one of my kids' houses, ain't I? And she's just called the cops on me."

"What?"

"Yeah, I'm literally sitting in the front room in Romford, while she's screaming to her children about what a mess I am. I just want to see my kids, man…"

"What?"

"Yeah, take a listen."

A short gap of noise before the phone signal drifted across the room. "You better leave, you fuckin' bastard. How dare you come here? Now. And just sitting in my chair like you own it. We don't need you and we don't want you…. They're… they're on their way. And you're *going to jail.* Restraining order for you! Ggggeeeetttt!"

The phone returned back to a familiar voice. Calm voice. "You hear that?"

"What, bro. Handle that. Why are you there? Come on."

"I'm sorry, Mike. I just needed to get my head straight. I'm struggling with cash flow. I owe some guys money, and I was caught stealing some stuff from the chemist and the pills were the wrong ones."

"I'm giving you money."

"Yeah, but it's not enough, man. I need 50 grand. Yesterday. They're coming for me. Remember Russia? The casinos? Mans are coming from there for me."

"Russia? You said Latvia. What is going on? Get out and let's talk."

"I'm sorry, sorry. I've got to see my kids. You know I love them. Trust…"

"Sir, excuse me," said a voice. "I believe you're violating your restraining order and have no rights to be here…"

"I've gotta go…"

Michael paused, frowning for nearly two minutes. He tried to call Lawrence back, but no answer. *It isn't right. Fucccck.* He had an important meeting to attend to — and all he could think of was how his personal life was crumbling in front of him. Lawrence, Madyson, Shanice, Paul, Daniel, Mum, Dad — relationships strained by his choice to try and perform a miracle proposition to help his community. And he was failing. Hard.

The Society of Black Politicians had somehow arranged a televised recording with Gerald James, and he wasn't ready to appear on camera as simply another loser with a big idea. He had to run with the B Didzy push and he publicly thanked him on his site and social channels. This was as big as it was going to get; he couldn't run from it, especially when it was pulling him in.

He jumped onto Mindsite and started watching a video somebody he half knew had posted, and it started with B Didzy shouting about black freedom. The video was edited hastily into old civil rights clips and Martin Luther King chants. There were crowds marching, shouting: "Back to Africa! Back to Africa!" "We want our reparations!" Then, the video turned to modern-day marches, with similar echoes of protest. "We don't need you; you don't need us!" one voice shouted. Then, a looter threw a stick into a shop window and the crowds followed and began to rob the shop. Soon, this one shop was a symptom of many as the protesters became rioters and buildings were now on fire. The text on the screen wrote, We're Taking What's Ours. Then it suddenly faded to black and Michael's face appeared. *This is our new leader. Follow him.*

Michael almost fell out of his seat. *WTF!*

It took Michael a short while to digest what was going on online and what was actually truth and reality. He called a quick virtual meeting with his PR and social team to prepare them for a media blitz. He was being picked up in a swanky black Mercedes and it would contain all the luxury you'd expect from a high-ranking political official, such as the prime minister. The car pulled up to its destination, he inhaled as he saw Melissa Grant standing there with the biggest smile on her face. He hoped she would allow him to lead the interview and not attempt to put words in his mouth.

Entering Downing Street was a privilege for anyone but it gave him a sense of miseducation and wrongful doings. An entendre of thought. A double mixture of the best and worst drink known to man. The prime minster's head of communications led them all into a dark part of the home, which blended a Victorian outlook in its original design, but had modern furniture added to it.

Soon, a voice he recognised, appeared into the surroundings.

"Michael. Michael Featherstone."

Michael turned around and watched as the smaller man, yet bulky in size, approached him and held out his hands to shake.

"Prime Minster, good to meet you."

"Call me Gerald, please."

Before Michael could answer, Gerald James moved onto the single chair, next to the microphone stand and waited for somebody to come to him. The head of communications quickly approached him and whispered in his ear. A makeup artist entered the room and added touches to James's face. She looked at Michael.

"Take a seat, please."

He didn't need makeup, he thought, but he had to sit down. It was happening now. There was no other media presence, and Melissa was strangely silent, lost in the awe of the situation.

"Okay, Michael. So…" said the head of communications, "this is how we do this. Melissa has explained to me why this is so necessary for us to record your interview with the prime minster. All you have do is ask your questions and the prime minster will answer. We'll then share the recording with Melissa and you'll distribute it accordingly. We appreciate you may want to share it with the public, which is fine but only once we've told Melissa and the Society of Black Politicians that it's fine to do so."

Michael nodded. He had a shortlist of questions in his pocket to ask the prime minster, but he knew he didn't need them. The questions were on the tip of his tongue everywhere he went.

"Gerald, I may call you, Gerald," he began.

The prime minster nodded.

"The main reason I'm, we're, here is so that my website, Goingbackhomesoon.org, encourages black people, or people of an African diaspora, can have a healthy lifeplan to their existence in the Western world. It is not an exercise of rebellion against those who may judge us, or we have to live besides, but it's an option of mental freedom and to escape any misunderstandings due to explicit, implicit or illicit racism and stereotyping. My first question is: are you okay with supporting my website and for what it stands for?"

Melissa nervously grinned as she waited for James to answer.

"Of course, I am in support of your scheme and website, but I hope that it is not a hoax to convince people, British people, to leave their homes for something they have no knowledge of and haven't looked into the conditions of leaving Britain and what it really means. I appreciate that each civilian does not experience equality in this country and may feel disheartened by this, but jumping at the first opportunity to leave could equally be as devastating. If you don't mind me saying, your website is very clear on the objectives of what you're aiming to do, but please be aware that not all civilians are as educated on what you're trying to achieve as you are."

"Yes, of course, Gerald. But you must understand that my website isn't something that one person has simply created to better its subscribers. It's to create and build a foundation of truth, one that is continuously denied by schools, employment, entertainment, business, etc. There's a theme of lost people in the West who need this. Is Britain ready to face an opinion of difference that isn't a protest or a hostile act? Can it truly survive if black people leave the UK in droves?"

Gerald James: "Well, there's two questions there… and with the first one, a difference of opinion is nothing new to politicians and in this democracy, it's what we expect. It's how we evolve. I encourage all those people to speak with their local constituency and develop relationships with their MPs, so their voices are heard. Too often we hear that minority voices are being swept under the rug, and that is not acceptable."

Melissa agreed. The thought of the prime minster being fully briefed on Michael's questions and website wasn't going to look good on camera. The world was used to the stumbling of the prime minster, not the articulate speaker he appeared today.

"And… the other question: black people leaving. I don't want black people, who were born here, or are citizens, or plan to become citizens to leave the United Kingdom. They help the country not only economically, but culturally, it helps us grow as people — and this is what the UK needs to become — a fully-fledged melting pot of strong races under one umbrella: Great Britain."

Michael wanted to gag. Gerald James was as cheesy as he expected the prime minster to be.

"Last questions, Gerald. And thanks for your time today, it's really been appreciated. But focusing on the possible exodus of two or three million people in the UK, what would the real outcome be for this country? Does it mean a better way of living for the working class people? Or does it mean allowing other foreigners to enter the country to fill that void?"

"Michael, Michael, Michael. As I said, I think your website is grand and has grand ideas, but an exodus isn't the best idea for anybody. It will leave confusion and heartbreak and will give the country a temporary feeling of befuddlement and anxiety. Any exodus needs to be managed by a number of parties and teams and I know you're leading this brigade but it's not been agreed legally as to whether this is the right thing to do. So while I acknowledge there is room for such ideas, I also believe it requires legislation to fully attain our attention and to be executed in a way that the orderly people of the UK know how. Thank you."

Shit. Not the way I thought it would go.

"Thank you, Mr. Prime Minster."

Melissa was sitting in the car looking at Michael and trying to work out his expression. To her, it was a massive victory and once the head of communications gave her the okay to circulate the interview, the media was going to have a frenzy with it. They would become famous — and the Society of Black Politicians would be able to justify its "irrationale demands" for government funding. But despite their best efforts, Michael wasn't happy. She'd seen the viral post from B Didzy and knew it would create more impact than anything she'd promised to Michael, but they had just come from 10 Downing Street — a memory and experience not to be sniffed at.

And while something was quietly troubling Michael, something was bothering Melissa, too. Her friend, Christina, was still finding it hard to convince Melissa that she wasn't permanently traumatised by a robbery that happen many years earlier. Melissa would note the references to reported crime as a personal victory for the good and wellbeing of ordinary people in the city, but for this to still be continuing every time they discussed politics or current affairs, Melissa suspected there was something else Christina wasn't telling her. For some reason, Michael's stubborn stance reminded her of Christina, and wondered if they knew each other, perhaps.

As the Mercedes pulled over to drop off Michael, Melissa looked up from her phone and said: "We've got the all clear. They're sending me the edit now and we can distribute it to all the media. Stand back, Michael. It's about to kick off! This is going to work wonders for your mayoral campaign!"

Getting out, he looked back at Melissa and said, thanks. Her effort was appreciated. Her attitude wasn't. Only he could take this Africa mission to where it really needed to go, but she had more of the immediate answers, he thought. But he *still* needed sustainable explanations for taking his people back home to Africa.

It'd been a long day and Michael was going to go straight to sleep. Ignore his phone and get some kip. The interview would hit the press circuits that night, and would reach the local and national news outlets. He was getting messages on his phone, but silent mode prevailed and he wallowed into a deep sleep that had been overdue.

He didn't even realise it was the morning until he heard a shuffling of feet besides his front door. He walked towards it and heard the voices, too, as he came closer. He looked through the door's view hole to get a better understanding — and there they were. Journalists, photographers, vloggers — all looking to get some airtime and footage with him. They must have seen the interview, he summarised, and he shouldn't have come home yesterday.

He tapped opened his phone and the notifications rallied up on his screen to the point where they trailed off and continued on for at least two minutes. He jumped onto his Mindsite page — and he didn't even need to post anything, people were doing it for him. He headed straight to the comments. *What did people think of the prime minster's words?*

"Saying the same old, same old."

"I like his suit."

"I thought he was handled those questions like a pro."

"Maybe he's black."

"True. Props to Michael for addressing the important issues."

"Good interview."

"What about Europe? Does anybody even care?"

It made Michael laugh. The different perspectives generated from the same interview. *Were people even watching and listening? Did they really absorb the crucial information?* He read on for a few moments before acknowledging there was nothing to tarnish his reputation with from the interview, and it had been reasonably well edited.

The notifications had finally settled and he noticed B Didzy had sent him a DM via Javaload and was asking him to fly to New York City to be on Didzy's TV show. *He is right,* Didzy had serious influence of popular culture, and could escalate the plight to stratsopherical heights. Michael paused. He wouldn't reply immediately. He thought if he could dig out his old freestyle and rapping tracks he'd made a few years ago, and get signed onto Didzy's record label it'd be all the success he needed. But the relevance wasn't there. Michael knew it, and he remembered something the famous musician, Rob Stagnoff, had said in an interview once, about how he didn't mean to become a global ambassador for the faminine issues in the third world, Rob just wanted to make music — and to some extent, Michael had connected to that sentiment. But Michael wasn't a successful musician — his tracks were terrible — but this was a dream coming true, albeit the order of it wasn't as he predicted.

Another message was from Melissa. He was still undecided about her and

SBP. She asked if he'd seen the video and what he planned to do next. He texted her back and told her about Didzy and his musical aspirations. She replied quickly with an confused emoji and he laughed, noting her mood as lighthearted. Her actual text wasn't, though.

"Don't do anything else with Didzy. He's simply trying to grab onto something that he doesn't honestly believe and knows the popularity it will cause, but won't help you directly."

"What about you and the SBP?" Michael responded, angrily.

"The Society was established based on the racism all of our qualified members have faced, and to leverage some equality in this systemic prejudicial world we exist in. If that's not representative of your cause, then we don't know what it is. Didzy is only about Didzy. His track record proves that, but yet for some, his ego is still attractive for the masses that wish to be him and follow his path to success, and lord be it, a level playing field."

Michael didn't know what to say, so he said. "Sorry."

There was a small noise gathering from outside the flat.

"Michael! Michael! What do you want to say about your interview with the PM?"

Crikey. He'd almost forgotten about them. He couldn't face them now. He looked at a nearby mirror and saw his reflection: it wasn't pretty. The shower needed his stinky body. The water would salvage what little bit of stress that was indicated on his face. Another message stopped his thought train. It was his mayoral campaign manager, Lisa.

"You need to pull out of the mayor of London race now," she said. "This prime minster interview is not going to help and it's going to ask more questions than to offer solutions. Call me now, please."

Wow! Do one good thing and the rest all fall down. But he partially agreed with Lisa. His goal wasn't to be the mayor of London — that was simply a platform for his African voyage. His goal was to rescue his people, not the entire city of London.

Chapter 18

1996

Cold and wet. Boy A. Back again, sitting on the floor of the dark interrogation room. He could hear the police officers in the hall, laughing and joking. They were drinking coffee and eating doughnuts, typically, and taking their time with him. It was only a matter of time before he was going to be beaten up until he told them everything he knew about an accomplice.

That time was quicker than expected. One officer laid into him, the other slapping his face. They assumed he was guilty, and he was, but the violence unjustified.

His face damaged. The cops looked on as if they knew they wouldn't be reprimanded for their actions. Boy A was thrown back into his cell. A stink-infested dark place where bugs roamed and good hygiene wasn't on the agenda. He knew he should just say something, but that meant a life of looking over his shoulder, worrying about if he was going to meet Boy B again — and he'd tried to rectify his bad decision.

"Man, fuck you! I ain't dones nothing!" He shouted. To no-one.

Boy B moved awkwardly on his bed. Deep in thought, he couldn't stop thinking about Boy A. God knows what happened next — even if they meet each other again. There was no reason to do another robbery so soon, knowing the cops were looking for them. Knowing that the heat would continue for another couple of weeks. He had to lay low and he was lucky his own mother had his back. It'd been a long one, and later on he'd weigh up the items he could sell, and get the cash for them as intended, but it'd have to wait. He was tired. Tired and smelling. *The girl. Damn. Why did he do it? Crap.* He would have to lay low for a long time. A real long time.

2018

As predicted, the interview with the prime minster had caused plenty of noise about Michael's African quest, so much so, that even being at home meant dealing with the press and the public. Everyone wanted to know timings, everyone wanted to know finances, everyone wanted to know everything. Michael hadn't heard much from Lawrence or his friends, and hadn't recently got any messages from Shanice or her mother. He tried to stay as proactive as possible, but his close circle seemed tired and bored of his so-called mission to Africa. Maybe they were losing interest.

He sat at his office and looked outside the window. The view was shite. *Straight up, lame.* Council blocks and entrances into a high street that sold bad chicken and chips for a pound. *Africa was surely better than this. We'd have more to dream about, than to dream about what we have to fight about,* he thought.

The SBP was surprisingly supportive of him pulling out of the Mayor race, but camera crews and newshounds still wanted their quotes. Michael didn't mind speaking to them as "no publicity was bad publicity", but he could only do it from the office; not from his home. His flat was his castle to dwell in, and he needed that space to regroup from the day's events. The office phone kept buzzing and he and his small team dutifully answered the calls, responding to basic questions, which were already on the site's FAQs page, to more in-depth ones that required some thought to answer. He couldn't be afraid, especially with people like We Know out there. He had to keep going, he knew that much.

The phone rang again.

"Hey, hey, Mike, what's up?"

It didn't register.

"Who's this?"

"Bryan. Who you think it is?"

It had been a while and there was no reason for Bryan to be calling, except to state the obvious.

"Yo, Bryan. How you keeping?"

"I've been fired."

"No shit. Haha."

"It's not funny, Mike. Balstec wanted you, not me — and I didn't bring any new business, so I'm at the dole queue."

"Dole queue?! You are incredibly funny."

Bryan gave out a soft laugh. "It's good to hear you laughing. And I see, things are taking off well for you. Meeting the PM and all."

"Well, you know," Michael didn't want to gloat. "It's just business. Nothing more."

"Well, it's definitely inspiring, mate — and I didn't think you would take it this far."

Michael knew Bryan wouldn't say the 'black' word, or mention Africa, as it made him uncomfortable, but he sensed a compliment when there was one. "Thanks, Bryan. What else is happening?"

"Err, the main reason I called was, err, to ask for a job…."

Michael spun on his chair, holding back the laughter. At the corner of his eye, he saw people outside his office door looking in and gauging what he was doing. Then he saw the police uniforms. "Bryan, I've gotta go…"

The office door smashed open and three police officers with batons strolled in — `and weighed him up and down.

"Get down onto the floor. You don't need to say anything…" said one officer.

Michael didn't even hear the rest of it. He was willing to cooperate. As a black man in London, he'd always mentally kept himself ready for a situation like this.

"Don't look at me, man."

They ransacked the office, going through each drawer, slamming everything in their way. They appeared exhausted with the search and didn't have a full understanding of what they were after.

"We understand you have drugs in this vicinity, and we have a warrant for your arrest," said another officer.

"No drugs here," said Michael, but he then thought of Lawrence. "Oh, shit."

"What was that?"

"Nothing. No drugs."

The search continued and the mess of the office flourished as the officers threw items on the floor and not in the place where they'd found them.

"Fuuuck!" shouted one officer.

"What?" said another.

"There's nothing here. Nothing."

"Err, sorry to bother you, sir. You can get up now. It seems we've been wrongly tipped off, and are truly sorry for the assumptions of drugs being on your property." There was a glimmer of sincerity in his voice.

Michael stood up. He was pissed but not angry. "No worries. You've got a job to do. Is there anybody I call to talk about this mess?"

"Speak with our customer services and they'll arrange it all for you. Again, we're sorry."

The police officers left the way they came in, but Michael knew the violation was intention. It was intended to frighten him and slow down his goals. The We Know party had better come with a stronger plan. *One messy office isn't going to stop me.*

While mentally he had absorbed the police situation and dismissed it as a weak attempt to throw him off his target, it had physically disturbed him. He sat down and sighed, aware he would have to tidy up and put everything to where it originally belonged and ensure it all made sense to him. The thought alone was tiring, something he didn't want to do. He shifted his attention to his phone, and looked up goingbackhomesoon.org on its brower. He jumped into the CMS of the website and saw the questions coming through from his Contact Us page.

"When will the petition be given in to Parliament?"

"When is the movement really going to take place?"

"What's next for us?"

"We're ready."

There was a sense of impatience and he had to deliver something substantial to keep the interest (and the money) genuine and rolling in.

His personal mobile phone rang.

"Hello."

"How were the police? Did they see the We Know pictures?"

"I knew it was you!"

"Yes, and it'll get worse if you don't shut your operation down. NOW!"

Michael hung up the phone. This person was becoming irritating. But did they have a point? *Focus, Michael, focus. Let me clean this shit up.*

Something about tidying up opened Michael's mind further. He thought about all the things had to deal with and how he was possibly going to delegate everything. It was a mammoth task, but he had to remember it wasn't above him, it just had to be done. He really needed to understand the scale of costs and revenue the business was accruing and how much turnover would be actual gross profit.

The office again tidy, but the handle of the front door was damaged, and it meant he could only lock it from the outside, not the inside. He wanted Lawrence to look at it, but giving his brother a call wouldn't achieve anything in the short term. Michael settled down and took a deep breath, and pressed numbers on his phone.

"Hello, Michael."

He breathed a sigh of relief upon hearing the familiar voice.

"Tyler, hey. Good to hear from you."

"You called me?"

"Err, yes, I did."

"Everything okay? I've got the bank statements and the site's transactions like you asked."

"I wanted to know how the money's doing. Am I really going to be able to afford all this?"

"We should do this in-person, Michael."

"Yes, we should. Give me an overview and what you think, then we can arrange to talk face-to-face."

There was short quietness on the call and Michael was unsure if he was going to like the news Tyler would tell him.

"Well, let me see. You have raised so far nearly £300,000 and the account is pending another £100,000 from B Didzy. You're doing real well, and momentum is picking up in revenue."

"What's the magic number again?"

"£3 million — for six months, and that only covers the initial expenses: the flights, transport, basic accommodation and pocket money for one million people. Roughly approximately a month after moving to Africa, the money will be gone."

"Shit," said Michael.

"What is it?"

"We're nowhere near the target and once people leave their homes, they'll expect a level of comfort — not to be thrown into a world of unemployment and what do we do next. There must be a sense of security, or else people won't do it. We need to attain some bigger loans and funding in principle which acts like a benefit system for those who are struggling with the transition."

"Sounds promising, but who do we ask — you've posted everywhere?"

"Not everywhere…"

All the platforms were being ignorant. The social media platforms that everyone ran to on their phones and desktops. You name them, Mindsite, Postya, Javaload, Squareview, HeyBrow and of course, search engine, Huddle — there were all conspiring to dish some dirt on Michael's name. It didn't matter if the images that were circulating were from his youth: a 15-year-old boy who was aggressively confronting another teenager. And the caption said, "Is this who you want to lead the revolution, black people?"

It's a cheap shot, they all said, back to Michael — friends and family. But it was a symptom of the the society they currently lived in. Nobody was safe when their name became a trending topic for the masses. Michael thought back to Tyler's cost estimate and how they were far behind their goals to fund this permanent excursion. Getting his subscribers to pay was one thing, but he had to get the interest of venture capitalists, CEOs to contribute some costs. Banks, too.

Money wasn't the issue today, it was his image, and what people thought of him — and whether he was truly investable — and damn, social media.

It'd be a problem if this picture didn't eventually disappear. He still hadn't responded to B Didzy about New York and the longer he left it, the less chance he'd be able to maximise the investment the project could attain. But Melissa's advice sat heavily with him — Didzy was an entertainer at heart, not an activist — and would rely on Michael to do the political upheaval it all required.

He needed to go home; he'd done enough to last him the day. The building was noticeably quiet and the steps of Allen approaching the office meant Michael's day wasn't quite over yet.

"I knew it was you," said Michael as Allen looked curiously at the door as he entered. "Long story."

Allen kept silent until he walked up close to Michael and gave him a hug. "Whatever, bro. I'm proud of you. This is all amazing."

Michael held the embrace and muttered, thank you. It was what he needed to hear.

Allen moved away first and took a seat on the spare chair. He took a firm look at Michael, analysing the body language and whether it was all taking a negative effect on his friend. "You got a lot going on, man. All from your little idea."

"I know, bro. I know. Sometimes I need to pinch myself it's actually in motion, you know."

"It's definitely happening. I can't go on Mindsite without seeing something about you or the campaign. Then there's the mayor stuff, the interview with the prime minster. Bro, what is going on?!"

"Just doing it, man. I can't do it alone but gotta lead."

"I hear you, man. You are definitely leading and I respect that."

"But what? I sense a 'but' coming."

"Nah, nope."

"Yes," said Michael.

"Nope — I came by just to check on you. Your home is swarming with journalists and TV crews and I thought this office would be as well. You know, it's crazy… We all need to catch up: Me, you, Daniel, Paul — gotta do it for Madyson."

The thought of Madyson made Michael suspire. So helpless when it came to her, and understanding what she was going through internally. He had failed her. "Yeah, Madyson. We owe her."

"We do."

"When are you free next?" Michael looked at his phone as he spoke and saw an incoming call. It was Shanice. He signalled to Allen.

"Hey baby girl, how you doing?" he said. But his expression soured immediately as it indicated trouble and more pain. "Wait? What? She's in hospital."

Allen shook his head. The timing far from perfect.

"She was in a car accident; and drinking. What? … My interview. What?... Where are you? Are you okay? … Good. Good… Don't cry… Tomorrow, says the doctor… You have help? You sure?... I'll be there as soon as I can… But call me later, okay… Love you!"

Allen's sympathetic stare meant Michael had to acknowledge it.

"Kids, man. Always some kind of drama," he said. "Natalie's been in a accident, but is okay."

“Drama keeps the heart beating, man,” said Allen.

“That’s one way to look at it.”

Another sound came from Michael’s phone.

“You busy, man?”

It was from Rebecca. She wanted to see him and she was not far from his office. Michael shrugged, whilst Allen nodded, thinking the drama would help somehow.

Rebecca looked upbeat as she entered his office. Her body language positive, clothing pristine. She was with her friend, Michaela.

“Hey Mike, it’s been a while. How are you doing? This is Michaela, I’m not sure if you remember her.”

Michael took a prolonged stare at Rebecca’s friend, but noted how attractive she was, but appeared uneasy and unnecessarily nervous. “Hi, Michaela. I would offer you seats, but Allen stole the remaining chair. Actually, Allen stand up. Here, you and Michaela can take a seat.”

“No, we’re okay,” said Rebecca.

“I insist.”

The women took their seats and waited for someone to take the lead in conversation. Allen sensing Rebecca wasn’t expecting him to be there.

“Mike, I’m going to hit the road. We’ll catch up later.”

Michael gave Allen a hug before showing him to the door and watched as he waved to the women and left to walk down the corridor before disappearing from sight.

Walking back into the office room, he wasn’t sure what Rebecca and Michaela had in mind.

"I can't believe you met the prime minster, Mike," said Rebecca. "That's so incredible."

"I know, it's still hard to believe it happened, but I'm not sure if it's a blessing or a curse."

"What do you mean?"

"This whole Africa experience — it's taking a life of its own, and I can barely look after my personal life as a result."

Rebecca put her head to the direction of the floor. Michaela watched intently but remained quiet.

"I don't know. I may have to close it down. I'm getting hate mail, my history is splattered all across social media. But nobody is really putting down significant investment."

"I know somebody who could help," said Rebecca.

"Who?"

"Umm," she paused, and looked at Michaela. She was thinking of Jason and whether she could ask him about somebody rich he always spoke about, but remembered Michael's feelings towards him. "Nobody you know, just some executive management people at work. I think they could be of use to you."

Michael wasn't sure what she was implying or if she really had any contacts to help him. Probably saying anything so they could rekindle their relationship.

"Umm, Becca. I'm going to wait in the reception," said Michaela, sensing she was in the middle of something.

As soon as Michaela left the office, Rebecca stood up and moved closer to Michael. He could feel her body heat as she stepped within his circumference.

"I just want to be a supportive friend to you, Mike. You know, we've been through a lot and I don't want to throw it all away."

He thought he replied to her so it was clear that she wasn't of benefit to his personal or professional life and she'd only be a burden or hindrance to a cause that she had no real experience with, and couldn't assist him with. But to Michael's surprise, he held her tightly, feeling the warmth on her mouth on his, and searching a familiarity of comfort and desire. She felt and tasted good and if it wasn't for Michaela being in the reception, he was positive they would have been having sex at that very moment.

"Michael," she pulled away first. "I've missed you…"

"I'm sorry, I don't know what…"

Rebecca was thrilled. "It doesn't matter. I'm here for you. I am." She headed towards the office door, and noticed its strange handle.

"Long story."

"I'll call you tomorrow, okay?"

He was unsure. "Yes, please."

A little bounce in her step and she knew she'd done the right thing. Michaela was looking at her phone, scrolling aimlessly.

"You look happy," said Michaela.

"Well, I have reason to be, don't…"

The reception door swung open and a man with tightly-fitted jeans walked through. He paused, and smiled at them both.

"Paul!" Rebecca yelled.

"Oh, hey…"

"Rebecca. Mike's girlfriend."

"Sorry, of course, of course." He took a glimpse to Michaela as he said it.

Rebecca leaned over to give him a hug, and Paul accepted it.

"You hear to see Mike?"

I know you, don't I?

"Yes, I'll go through. Sorry. Life treating you well?" Paul asked.

It's him, isn't it?

"All is good. We were just leaving," said Rebecca. "We can't chit-chat, I'm afraid."

"No worries, but good seeing you again."

"Yes, definitely."

Michaela turned her head away and pretended not to hear what they were saying. She caught brief eye contact as Paul waved to them before heading down the corridor.

Seeing Paul enter his office, Michael said: "I just want to go home, bruv. Seriously. Everyone's been here already."

"Wanted to see you in-person, my boy."

"It's 8pm. I need to go."

"I know you do, but listen. I was watching the London news this evening and they were talking about you, the business — and questioning if it was a legal enterprise, or not. Private or charity. Mate, they're throwing down the gauntlet at you…"

"Bro, I know, I know. You don't need to tell me."

Chapter 19

1996

Boy A was dishevelled. In his cell. His mind working overtime.

"Lawrence, what are you doing?" said the police. "You're going down for this. Tell us who your accomplice was — and you may get a lighter sentence. Don't be a fool!"

He was already a fool. He was there. In jail. Tricked by his friends, linking up with another ends guy as a way to prove his masculinity. He went in too deep and couldn't see the way out.

"We're talking to you, Lawrence. You sit in silence and you'll rot in silence."

It was last thing he remembered them saying. It was the last thing he remembered about this moment in time, before being sentenced and locked away.

Boy B was smiling. His mum had even checked with him to see how much money he got from the stolen goods.

"Got quite a bit, Mum. Here's £200."

"Well done, Paul. I always knew you'd be the smart one."

2018

It was the video call that he never wanted to do but realised he had no choice. Tyler, Melissa, Miles, Daniel, Paul and his PR team had joined the call. The air was sombre, and the realisation of Michael's abrupt call meant something was up. They were aware of the pressure around him, and the need to control the surrounding forces that were causing the pressure.

"Hey guys, it's been a journey and thank you all for joining the ride. I wanted to let you know that I've made an important decision regarding goingbackhomesoon.org. I've made this decision independently and want to ensure you that nobody has influenced this decision. The need for our people, black people, to fully recognise their self-worth and gain supreme self-esteem will only come from experiences such as the one I had in mind, and I'm sure somebody else will follow my lead, but I want you all to know that 'Goingbackhomesoon' is *officially closed for business.* We won't be taking anybody anywhere and we won't be a company anymore. I've decided I'm not the right person to do the leading of such an experience, and have realised it takes a big team to pull off such a thing. Meeting all the people I did on this journey has been amazing, and the support along the way, has given me confidence in the intelligence of our people, but yet, I don't feel we're in the position where we want to be just yet. All the money raised will be returned to those who put their cash forward. We will have a press conference shortly to further address my reasons for closing the business. And it is, was, a business. It wasn't a free ride, but it was a qualified opportunity for us to regain our warrior and royal heritage again. I'm sure we will soon. I hope this doesn't come as disappointing news, but it'll allow me to concentrate on my personal issues and friends and family who need me."

Everyone on the call stayed quiet.

"I had fun with the prime minster, B Didzy and you guys, but I've gotta let it go. The mission has been misunderstood. There's so much work to do, but in what we did we achieved a lot. Thanks for staying with me on this journey, guys. Really appreciate it."

Melissa realised she was on mute, and said a short prayer to herself. She tapped her phone to send a message to the WeKnow perpetrator who had harassed Michael to let them know it was over. They had finally gotten to him. The idea of getting SBP to a higher exposure was great, but to be a part of such a ludrious decision or 'mass exodus' was something the Society couldn't support, but to tell Michael this meant he never would have trusted them.

Michael paused before continuing. He thought about Madyson and wondered if he was letting her down. Why she died so young. *What was her meaning in life really meant to be?*

He had heard from Lawrence recently, too — and he knew he had to support his brother where he could. Working together for his business wasn't the answer, but just quality talks and some feeling of respect for each other. Lawrence admitted he had money troubles and had to borrow money, and that he served a short sentence for breaking the restraining order from his ex-partner. He would speak to his kids, just by phone only. Lawrence knew that Madyson had HIV as she revealed it to him secretly after confessing that she had a crush on Paul, but wasn't clear if she'd slept with him or not.

Lawrence admitted he had a drug problem that he would get sorted out, and he used it for depression reasons only. But he would stop.

Allen told Michael that he was living again with his fiancée and they were doing their best to make it work.

Chapter 20

2025

Located at the westernmost point of the Africa continent, he had made it. It was the gateway he'd envision all those years, through all of his efforts to build it as a landing base for everyone like him. With palm-fringed beaches, and some of the best wildlife-spotting opportunities you'll find anywhere, it should have been a tourist's haven, but it wasn't. It was now his home. Senegal.

"Saleem aleekum, brother."

"Lekum salaam, bro."

Michael was learning. French and Wolof were on his language list, determined to understand the people and the culture better, but as he travelled Jola was commonplace, too, especially in the Casamance region in the south of Senegal.

"Jërejëf, oui." He often found himself saying as he progressed to building a relationship with the native people. The initial visit had developed from a three-month research one to a 12-month journey, where self-discovery had became the theme of the day throughout the experience. Tempted as he was to venture across different parts of Africa, he wanted to stay close in Senegal and see the effects of its history and how it really triggered the economy and culture that now existed in front of him.

He didn't need a visa at first due to Senegal's ECOWAS status, and on Yemi's advice before he set off to Africa, Michael hired a local guide and driver to unearth everything there was to know about the country, so he didn't remain in tourist mode during his time there. It was, of course, costly to do so, but he was prepared to be ripped off at first, until he gained knowledge of standard versus tourism prices.

Fully vaccinated before arriving, he continued with booster top-ups at the local hospital. The state of the hospitals also conjured a vision of how the majority lived, but the area of Dakar was surprisingly robust, plentiful and full of business-minded individuals trying to look after their families, the same way people across the world were. The sense of good living to those who'd lived there their whole life was one of humility and commonality. The goal to be better than the next man wasn't fully recognisable, there wasn't any obvious remorse, just humble people, who were self-aware and knew about the West and what it offered, and what it also took away.

Senegal was hot and humid, and light clothing for Michael was a must. But as advised, he kept his skin on-display to a minimum, fearing malaria at every turn. Sandals at times, but the good ones, not the overly-exposed types. And not all areas of Senegal liked the heat, as torrential downpours often lingered in the south around the months of June to November.

Often called the "Englishman" by the locals, Michael didn't let it get to him. It's what he was. *British, yes. English, unfortunately yes, too.* No escaping it. Explaining his West Indian heritage to an African was like pretending an orange was an apple, his cultural make-up was undoubtedly English. He kept quiet about what he had been doing in England, and nobody appeared to recognise him from any social media channels in Senegal. He was really starting over, but to add his growing knowledge and influence where plausible.

As time went on, Michael soon realised what his purpose being there was. *Water.* He couldn't drink the tap water. And it frustrated him. The basic requirement and privilege he'd been used to in England wasn't recommended in Senegal. He could wash and rinse after brushing his teeth with tap water, but he had to boil the water if he intend to drink it. This gave him his idea, and what he was going to do about it.

As well as water, Senegal had new development challenges to mitigate, due to the socio-economic impact of the coronavirus pandemic. The need for increasing and protecting human capital for productivity growth was one area; lowering energy costs, reducing the carbon footprint, and optimising the energy mix was another. But the list made Michael realise that the fundamental area was water, and while Dakar was better off than other cities, towns and villages, it was something he had to do, which had the potential to help many people.

He'd read about how an organisation called WUWCO and how it worked to serve women in Catholic regions of Senegal and he called them immediately. He could have called other irrigation and water companies in the country, but wished to avoid the political nature of donating a big wad of money and only half of it reached the intended people. He read how WUWCO had provided wells of water to many at-risk communities and he learned the difference in terms of scale and effectiveness.

The simplest wells had traditionally been hand dug. Often these well types were 50 or more feet deep and used when ground water was generally abundant. But they were dangerous to build and cost many lives of unskilled labourers. And they were also easily contaminated as they were often uncovered. Other suggestions included the 'Shallow Wells', or the 'Well Pump Installation' — the latter waiting on the concrete pad to dry, so the pump mechanism is lowered carefully into the hole and a hand pump is attached. The working team would make note of how much water flowed and then ensure when it was safe to drink.

The WUWCO group visited the small Muslim community of Keur Mbar, in the rural heart of Senegal and began the Well Pump Installation process, using Michael's finance to kick start the project. As a result, a well of drinking water, based on solar energy, and a water tower were built. In addition to a drip irrigation system being completed, too. A mango plantation was developed in the village that was to be irrigated with water from the well, meaning it would allow the water to be used beyond simply its drinking benefits. Before the well was built, people living in the village had to walk 10 kilometres to obtain drinking water. And Michael stayed around and visited the village regularly to ensure the local community was actually invested in the work going on around them. Michael asked the village to arrange and pay for the initial geological survey work to be done to help with the foundational ad planning work of the well. It was just a few hundred US dollars but it made the village community mobilise themselves and to be organised around the project. Michael knew he wasn't just doing this for his own ego, the thought of self-sufficency, and in the long run, meant this initial commitment to the well would will be valued and cared for by the community.

After the well was installed, the drill team explained how the pump worked, and how to keep the area clean, and what to do if it was ever broken. Maintenance support was on hand, whereas simple repair work could be costly if unskilled people tried to fix it alone.

Michael found it hard to believe at first that the clean water a developing community desperately needed was often right underneath them. And how relatively small the investment to make such a dramatic difference in so many lives was. Thinking about it, he understood, however, money was at the root of every service, but it was the deeper thought of upmanship and capitalism that meant the money was unequally divided and left people without basic, essential amenities and poor living standards.

The deep wells, which would serve large communities with clean, safe water, was on his agenda, and Michael read how some wells had to be over 900 feet deep and geography reduced the local requirements to sustain such quality of water. It led to the big boys and their big trucks getting this delivered — and meant the popular and busier towns and cities were first port of call.

It reminded him of London and how cornershops seemed to have access to everything, not just the major supermarkets. And it all made sense. Distribution was key.

After returning the money back to the subscribers and paying off any company-associated costs, Michael wasn't left with much. He had enough cash to live on very basic means for a year, and after six months in Senegal, he was given a lifeline and some faith in humanity.

Simon from Balstec offered him some money, well, a lot of money, and didn't want it back. Simon simply called it "respect money" — respect to Michael for leaving England to start the Africa process, and then listing it on social media as a work in progress. Simon had watched Michael throughout the Africa journey since they met at his farmhouse. Balstec had enough money to help people in Africa but it didn't have any relationships of value there. Michael was going to be their connection. The company didn't want any branding tied to anything Michael did, they just insisted the money was used correctly and where his heart took him to. It was the best phone message Michael had ever received.

He was aware he had left people behind in England, but he accepted that his influence or his presence there only meant more hassle for the ones he truly cared about. Shanice, in particular, would only understand this later in life, and with her mother fully healthy, he didn't want to add any more emotional stress to their lives. He would help other people where he could: that was his goal in life.

On an excursion to Keur Mbar, Michael was told the village was only three metres above sea level, and if the sea nearby rose to two metres, its surrounding areas would be underwater and the population would have to be moved. As they built the well, problems such as erosion of coastal areas could become an issue. However, it was the tenacity of the local villagers that convinced him to build the well. They had survived flooding and would continue to do so, as it was uncommon and they were developing ways to combat it. And it was their home: and they needed to be there, with clean water to drink. Michael knew this was why he had the Balstec money — decisions like this. It became an easy investment and one he wouldn't regret. He just loved the people of the village and their fight to live the way they wanted to.

"Shall we get out and see how they're doing with the well?" asked Michael to his passenger as he got out of the car.

"Yes, let's do it."

Michael took Rebecca's hand as she walked around the vehicle and smiled at him. Their journey together was starting again and they couldn't have been more happier.

THE END.

Going Black Home

Patris Gordon

Going Black Home

Patris Gordon

Going Black Home

www.ingramcontent.com/pod-product-compliance
Lightning Source LLC
Chambersburg PA
CBHW031154020726
47499CB00002B/356